Tenderness softened his dark eyes

Gavin's breath brushed Lindsey's cheek as he leaned close to her. "Try to hang in there, okay?"

"Okay." The look in his eyes destroyed her resolve to remain uninvolved with him.

He had a tough exterior that made him appear fearless. Emotionless. But she knew what it was like for him to lose control. Gavin had deep emotions—feelings he channeled into work instead of sharing with a woman.

"So you're not giving up?" Lindsey asked, knowing her heart lay in her eyes.

"No." His fingers wiped away a tear she hadn't realized she'd shed. "You have to trust me, Lindsey. I'll find our son."

Dear Harlequin Intrigue Reader,

The recipe for a perfect Valentine's Day: chocolate, champagne—and four original romantic suspense titles from Harlequin Intrigue!

Our TOP SECRET BABIES promotion kicks off with Rita Herron's *Saving His Son* (#601). Devastated single mother Lindsey Payne suspects her child is alive and well—and being kept from her deliberately. The only man who'd be as determined as she is to find her child is Detective Gavin McCord—*if* he knew he'd fathered her missing baby….

In *Best-Kept Secrets* (#602) by Dani Sinclair, the tongues in MYSTERY JUNCTION are wagging about newcomer Jake Collins. Amy Thomas's first and only love has returned at last and she's ready to tell him the secret she's long kept hidden. But would revealing it suddenly put her life in jeopardy?

Our ON THE EDGE program continues with *Private Vows* (#603) by Sally Steward. A beautiful amnesiac is desperate to remember her past. Investigator Cole Grayson is desperate to keep it hidden. For if she remembers the truth, she'd never be his….

Bachelor Will Sheridan thinks he's found the perfect *Mystery Bride* (#604) in B.J. Daniels's latest romantic thriller. But the sexy and provocative Samantha Murphy is a female P.I. in the middle of a puzzling case when Will suddenly becomes her shadow. Now with desire distracting her and a child's life in the balance, Samantha and Will are about to discover the true meaning of "partnership"!

Next month more from TOP SECRET BABIES and ON THE EDGE, plus a 3-in-1 collection from some of your favorite authors and the launch of Sheryl Lynn's new McCLINTOCK COUNTRY miniseries.

Sincerely,

Denise O'Sullivan
Associate Senior Editor
Harlequin Intrigue

SAVING HIS SON

RITA HERRON

TORONTO • NEW YORK • LONDON
AMSTERDAM • PARIS • SYDNEY • HAMBURG
STOCKHOLM • ATHENS • TOKYO • MILAN • MADRID
PRAGUE • WARSAW • BUDAPEST • AUCKLAND

To Tashya for all your great suggestions!
Thanks for letting me write this one.

Rita

ISBN 0-373-22601-2

SAVING HIS SON

Copyright © 2001 by Rita B. Herron.

Visit us at www.eHarlequin.com

Printed in U.S.A.

ABOUT THE AUTHOR

Rita Herron is a teacher, workshop leader and storyteller who loves reading, writing and sharing stories with people of all ages. She has published two nonfiction books for adults on working and playing with children, and has won the Golden Heart Award for a young adult story. Rita believes that books taught her to dream, and she loves nothing better than sharing that magic with others. She lives with her "dream" husband and three children, two cats and a dog in Norcross, Georgia.

Books by Rita Herron

HARLEQUIN INTRIGUE
486—SEND ME A HERO
523—HER EYEWITNESS
556—FORGOTTEN LULLABY
601—SAVING HIS SON

HARLEQUIN AMERICAN ROMANCE
820—HIS-AND-HERS TWINS
*859—HAVE GOWN, NEED GROOM

*The Hartwell Hope Chests

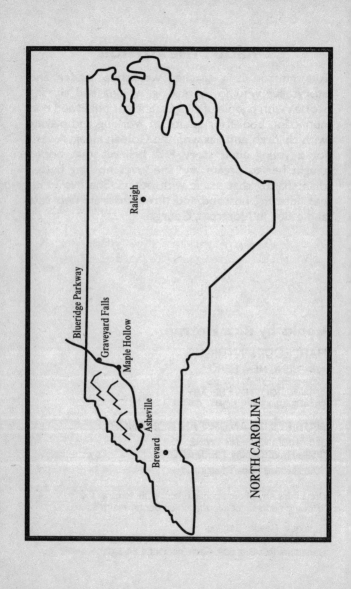

NORTH CAROLINA

Raleigh

Blueridge Parkway

Graveyard Falls

Maple Hollow

Asheville

Brevard

CAST OF CHARACTERS

Lindsey Payne—A woman who has loved only one man in her life—the same man who unknowingly gave her a son. But now their son is missing.

Gavin McCord—A man who thought he was protecting the love of his life by pushing her away. Did he push her into the arms of danger instead?

Dr. William Cross—An old-fashioned doctor who runs a small-town birthing clinic—is he hiding something?

Janet Quinn—The nurse who helped deliver Lindsey's baby, then disappeared. Could she have stolen Lindsey's child?

Andy Atkins—A mentally challenged orderly who claims another woman gave birth the same night as Lindsey. But is he reliable?

Lamar Forbes—The sheriff who insists his small town is a haven from big city crime—until someone tries to kill Lindsey Payne.

Christopher Little—A lawyer with a big bank account and a very closed mouth. How far would he go to protect his clients?

JoAnn Haney—Lindsey's best friend. She's desperate to have a baby—but how desperate?

Jim Faulkner—Lindsey's ex-husband. She put him in jail; is he out for revenge?

Yvonne & James Faulkner—Lindsey's ex's parents; they hated Lindsey for putting their son behind bars.

Danny Swain—A prisoner who threatened to get even with Gavin. Could he have orchestrated the kidnapping from his jail cell?

Dwight Johnson—His son died under Gavin's care—could he have taken Gavin's son as a replacement?

Dear Reader,

What is every woman's worst nightmare? To lose a child or have a child kidnapped.

Real-life stories about missing children are a common occurrence, yet the mystery, the suspense, the emotions are universal. Every time I see a newspaper article or TV clip or a picture of a missing child, my heart wrenches for the family. And each time, I hope for a happy ending.

Having three children of my own, I can't imagine missing any part of their lives—so my heart certainly went into writing *Saving His Son*. But in my version, you get the happy ending...plus a little romance!

Hope you enjoy.

Please write me at P.O. Box 921225, Norcross, GA 30092-1225 for updates on other releases.

Sincerely,

Rita

Chapter One

"Your baby is alive."

Lindsey Payne's hand trembled around the phone receiver as the hoarse voice faded into nothingness. It was the second time the person had called in two days, the fourth call this week. Could it be possible? Could her son really have survived?

"Who is this?" she finally croaked. "Why are you doing this to me?"

The harsh click of the phone cut her off, jarring her senses into a thousand frayed nerve endings. Just like the other times. Tears spilled out of her swollen eyes as grief consumed her. Her baby would have been six weeks old today. If he had lived.

She'd been so distraught in the hospital the doctor had prescribed sedatives, but by the end of the first week, she'd weaned herself from the drugs and the memories had surfaced. Blurred memories which raised questions in her mind. Someone had tried to kill her in the hospital. At the time she hadn't cared. She'd been in too much pain to fight.

Later, when she'd told the hospital staff, they claimed she'd been hallucinating. She'd pleaded with the local sheriff to listen, but he'd insisted nothing ever went wrong at Maple Hollow's birthing clinic. That she should try to move on with her life. And she'd tried.

Then the phone calls had started, making her wonder if her baby was alive. He was out there somewhere crying for her. Needing her.

Or maybe she was going crazy. Maybe someone was feeding off her grief, and she kept hanging on to their twisted words out of a misguided need for hope. But who would do such a horrid thing?

"Lindsey?" Her neighbor JoAnn stood in her den, her face pinched with worry. "I knocked but you didn't answer, so I got worried and used my key. Are you all right?"

Lindsey nodded, grateful for the numbness settling over her. "I'm fine, thanks for thinking of me."

JoAnn placed a basket of muffins on the sofa table behind her and moved into the doorway toward Lindsey. "Did you receive another phone call?"

JoAnn's intuition startled her. "Yes."

"I'm sorry, Linds," JoAnn's voice broke. "I don't know who would be so cruel. Maybe you should change your number."

Lindsey knotted her hands in her lap. "No, if the caller knows something about my baby, I want to talk to them. I just wish whoever it is would stay on the line long enough for the police to trace them."

The compassion in JoAnn's expression almost triggered another onslaught of tears. "Why don't you visit the class today for bike day? We're taking the kids on a picnic."

Lindsey remembered the excitement over bike day from her own special needs class the previous school year. She'd taken a year's leave of absence to stay home with her baby. Now, she wondered if she should return sooner. "It sounds like fun. Maybe I will come by later."

"I'll see you there then." JoAnn turned to leave, pausing in the shadowed hallway. "And Lindsey, try to eat something. You're getting way too thin."

Especially for someone who'd recently had a baby.

The unspoken words hung in the air between them. She and JoAnn had joked about the extra pounds Lindsey had gained during her pregnancy. She'd worried she wouldn't be able to shed them. So far, losing weight hadn't been a problem.

When JoAnn left, Lindsey headed to the shower, bystepping the white wicker bassinet she'd purchased for her infant's arrival home. The pale yellow blanket still lay folded at the foot of the mattress, the Winnie-the-Pooh mobile dangling above the eyelet headboard. She should move the bassinet to the nursery with the other baby furniture but couldn't bring herself to part with it yet. She'd planned to keep her son in her room at night so he'd be close by when he woke. Now, the empty cradle reminded her of her the aching void in her life.

She should at least move the bassinet to the den so it wouldn't be the first thing she saw every morning. Inhaling a calming breath, she hauled it to the front room, then hurried to shower. Visiting the school would do her good. The kids needed her. And she desperately needed to fill her time with something besides her own troubled thoughts.

The hot water felt heavenly on her skin as she washed the last strains of fatigue and tears from her face. After toweling off, she pulled on her robe and poured herself a cup of coffee, her gaze resting on the mail that had arrived the day before. The stack she'd been too apathetic to open. The sympathy cards she could no longer bear to read.

A pale blue envelope drew her eye, her stomach clenching at the distinct size and shape. Had someone sent her a congratulations card? Someone who didn't know about her loss...?

Her vision blurred as she ripped open the envelope and stared at the blue teddy-bear shape. Her baby's autopsy report had been placed inside. Blood type: O positive. It couldn't be—she had type A; Gavin, B.

The card fluttered to the floor as Lindsey doubled over. Could the hospital have made a mistake? If even the remotest possibility existed that her son was still alive, she had to find him. An image of Gavin's handsome, dark features flashed into her mind, the anguish of his parting words even more visceral since she'd lost their son. No, she couldn't turn to Gavin.

She'd go to the sheriff, beg him one more time to take her seriously and investigate her son's death.

THIRTY MINUTES LATER, Sheriff Forbes greeted her with a nod, the wrinkles around his eyes more prominent beneath the glare of the overhead light. His thick gray hair stood in tufts on his head, his bushy eyebrows due for a trim. He needed to retire, to be fishing with his grandchildren somewhere, not running the town. "How're you doing this morning, Ms. Payne?"

"I'm okay, but I need to talk to you."

The sheriff gestured toward his office, grabbing a cup of coffee off the scarred linoleum counter as he passed. He offered Lindsey some, but she declined, knowing the caffeine would only add to her shakiness.

"What can I do for you this morning?" Forbes lowered his wiry frame into the vinyl chair behind his cluttered desk, folding one leg to rest across his knee.

Lindsey lay the card on the jumbled mess. "I received another call this morning."

His eyebrow shot up with concern. "Did you recognize the voice? Was it a man's or a woman's?"

"I couldn't tell, it was too muffled. Then I received this autopsy report in the mail."

The sheriff wrapped a handkerchief around his fingers, opened the envelope and scanned the contents. "I'll have it checked out, but I doubt we can trace it. The card is generic, no return address. Probably won't be any prints either."

"Even if you can't trace the card, the autopsy proves my baby is alive," Lindsey argued.

The sheriff's gray eyes filled with pity. "It doesn't prove anything, except that someone's playing a sick joke on you, Ms. Payne. For all we know this report isn't even legitimate. Someone could have stolen the autopsy report or doctored it to make you think this baby wasn't yours."

"But why would someone go to such lengths? And doesn't that report make you wonder if something is wrong?"

"It makes me want to find the creep and teach him a lesson for planting false hopes in your head." He rose, hooking one thumb in his belt loop. "Look, I've known William Cross since we were kids. He's the best doctor in these parts. There's no way he'd lie to you about something this important." His voice grew more confident. "Why, he's delivered half the town and no one's ever had a complaint."

"That doesn't mean something didn't happen that night," Lindsey said with conviction.

"Even William was upset over losing your little boy. I haven't seen him so distraught since Mrs. Cornell miscarried her twins." His foot jerked up and down. "He hates it when deliveries don't go smoothly, but he's only a doctor. Sometimes the good Lord works in mysterious ways. We have to accept his plan.''

Frustration swelled in Lindsey's chest. ''So you won't consider the possibility this report isn't real?''

The sheriff's grave expression infuriated her. ''There's nothing to investigate. I don't for a minute think William would tamper with medical records. He could lose his license.''

''What about the medical examiner? Isn't he related to Dr. Cross?''

''Yeah, but you're way out on a limb. If something had happened with your baby, there'd be witnesses. Don't you think someone would come forward?''

''There is a witness. The person who keeps calling me. Maybe they're afraid to come forward.''

Forbes clicked his teeth. ''Ain't a soul in these parts afraid of Doc Cross. Just listen to yourself, sounds like you lived in that big city too long. Crazy things like you're supposing don't happen in Maple Hollow.'' He moved around the desk to comfort her, but Lindsey backed away, almost stumbling over the small bookcase in the corner.

''Why don't you let Doc give you some nerve pills or something to help you through this?''

Lindsey turned and headed to the door. ''I don't need pills. I want answers.'' Without even looking back, she slammed the door, then hurried outside. Heat rolled off the pavement in waves, sucking the air from her lungs.

But she couldn't give up.

How many times had she lain awake in the darkness thinking of her son? She could almost feel him in her arms. She could hear him crying for her, she knew he was out there somewhere. He needed her. And if Forbes didn't intend to help her find the truth, she'd find someone who would.

Gavin McCord's handsome face flashed before her. Emotionless, calm, a tough cop—afraid of nothing, He would never let anything stop him from doing his job. She wrapped her arms around herself, aching for his comfort, but he was the last person on earth she wanted to ask for help. Although he hadn't known about the baby, when she'd tried breaking the news about her pregnancy, he'd cut her off as if he'd guessed her news. His parting words haunted her. "I'm not cut out for marriage, Linds. Don't want a wife or kids—ever."

Well, that was fine. She didn't want a husband, either. She'd had one, and he'd been trouble. First she'd discovered his gambling problem, then he'd embezzled funds from his own law firm. When she'd divorced him and decided to testify against him, he'd tried to kill her. Gavin had been assigned to protect her. That last night before she'd testified, they'd both crossed some invisible line…they'd slept together and made a baby. Only Gavin hadn't wanted a relationship…

She refused to beg for Gavin's love. But she needed his expertise right now and she *would* beg him to find her son if she had to.

"ANOTHER CASE well done." Gavin's superior, Lieutenant Peterson, slapped him on the back.

Gavin shrugged. "Yeah, one dealer down. A zillion more to go." He rolled his left shoulder to relieve the throbbing sensation that had escalated in the last hour. He'd taken a bad punch, had a few bruises to show for his work.

"You're getting cynical in your old age," Peterson said with a wry laugh.

"Goes with the territory." Gavin bit off the end of a stale eclair, frowning as the white creme squished out the sides and dribbled over his fingers.

Peterson dropped a folder on his desk. "Get that report on my desk before you leave, McCord. Then what the hell, take a day or two off. You deserve it."

"Don't go overboard," Gavin drawled sarcastically, wiping his fingers on a napkin. "I've only been under-cover for three weeks, with no sleep I might add."

"You do look like hell," the lieutenant added.

Gavin rubbed a hand over three weeks' growth of beard. Too tired to get up, he lifted his booted feet, planted them on the top of his desk and leaned back in his chair as Peterson loped out. He thumbed through the papers, stacking a few of them in his To Do pile, when a plain manila envelope caught his eye. He picked it up and studied the envelope. No return address. No postage meter or stamp. Hmm, odd.

His curiosity piqued, he ripped it open and removed a sheet of paper, his eyes narrowing when he noticed letters cut from a newspaper forming the words *An Eye For An Eye*. "Son of a bitch," he muttered. "Who in the hell sent this?"

Not that he didn't have enemies. Jeez, the problem was he had too many.

LINDSEY STOOD outside the Raleigh police department, her stomach twisting.

Gavin might not relish seeing her or hearing she'd given birth to his baby, but he thought like a cop, acted like a cop. He would take her case. She'd make it plain she hadn't come to him to resume a personal relationship, the same way he'd made it plain he didn't want one with her. Other than that one night of incredible sex.

But she wouldn't repeat her mistakes.

And if Gavin hated her because she hadn't told him about their son, well…she'd get over it.

Right now, her son was the only person who mattered.

GAVIN WAS STILL contemplating who might have sent the unnerving note, *An Eye For An Eye,* when the door screeched open.

"Someone here to see you, McCord."

All thoughts of the anonymous note flew from his mind when Lindsey Payne stepped through the door—what was she doing here? He thought she'd disappeared from his life forever.

Peterson waved her in and left, and Gavin clamped his jaw tight, fighting his gut reaction—lust. Need. Want. For a woman he couldn't have.

She moved toward him and his breath hitched in his throat. She wore her silky blond hair pulled back in a ponytail, accentuating the starkness of her high cheekbones. Dark smudges curved beneath her eyes and a denim jumper hung on her slender frame as if she'd lost weight. Her pale complexion alarmed him. Even so, she was still the most beautiful woman he'd ever laid eyes on. He'd dreamed about her too many nights to even count.

Lindsey tipped her head, her smile weak. "Gavin."

He straightened, instinctively aware something was very, very wrong. Her once vibrant eyes were hollow and empty, sending his protective instincts kicking in. Even when Lindsey had been threatened by her ex, she'd been a fighter. The strange mixture of courage and vulnerability had been one reason he'd been unable to resist her that last night. Now, she looked almost fragile.

"What's wrong, Lindsey? Faulkner hasn't been harassing you, has he?"

She sank into the hard wooden chair. "No, not exactly."

Gavin filled a cup with water and handed her the cup. "Here, drink this and take a deep breath. You look awfully pale."

"I'm okay." Lindsey accepted the glass and drank, her hands shaking.

He gave her a moment to gather her thoughts. "Why are you here, Lindsey?"

She bit down on her lower lip, a small nervous laugh escaping her. "Don't worry, Gavin. This is not a social call. I didn't come back—"

"I didn't mean it like that." His heart squeezed at her cryptic tone. The Lindsey he knew never sounded cynical—not like him.

She inhaled a fortifying breath and he gestured toward the door. "Do you want to go somewhere and talk?"

Her brown eyes studied him pensively, and he remembered too late she'd asked him the same question the last time she'd seen him. He'd just testified against a murderer, only the man he'd testified against had threatened retribution to him and everyone Gavin knew. He'd immediately relived his childhood fears. Only this time he wasn't the kid. He was the man whose loved ones had been threatened. He'd panicked and told her he didn't want her. Didn't want a relationship. Marriage. A family. Ever.

"Your office is fine. I came here…to ask for your help." Her voice sounded stronger, but her fingers fumbled over the handles of her leather purse as if she were reconsidering the idea.

He stroked his beard with his chin, faintly aware her

hand followed the movement. "What kind of help do you need? Money? Legal advice?"

"No." Her eyes darted toward the closed door. "I need your services as a detective."

"You came here to report a crime?"

"Sort of…yes." Her back stiffened as if she didn't know where to begin.

He'd seen the same nervous reaction when she'd confessed about her ex-husband's illegal activities. "Take your time, and tell me what happened."

She nodded, seemingly grateful for his encouragement. "I…I had a baby a few weeks ago."

His heart thundered in his chest, his mind automatically ticking away the months.

The air caught in his lungs.

"But the doctor told me my baby died. I think he may have lied," she continued in a shaky voice. "And I want you to help me find him. Or at least find out the truth. To find out if my baby is alive."

The air caught in Gavin's lungs. He leaned against the front of his desk and folded his arms. "Tell me something, Linds."

She lifted her heart-shaped face to stare into his eyes. "What do you want to know?"

"Was the baby Faulkner's, or…was he mine?"

Chapter Two

Lindsey bit down on her bottom lip, her stomach churning. All the way to the precinct she'd stewed over what to tell Gavin. Should she lie? Tell him the baby was her ex's?

Gavin had claimed emotions muddied a man's judgment. Would it be better if he didn't know the truth?

"Lindsey?"

She was a terrible liar. And if he knew the baby was his, maybe he'd search even harder for him.

He leaned so close his breath brushed her cheek. "Is the baby Faulkner's or mine?"

She looked into his eyes, the dark smoldering depths lurking with questions, and she heard the tension in his husky voice. He deserved to know the truth.

"The baby is yours."

His dark gaze pierced her to the core. "You're sure?"

She nodded slowly, her voice low. "He was six weeks early." She glanced down at her hands and knotted them in front of her. "The last time I slept with Jim was the night before I signed the final divorce papers. He came by to try to make amends. I felt guilty over our failed marriage." Lindsey shrugged, trying to remember all the reasons she'd given in to Jim that night. The next day he'd threatened her, had thought he'd won her loyalty back, but she'd seen through his manipulation and felt ashamed for letting him use her. She had to testify against him.

"When was that night?"

"Two months before…before that night with you. Besides, Jim always took extra precautions. He was adamant about that…. He…didn't want children."

Silence descended upon them with a chilling bleakness. Gavin dropped his gaze to the floor, then leaned back, half sitting, half propping himself on the front of his desk. His dark blue shirt stretched tight across his massive shoulders. "Why…Why didn't you tell me?"

"I tried to. I called and left messages but you never returned my calls." Anger, swift and hard, pressed against Lindsey's vocal chords. "I didn't expect anything from you, Gavin, not money, not support, certainly not marriage. I know we were both upset about Jim finding the safe house and we let things get out of control. Still, I thought you had a right to know. But you avoided me and when I came to the courthouse…"

"Jesus." He reached for her, his expression pained, but she shrank away. "I had no idea that's why you'd come."

Lindsey stood and backed away from him, wrapping her arms around herself, her voice brittle, "No, don't…don't touch me, Gavin. Don't make excuses." She let the anger and pain from all those lonely months drive her. "The day I finally cornered you at the courthouse, you wouldn't even talk to me. I'd even written you a letter, but you said you didn't want to see me again, that you didn't want marriage or babies. *Ever.* So I threw the note in the trash outside the courtroom that day."

His gaze jerked back to hers, pinning her with the force

of his emotions. Hurt, anger, remorse. He started to speak, but Lindsey cut him off.

"I didn't come here to renew our relationship. I know the one night we shared meant nothing to you, and I didn't intend to trap you into marriage or make you accept responsibility for a baby you didn't want."

A vein pulsed in his forehead, but he didn't argue.

"I'm not asking anything from you now except to find out if my son is alive."

"Our son," he said in a deadly calm voice.

"Yes, our son." She raised her chin a notch, forcing herself not to think about the pain he might be feeling. "All I want is for you to help me find my son and bring him home. Then we'll be out of your life. Forever—just like you requested the day I tried to tell you I was pregnant."

His shoulders went rigid and for a brief minute, fear knotted her stomach. She'd seen Gavin wrestle her ex-husband the night he'd attacked her. But Gavin had never been anything but gentle toward her. He rolled his shoulder as if it hurt, the overly long strands of his hair brushing his collar. He looked as if he hadn't slept in days, too. She wondered what kind of case he'd been working on, then felt like kicking herself for caring.

As if he sensed her fear, he suddenly dropped his gaze and walked around to his desk, sat down in his chair and dropped his head forward into his hands. Lindsey caught herself swaying and sank back in the chair. The sound of the clock ticking droned in the background, amplifying the tension between them.

He fiddled with a pen and some paper, avoiding her gaze, then finally replied in a low, controlled tone, "All right. Start from the beginning and tell me everything that happened after you left Raleigh." When his chin lifted,

Lindsey saw the pain in his eyes but she also recognized the calm, take-charge cop who'd protected her after her husband's attack. The man who'd won her heart with his brooding macho manner. The man who'd broken it later. Had she made a mistake by coming to him for help?

GAVIN'S HEAD throbbed from trying to contain the rage building inside him. But he'd seen the flicker of fear in Lindsey's eyes and shame had filled him. Her first husband had been a violent man. He had to channel his anger into something productive. Even if he died a slow painful death on the inside.

He had a baby. A son.

A little boy who'd died or been kidnapped before Gavin had even known he existed. He'd left Lindsey alone to deal with the pregnancy, the birth of his child, the baby's death. He'd sent her away to protect her, yet he'd left her vulnerable and unprotected.

"Tell me everything."

Lindsey twisted her hands in her lap. "My baby died a few hours after he was born. At least the doctor said he did."

"What do you mean, the doctor *said* the baby died? Why don't you believe him? Did you see the baby? Did he look healthy?"

"Yes, I held him, but they whisked him away because there were complications."

"With the baby?"

"With me, with both of us," she whispered, staring at her hands. "I went into premature labor. I developed eclampsia and the fetus was in distress so they had to perform an emergency C-section." Her hands stilled, straightened, curled to dig into her palms as she struggled with the memories. Seconds later, she continued in a shaky voice, "I had a boy. But I was drowsy from the anesthesia and couldn't stay awake. The next thing I remember, I woke up and the nurse told me he...he didn't make it." She paused again, then met his gaze, her big brown eyes pleading with him to believe her. "I was so hurt, so stunned I couldn't believe what she was saying. Then I went into shock."

His throat tightened.

"The doctor gave me a sedative, and I guess it knocked me out, but later that night, I woke up and saw someone in my room. A man...he tried to kill me."

His head snapped up. "What?"

"Someone tried to smother me with a pillow. I thought it was the doctor at first—"

"You think the doctor tried to kill you?"

"Yes...no, I don't know." Lindsey sighed and shifted in her seat, then tucked an errant strand of hair behind her delicate ear before continuing. "All I remember is that he was wearing surgical scrubs."

"Did you recognize him? A voice maybe? His eyes?"

"I didn't see his face, only shadows. It was dark and I was groggy from the pain medicine." Her face lifted, her eyes big and wide. "But the staff claimed no one had been in my room. They insisted I was hallucinating."

Which was possible. He'd seen firsthand the bizarre effects drugs had on people. But Lindsey was normally stable, not an irrational female who invented things.

She fumbled with her purse again, her hands trembling as she removed a paper and handed it to him. "A week after I was released from the hospital I started receiving strange phone calls telling me my baby is still alive. This came in the mail today."

He reached for the file, surprised to find an autopsy report. "You hadn't seen the report before?"

"No, I asked about the autopsy, but the doctor never showed me the report. He claimed my baby died of heart failure. But the blood type doesn't match mine or yours."

A knot of anxiety tightened Gavin's stomach as he studied her expression. Her story seemed bizarre—could it be true?

"I think someone switched my baby with the infant that didn't make it. And they tried to cover up the switch."

"Sounds pretty sinister. Why would someone switch babies?"

A defeated expression darkened her already dull eyes. "Maybe someone kidnapped my baby or adopted him out. Or maybe someone wanted to hurt me or get back at me…" Her voice broke, a wave of tears gushing out.

He ran a hand over his beard stubble, fighting the urge to fold her in his arms. When another tear slipped down her cheek, he lost the battle and actually reached forward. She stiffened immediately and he dropped his hand, trying to decide if she hadn't accepted the truth about the infant's death or if the odd events could have happened the way she described. If their child could be alive…

"Did you go to the local police?"

"Yes, but the sheriff in Maple Hollow is as old as Methuselah. He's been best friends with Dr. Cross since grade school." She pressed her fingers to her temple. "He assured me nothing strange or illegal ever occurs in Maple Hollow. That Dr. Cross would never lie to a patient."

"You don't believe him?"

She shook her head. "I'm not imagining the phone calls, Mac. Or the fact that someone sent me this report."

Lindsey had slipped and used the nickname she'd whispered that night in bed, but she didn't even realize it. He stared at his dirty boots. He'd break her heart if he investigated and discovered the doctor had told the truth.

But they were talking about his son here. How could he not believe her? Not investigate?

He shifted, agitated. "Maple Hollow isn't in my jurisdiction, Linds. If the sheriff doesn't suspect any wrongdoing, he won't welcome a stranger poking around. Besides, missing persons are usually referred to the FBI."

She stood so abruptly her chair teetered backwards and hit the wall with a loud thump. "Then you won't help me?"

Panic rolled through him at the wild, stricken look in her eyes. "I didn't say that."

"But you're not going to, are you? You think I'm some irrational female. That I'm crazy, that I'm making this up."

"I never said that either." He clenched his jaw, lowering his voice to a soothing pitch. "I've never known you to be irrational." And he hadn't. The woman was made of steel—she taught handicapped kids, for God's sake. And she'd stood up to her ex-husband in court and in front of the man's family. She had to be tough. But he'd be crazy to get tangled up with her again. Hell, he'd never gotten over her the first time.

"Will you help me?"

The desperation in her voice tore at his soul. "Of course, I'll help you. You're talking about our child." In his mind he pictured her round with his baby. The pain was so intense his knees almost buckled. "Did Faulkner know you were pregnant?"

Lindsey paused, the strain of the day obviously wearing on her. "No."

"You're sure? Have you had any contact with his family at all?"

Lindsey sighed. "His mother phoned me a few times before the trial and asked me not to go through with the charges. Then she called once or twice afterward to try and persuade me to recant my testimony. But after I moved from Raleigh, I never heard from them.''

''So, they didn't know about the baby?''

''I don't think so. I moved the day after I saw you at the courthouse.'' She toyed with a fingernail. ''Besides, I never told anyone the name of the baby's father.''

Including him. Their gazes met, held. He gritted his jaw, the pain once again almost unbearable. Lindsey threaded her fingers together in her lap, looking tired and drawn and too damned thin.

''What about the staff, you said they didn't see anyone go in your room?''

''That's right. Only, I went back the week after I was released from the hospital to talk to Janet, the nurse who helped with my delivery, but she'd taken a leave of absence.''

His voice softened. ''Even nurses go on vacation, Linds.''

Her face jerked toward him and he saw fear in her eyes, the same fear he'd seen the night he'd crossed the line from duty to pleasure. The night they'd created a son.

''Maybe, but it seemed odd that no one in town knew where Janet went on vacation. Maple Hollow's so small everyone usually knows everyone else's business.''

He mulled over that piece of information, trying to piece together a reason someone might kidnap their baby and make her think the child had died, but guilt slammed into him. If he'd been there to take care of her, maybe he could have prevented her premature labor, or if he'd been at the hospital, he could have seen his son himself, protected him...

''What about the other members of the staff?''

''A terrible explosion occurred that night at a local factory. Except for Dr. Cross and the nurse, all the emergency workers were called to help.'' She paused.

''Something else odd, happened, too. I heard a girl crying in one of the other rooms at the clinic.''

''Another patient maybe?''

She threw up her hands in frustration and paced to the window. ''I thought so, but the doctor claimed I was the only patient that night, that I imagined the other woman.''

He narrowed his eyes. ''You're sure you heard someone else?''

''I'm positive. You know the kids I taught said I had eyes and *ears* in the back of my head.''

He smiled at the memory. A natural with children, Lindsey would have been a wonderful mother. ''Could the woman have been someone from the explosion?''

''No, they transferred all the injuries to the county hospital. The clinic isn't equipped for major medical emergencies.''

Gavin stood, walked to the window beside her and stared out at the busy street. Thick traffic crawled by, horns honked intermittently, the wail of a siren burst into the strained silence. Sun splashed off the concrete, flickering from a beautiful blue sky. But Gavin had never felt more dismal in his life.

''What's the sheriff's take on things?''

''He thinks Dr. Cross invented medicine. He can't believe anything bad about him.''

''But you're convinced Cross is involved?''

''I don't know what to think, Mac, but I *feel* my son is out there, I hear him crying for me at night in my sleep. I have to know the truth about what happened.''

His gaze dropped to her arms where she'd cradled them around her. His voice softened with sympathy. ''Even if it turns out our baby died like the doctor said? Do you want to know that, too, Lindsey?''

''Yes, even then.'' Lindsey choked back the tears clogging her throat. ''Whatever you find out, I'll deal with it. But knowing the truth is the only way I can put this ordeal behind me and get on with my life.''

Gavin nodded, his own throat thick. ''I'll talk to Peterson. I'm due a few days vacation. Then we'll get out of here.'' She nodded and he crossed the room and forced himself to leave without touching Lindsey when he wanted to drag her in his arms and hold her, apologize for letting her down, promise her everything would be all right.

But he'd learned the hard way he couldn't make promises he might not be able to keep.

GAVIN PULLED INTO into the parking spot in front of his apartment, climbed out and waited on Lindsey to meet him at the door, a bad feeling lingering in his gut. The lieutenant had given him leave, no problem. His partner, Simon Durango, had agreed he should go. But the sight of Lindsey reminded him of the lonely hole in his life. The long days and nights he'd spent remembering her touch, the feel of her lips on his, the feel of her naked body beneath his. He'd admired her strength, had needed it that night they'd made love as much as she'd needed his.

He'd never gotten over her. He probably never would.

But he'd hurt her terribly. She must hate him. And who could blame her?

''Gavin?''

He jerked his head toward the shrubbery lining the far end of the complex, scanning the lot. ''Come on, it shouldn't take me long to pack.'' He unlocked the door and gestured for her to go in but she stood ramrod straight.

Those dark eyes watched him warily. "I can wait out here."

"At least come in and sit down," he said softly. "You look like you're going to collapse."

"Thanks, Mac." Sarcasm laced her voice. "I'd forgotten how charming you can be."

He winced. She'd been feisty and determined to do the right thing by testifying, regardless of the consequences to her safety. He'd wanted her the minute he'd laid eyes on her, but he'd fought the attraction, knowing she was off-limits.

"Do you mind if I use your phone while you pack?"

He shook his head, hating the awkwardness between them but knowing he'd drawn the boundaries. "It's—"

"I know where the phone is," Lindsey said quietly.

He nodded curtly, remembering the night they'd spent together. When her husband had discovered the location of her safe house, his hired hands had come after her and they'd tried to kill her. Gavin had apprehended them just in time to save her. They'd rushed to another safe house, an isolated cabin in the mountains. Emotions had been high, adrenaline pumping from the danger. Things had gotten out of hand. They'd made love. And he'd planted the seed that had become their son.

Now Lindsey had returned because their baby was missing.

A wave of nausea hit him but he welcomed it. After deserting them and leaving Lindsey vulnerable and alone, he *deserved* the pain.

Lindsey turned away, so he headed toward his bedroom to pack. She was absolutely right. They couldn't get personally involved again. He'd go to Maple Hollow, check out her story and pray he could help her discover the truth about their baby. But he'd keep his distance. Because he didn't deserve her or a child, and this time when he walked away, it would have to be final.

LINDSEY SURVEYED Gavin's apartment as she punched in JoAnn's telephone number. Two cardboard boxes with half-eaten pizzas were piled on top of a half dozen empty soda cans. A couple of crushed beer cans lay in the corner as if he'd tossed them toward the trash can and missed. Dust covered his collection of trains on the oak bookcase.

He obviously hadn't been home much lately or hadn't been taking care of his place, the same way he hadn't been taking care of himself. His unshaven face, long hair, rumpled jeans and shirt attested to the fact he'd been out on an assignment. Not that he'd ever been neat, but the dust on his beloved trains definitely hinted he'd been distracted.

A beep interrupted her reverie, and she realized JoAnn's message machine had played all the way through. "Hey, Jo, it's me. Sorry I didn't make it by the school but something came up. I'll talk to you later."

She hung up the phone and rubbed her neck, then stretched out on the sofa, ignoring the temptation to tidy his room. Exhausted, she closed her eyes, fighting the emotions coursing through her. The shower kicked on, and she envisioned Gavin standing naked under the hot water. She could see his dark hair full of lather, water trickling down the wide planes of his chest, soap bubbles beading on his taut thighs…

She smiled, letting the image erase the haunting memories for the last year. Gavin had been the only man she'd slept with other than her husband. She didn't give herself lightly, didn't jump from one man's bed to another. But during the weeks she and Gavin had spent together, she'd recognized a strength of character that had been missing in her husband. Maybe it had been the circumstances, the danger, the close quarters, but she'd fallen for him quick and hard. And the spiral downward after his dismissal had been devastating.

WHO WAS JOE? Gavin hadn't meant to eavesdrop. He'd simply picked up the phone to check his voice mail when Lindsey had spoken the man's name. Was he a new boyfriend?

He tugged on a pair of well-worn jeans and a black T-shirt, pulled on dark socks and his boots, then jerked the ends of his black hair back into a low ponytail, securing it with a leather tie. The discoloration streaking the side of his temple and his bloodshot eye made him look like a hellion, and the cut at the hairline of his forehead should have had stitches. Not exactly the image he wanted in front of the woman he still lusted after. Or her boyfriend.

For the first time in his life, he wondered what a child would think about him. *His* child. He certainly didn't look like anyone's father.

Feeling edgy, he tossed some clothes into a duffel, grabbed his shaving kit and toiletries, checked his gun and stashed some extra ammo in his bag. Not that he planned to use the Glock, but he never went anywhere without his weapon.

SOMEONE WAS watching her.

Darkness bathed the cold room and shadows streaked the whitewashed walls in hazy diagonal lines. The scent of despair hung heavy in the air. The steady drip of the IV. Fresh tears sprang to Lindsey's eyes and ran down her face. She wanted to scream, but tears clogged her throat. A slight shuffling sound startled her. Someone's feet dragging. She wasn't alone.

Janet, bringing her baby.

No, her baby...was gone. God, noooo...

The sound again. She turned her head. A sliver of light. The door closed. A shadow blocked the doorway. The doctor? Breathing rattled through the claustrophobic room. The shadow inched toward her. Her eyelids felt heavy. She tried to distinguish a face. She had to talk to the doctor. Force him to tell her where he'd taken her baby. Admit that the nurse had made some awful mistake.

He was holding something. A pillow. A chill slithered up her spine. She tried to pull herself from sleep. The pillow closed over her face. Pressed against her eyes. Blocked the air from her lungs. She heaved and tried to kick. But she was so tired.

And just as the inky darkness swallowed her, she heard a baby crying...

Chapter Three

Lindsey jerked upright, her heart hammering in her chest.
The sun had set while she'd slept, and early evening shadows engulfed the musty room. Blinking furiously, she finally focused and realized Gavin stood beside her. Relief
poured through her. But the silhouette of his handsome
face did nothing to alleviate her anxiety over the nightmare. And over seeing him again.

"Bad dream?"

She nodded.

"About that night?"

She nodded again and brushed her hair away from her
face. "I could hear our baby crying for me."

He stood so still, studied her with such anguish that
Lindsey ached to touch him. To feel some sort of stability
in her rocky world. He had shaved and showered and
smelled like soap and that minty aftershave she'd always
loved. His damp ponytail was infuriatingly sexy and his
bruised eye simply added to his dangerous appearance,
the kind that twisted a woman's insides with fear and
want.

Irritated that he still made her ache for him, she drew
back. "You should have made some noise or something."

"I was afraid I'd startle you."

"It's been a long day." She fingercombed her hair, then stood and brushed at her dress. "Are you ready?"

His dark eyebrows shot up. "Are you sure *you're* ready? You look as if you need a good night's sleep before driving."

"What I need is to find my baby." She moved toward the door. "And the quicker the better, so we can both get back to our own lives." Separately.

He frowned, then grabbed his duffel bag and headed to the door. "All right. Let's go."

She nodded, wondering at her sanity for asking him to her home. At least now she had no memories of him in her rental house. But once he stepped inside, his image and scent would linger in every corner. Then how would she ever be able to forget him?

HOURS LATER they drove past a neighborhood that could have been lifted from the set of *Andy Griffith,* then veered onto a side street which curved slightly around the mountain. Lindsey stopped by the cemetery, but Gavin shook his head, not yet ready to face the tiny gravemarker which marked his son's fleeting existence. When they'd stopped for coffee at a small diner, she'd bought fresh flowers from a stand outside the café. He watched in agony now as she lay the beautiful flowers on the small plot, her soft sobs wrenching in their sweetness.

He had to find out if the baby in the grave was his son—they could exhume the body. But he couldn't justify disturbing the sanctity of the child's grave without definite proof of foul play. Judging from Lindsey's emotional state, he didn't think she was ready for the suggestion either.

After what seemed like an eternity, she returned to her car and they drove down a dirt road, finally stopping at the end of the narrow drive where a tiny white house sat bordered by a picket fence, a whiskey barrel full of pansies and a front porch with a porch swing. Gavin instantly pictured a tricycle and kiddie pool in the front yard, Lindsey wearing a Little League Mom's shirt holding a baby on her hip. A picnic table on the back deck, lazy Sunday afternoons, a bunch of rugrats running through the sprinkler. His son sporting a baseball hat.

His son.

Lindsey thought that night with her hadn't meant anything to him. Hell, it had meant too much.

All the more reason he and Lindsey didn't belong together.

He'd seen too much meanness in his life. He couldn't take his kid fishing like Andy had Opie and pretend the world was a good place.

His gaze swept the property and he frowned. Situated off the main turnpike, the cabin was isolated and tucked into the woods with a thick bed of trees backing the property. He tried to remember the distance between her house and the last one they'd passed. At least a mile. Too far to yell for help if she were in trouble. And those woods would make an excellent hiding spot for someone who meant her harm. He kept his headlights on while she walked up the porch steps and opened the door. Thank God, she did use a key.

He killed his engine and followed her. When he went inside her house, he felt as if he'd suddenly come home. The scent of lilac and something that smelled faintly like baby powder drifted to him. Lindsey faltered beside a small bassinet, and she lay one hand on top of a baby blanket. A tiny white bunny rattler stood propped inside the baby bed, a miniature squeaky toy in the shape of a boat at the foot.

His gut tightened painfully, his feet refusing to move. He didn't know what he'd expected—that she'd disposed of all the baby paraphernalia, maybe. But the sight of the empty baby bed and toys was almost more than he could bear. He couldn't imagine the depth of Lindsey's pain. His own immobilized him.

He lay his hand over the small train whistle in his pocket, the one momento he kept from childhood. His mother had given it to him on one of their trips. She'd told him to blow on it if he ever got lost and she'd know where to find him. He wished his son had a whistle now.

"I should move the bassinet to the nursery with the other stuff," Lindsey said in a low voice, gesturing toward a closed doorway in the hall. "But I...I can't. I feel like if I put the bassinet away, I'm totally giving up hope that our baby is alive."

Gavin's throat completely closed so he simply nodded that he understood.

Lindsey slowly faced him, obviously struggling for composure. "Are you hungry? I can fix us soup or a sandwich before you check into a hotel."

He'd thought he might be staying at her house, but he understood her need for distance—her house seemed too small for both of them. The only spare bedroom was probably the one she'd converted into a nursery. He certainly couldn't bring himself to sleep in there...not without his son.

"Gavin, do you want to eat?"

He hated to put her to work. Then again, she looked as if she needed something to do to take her mind off her sorrow. "Sure. Whatever you've got is fine."

She drew in a deep breath, then slipped into the kitchen.

He surveyed the room. A blue ruffled sofa with mauve throw pillows faced a small TV and entertainment center.

CDs were stacked haphazardly on a pine end table, her favorite Bonnie Raitt CD on top. Decorating and teaching magazines littered a Shaker-style coffee table, with two additions he'd never seen in her apartment in Raleigh— parenting magazines, and a book of baby names.

Tension thrummed through him, her pleas all too real. He stepped in the kitchen doorway. "Lindsey?"

Lindsey's soft voice penetrated the silence, "Yes."

He slowly raised his gaze to hers, grimacing at the pain in her eyes. "Did you give our baby a name?"

"Cory," she said in a shaky whisper. "I named him Cory Adam." She paused and he sucked in a sharp breath. "My dad's name was Adam. I hope you don't mind."

He shook his head. His last name was McCord—she'd taken part of his name and given it to their son even though he had sent her away.

Lindsey turned back to the stove and he sat at the table, hurt and anger rolling through him in waves. There was no way he could sleep tonight until he talked to the doctor who'd delivered his son. He'd stop at the hospital before he found a hotel. Could Lindsey be right? Could someone have lied about their baby? Could their son, Cory, still be alive?

THE SCENT of alcohol and antiseptics assaulted Gavin as he entered the small hospital, reminding him of the night he'd rushed Rodney Johnson to the ER. The boy had been in trouble and Gavin had thought he could help him. Instead, the teen had dogged him right into a bust and been shot in the crossfire.

"Dr. Cross isn't here," the red-haired receptionist said from behind a small window.

Damn, he should have called. "What time will he be in tomorrow?"

"Around nine. He has rounds over at County first."

"What about Janet Quinn?"

"She's not here either." Impatience flared in her voice. "Is there anything I can do to help you? Is there an emergency?"

"No, I wanted to talk to them about Lindsey Payne."

The woman's eyes widened perceptibly. "Why are you asking questions about Miss Payne?"

He decided to use a personal angle. "I'm a friend, and I've been worried about her since she lost the baby."

The woman's expression immediately turned sympathetic. "I know what you mean. She took the news so hard, poor thing."

"Were you here the night she delivered?"

"No, we had a terrible explosion that night at the plastic factory in town. Everybody but Janet and Doc Cross had to help at County. Must have been sixty injuries."

"Lindsey was here several days. Did you treat her at all?"

"Oh, yes. I pulled late shift the next two nights. Wound up sitting with Ms. Payne until her sedatives took effect. She was so distraught." She pursed her lips, shaking her head back and forth. "Poor thing, so alone. The baby's daddy didn't even show up."

Gavin gritted his teeth, fresh guilt assaulting him. He considered telling her he was the father, but she saved him by continuing, "Frankly, I think the girl had a breakdown myself. Don't blame her, bless her heart. She claimed some crazy things after she lost the baby. I think she ought to see a shrink."

Gavin had heard enough. He glanced at the clock and the near-empty facility and realized there wasn't much more he could do until morning. Tomorrow he'd return with Lindsey and ask for a tour of the place. He'd question the doctor and gauge his reactions. For now, though, he'd find the hotel, call Simon and tell him to run a check on this missing nurse, Janet Quinn.

A few minutes later, he pulled up to the local sheriff's office, but discovered it was empty. He'd hit another dead end. Scrubbing his hand over his face, he cursed silently. Obviously the police department operated on a nine-to-five schedule. Didn't they have crime after dark?

Frustrated, he drove toward the small hotel he'd seen when they'd driven into town. Seeing the white-haired little man who ran the place, he tried to imagine someone in Maple Hollow doing the things Lindsey had described. Faking an autopsy report, telling her her baby had died when it was alive, but the images didn't fit.

The furnishings in the small room were sparse; a double bed with a faded orange flowered spread, a battered maple dresser, a bathroom with yellowed tile and a pea-green shower curtain hanging askew. He sank onto the double bed, not surprised when the shaky bed squeaked, the mattress bowing with his weight. Lying on his back, he crossed his ankles and folded his hands beneath his head and stared at a cobweb in the corner as the day's revelations paraded across his mind. He had a son. He'd lost his son. Was he alive? Missing? Could the nurse be right? Could Lindsey be so emotionally distraught she simply couldn't face the horrible truth? Did she need a counselor instead of a detective?

Had someone tried to kill her in the hospital?

He sprang off the bed. If someone had meant to harm Lindsey, they could come back any time. And once again he'd left her completely alone and unprotected.

LINDSEY FINALLY DRIFTED into a fitful sleep, the day's tensions clawing at her body. But in her dreams, she heard her baby's cry again. He was out there somewhere. He needed her. She had to keep searching. Had to believe he was alive.

She tossed and rolled, her throat aching, her mouth dry. A strange smell penetrated her nostrils, burning her windpipe, making her head throb. She opened her eyes, but the room spun. The air swirled around her, stifling. Hot. Perspiration beaded her face. She sniffed, suddenly alarmed at the strong pungent smell.

Gas.

She flung back the covers and rolled off the bed but her legs wobbled when she tried to stand and the room rocked back and forth. She screamed Gavin's name, only the sound came out as a croak, and she remembered he'd gone away again. The smell grew stronger, the air choking her. Her body felt sluggish. Her head ached. The room swayed, then blurred again, and she dropped down onto the carpet. She had to crawl out, escape. But a wave of darkness engulfed her as she pitched forward, and she cried out, afraid she couldn't make it to the door.

Chapter Four

Gavin had parked along the street in front of Lindsey's and had almost dozed off when he suddenly jerked upright, the hair on the back of his neck prickling. Out of the corner of his eye, he thought he detected a movement. A hazy shadow caught in the early morning light slipped into the woods behind Lindsey's house. Barking broke the silence, and he saw a dog running into the woods. Relieved, he leaned his head back against the seat but just as sleep pulled at his eyelids, a screeching sound erupted that made his blood run cold. His eyes jerked open and he bolted out of the car.

A front window stood ajar, sending his mind into alarm. He raced to the front door and knocked, then rang the door bell, tapping his foot impatiently. Seconds passed like a time warp set in slow motion. He pounded the door again and called Lindsey's name. She still didn't answer.

His stomach lurched. Something was definitely wrong.

Frantic, he jiggled the door, but it wouldn't open so he climbed inside the window. As soon as his feet hit the floor, he smelled gas. Jesus. Where was Lindsey?

He raced through the small den and found her lying on the floor, a white swirl of fabric clinging to her slender legs, her long hair shadowing her face. She looked pale and thin and so still his heart slammed into his throat.

"Lindsey!" He pressed his hand to her clammy face, and she moaned. His breath whooshed out in relief. She was alive. Adrenaline shooting through him, he slid his arms beneath her limp form, unlocked the front door, and carried her out into the fresh air.

Clutching her to his chest, he stumbled outside, then sank onto the grass near his car. An owl hooted in the distance. A dog barked again, loud and demanding. Shadows flitted across the yard as the leaves on the trees rustled. Was someone behind them? In the house?

She moaned again and, for a brief second, opened her eyes. She was trembling, her eyes dazed. He stroked a tendril of hair from her face, gently cradling her chin in his hand. "Lindsey, baby, are you all right?"

She coughed and clutched his arms, angling her head to look up at him as she rasped for air.

He stroked her back with his palm, trying to help her breathe. "Are you okay? Was someone in the house?"

"I don't know. G-gas. I could smell it."

"I know, so did I." His gaze shot to the house. What if it exploded? He picked her up and gently laid her in the back seat of his car, tenderly checking her face and arms and legs. "Are you all right?"

She wheezed again. "Feel dizzy."

"I'll call an ambulance. You do have one in this little town, don't you?"

"Yes, call the fire department," Lindsey rasped. "They'll send one."

He rubbed his hand over the side of her face, then pulled off his jacket and lay it over her, drawing the sleeves around her shivering form. "Just lie here and try to relax."

He grabbed his cell phone and quickly dialed for help. "Send an ambulance right away! Yes, she's conscious. 3499 Pine Hollow Road. Lindsey Payne. I think there was a gas leak in her house. Yes, send the sheriff and the fire department, too." She closed her eyes and his breath caught in his throat. "Hurry!"

He quickly checked her pulse. Faint, but her blood stirred slightly. He dragged her in his arms, lowered his head and listened to her breathing. Shallow, but steady. "They'll be here soon, Lindsey," he whispered, "Don't worry, darlin'. Everything's going to be all right."

He rocked her in his arms praying for the EMTs to arrive, all the time wondering if he'd just told Lindsey a lie. If someone had intentionally tampered with her gas line, they'd meant to harm her. And if they were trying to hurt her because she was asking questions about her baby, neither one of them was going to be all right—not until they found their child.

Ten minutes later, the wail of a siren rent the air. He strained to see over the hump of the road, exhaling with relief when he spotted an ambulance and fire truck racing toward them. The paramedics jumped out and raced toward him. "Hurry!" Gavin yelled.

"We'll check out the gas leak," one of the firemen said.

A young blond paramedic placed an oxygen mask over Lindsey's mouth and nose while another one took her vitals. "Blood pressure's low, pupils dilated slightly."

"She's going to be okay," he said. "But we should take her in for some blood work. Make sure her cell count is normal."

Gavin nodded. A sheriff's car pulled up the long winding drive, its blue light swirling through the pre-dawn sky. The car raced to a stop and a tall, gray-haired man wearing a tan sheriff's uniform lumbered out, his face drawn. Even with the early morning sun deflecting his view, Gavin felt the man's intense scrutiny trained on him. Felt those cop's assessing suspicious eyes.

"What happened here?"

"Gas inhalation," the paramedic explained. "We're taking her to the hospital for tests."

The sheriff hitched up his pants with his thumbs. "I'm Sheriff Forbes. Who might you be, Mister?"

He stuck out his hand. "I'm a friend of Lindsey's, a detective from Raleigh. Name's Gavin McCord. I'm glad you came, Sheriff."

The sheriff shook his hand firmly, glaring at him as if he recognized his face from a Wanted poster. "You here when this happened?"

He was going to treat him as a suspect. Gavin understood the drill, but he sure as hell didn't like it. "I drove over, saw a window open and got worried."

A vein pulsed in the man's high forehead as he chewed over Gavin's words. "Mighty early for a visit, ain't it, son?"

"I was worried about her," Gavin explained. "I thought I'd drop by and take her to breakfast."

"All the way from Raleigh?"

Gavin forced himself to bank his anger. The old coot was just doing his job. He'd do the same if he were the officer in charge, but the sheriff was wasting precious time interrogating him.

"No, I came down yesterday, I spent the night at the local hotel. You can check with the manager. I arrived around 11:00 p.m." He stole a glance at Lindsey, aware she was lying way too still for comfort.

The sheriff nodded, chewing his lip sideways. Gavin stroked Lindsey's hand, gently turning her chin so she could see his face. "You're okay, sweetheart, we're taking you to the clinic."

A moment of panic surged into her eyes and he grimaced, realizing the memories the place would resurrect.

"We're ready to move her," the paramedic cut in.

Gavin nodded. "I'm going with you."

One of the fireman walked toward them, his face furrowed. He held up a wire and pair of wire clippers. "Looks like the line was cut intentionally."

Anger swept through Gavin.

"Sir, we need to go," the paramedic said.

Gavin nodded and climbed in the ambulance. "Check out that wire," Gavin told the sheriff. "See if you find any prints."

Forbes frowned. "Just who do you think you are?"

Gavin's hands shook as he yanked his badge from his pocket. "A detective from Raleigh. I'm here to find out what happened to Miss Payne's child."

"You're out of your jurisdiction."

Gavin glared at him. "I've never let it stop me from solving a case before. And I don't intend to this time."

"Look, mister, the lady's baby died of natural causes. Now she's so distraught, she may have tried to kill herself."

Fury ran through Gavin's blood, hot and explosive. "Lindsey asked for my help yesterday. There's no way she'd attempt suicide today. And if that wire was cut intentionally, it proves someone tried to hurt her."

The sheriff stared at him in disbelief. The EMT closed the back door of the ambulance and Gavin sat down beside Lindsey, cradling her limp hand in his. As they pulled away, he prayed Forbes was one of the good guys, that he'd come up with some answers. Because if Gavin found out who'd done this to Lindsey, he would be tempted to forget the law.

He'd kill him with his bare hands.

LINDSEY AWAKENED, dazed and disoriented—where was she? A dark husky scent invaded her senses. Her house? No, the hospital. Glancing through the dim light, she tried to focus, then recognized the worry lines around Gavin's troubled eyes. His jaw was clamped shut, his expression bleak. Still, his handsome face served as a source of comfort in the chaotic turmoil surrounding her life.

She allowed herself to savor his presence for a moment, trying to imprint his image on her brain so she could summon it after he left again. And he would leave again. It was only a matter of time. "Ga—"

He pressed a finger to her lips. "Shh, it's okay. You're in the hospital, Linds."

She frowned. "What happened?"

"Your house had a gas leak. Did you forget to turn off the burner after you heated the soup?"

She shook her head, searching her memory.

"The sheriff's checking it out." He finally released the bedrail and raked a hand through his hair. "The doctors ran some tests, a chemical profile to trace any elements you might have inhaled."

"Dr. Cross?"

"No, Dr. Avery." He tipped his head toward the door. "He said Cross should be here any minute, though."

Lindsey fiddled with the oxygen tubes. "I don't understand what's happening, Gavin. Not any of it."

"I know." His jaw tightened. "But I'll figure it out. I just need a little time."

A nurse bustled in to check Lindsey's vitals. "Mercy,

Ms. Lindsey, didn't think we'd be seeing you again so soon.''

"Neither did I," Lindsey whispered.

"The doctor wants to monitor your oxygen saturation for a while, hon, but so far, things look good," the nurse drawled in a thick Southern accent. "He'll probably let you go home in a while."

"Thanks, Brenda Leigh. I really don't want to stay overnight."

"I know, honey-child. Now get some rest." She fluffed Lindsey's pillow, then slipped out the door.

Gavin gently stroked a strand of hair away from Lindsey's forehead. "I'm going to talk to the staff for a minute. Will you be all right?"

Lindsey ached to reach out and hold on to him but refused to allow herself the comfort. So she simply nodded, then closed her eyes and gave in to the exhaustion. But as soon as sleep claimed her, she heard her baby's cry.

"ROCK-A-BYE-BABY in the treetop…"

He listened to the baby's cries and watched in silence as she cradled the little boy in her arms and rocked him back and forth. God, how she loved to sit in that rocker. Especially lately. As if the soothing motion could lull her own pain. She sang softly, the same lullaby she'd sung to her first son. The son she had lost…

A cold fist pressed against his heart. He would do anything to alleviate the terrible suffering she'd had to endure the past few months. The infant gurgled, batting a tiny hand at the tendrils of hair floating around her heart-shaped face, and he smiled as she traced a finger over the baby's pointed little chin.

She was going to want to keep the child. Forever. Of

that much he was certain. No matter what his boss had to say.

He chuckled, thinking of the years he'd devoted to his employer, giving up his own needs and beliefs sometimes to please him. Well, no more.

A dark laugh escaped him at the irony. He would never have thought of the plan by himself. No, the boss had the devious mind. But he'd walk away the loser this time.

He stepped outside and lit a cigarette, watched the embers spark to life, the ends curl and sparkle with orange fire as he took his first draw. Tapping the ashes onto the weed-filled grass, he inhaled the chill of the mountain air and the scent of honeysuckle as he pondered his plan.

The baby was safe and sound, but Lindsey Payne and that cop-boyfriend of hers were not. They wouldn't get the baby back. And neither would the man who'd ordered him to take the baby from his mother's arms.

The little boy cried out softly and he glanced through the window. She patted his back, the old chair creaking and groaning as she rocked and sang. No, the little boy was where he belonged. And he'd do anything he had to do to make sure he stayed there. Including kill the Payne woman and that nosy cop. And he'd even defy his boss if he had to.

Chapter Five

The small hospital room seemed oppressive. Gavin would trade his life to turn back time and change the circumstances that had led to this moment.

But what could he have done differently? Agree to a relationship with Lindsey when he had nothing to offer her? Put her and the baby in danger by exposing them to the criminals who sought revenge on him? Make her see the truth, that he wasn't worthy of being a husband or a father when he carried the blood of a teenager on his hands? And now he was responsible for his own son's fate. It might even be too late. They might have lost their son forever.

No, he'd done the right thing by pushing her away.

But if he'd listened, if he'd only allowed her to tell him about the baby…he could have done something, hired someone, to ensure her and his son's safety.

The dark troubling thoughts wrestled with guilt and remorse in the hollow places of his mind until he thought his head would explode. Lindsey's breathing grew deep, and he realized she'd fallen asleep. He went in search of the nurse. He couldn't change the past, but he damn well could change the future. And if his son was alive, he'd bring him home and plant him in Lindsey's arms or he'd die trying.

He found the nurse at the nurses' station, catching up on files.

"Poor Lindsey," Brenda Leigh said sympathetically. "I hope she's resting now."

"She is. Have you worked here long, Brenda Leigh?"

"Just a few months, transferred from County, that's the main hospital." He followed Brenda Leigh down the corridor. "We refer patients to County if there're complications we aren't equipped to handle. Minor emergencies, deliveries, routine cases we take care of ourselves." Gavin nodded, his gaze surveying the clinic. It was small and ill-equipped compared to the more modern facilities around the Raleigh area with its Research Triangle Park.

A waiting room that would hold no more than five people, one receptionist, a closed door that probably lead to the exam rooms—something about the place made the hair on the back of his neck prickle. A young woman, eighteen at best, sat alone with her hands over her swollen stomach, leafing through a baby magazine. The set-up reminded him of the homes for unwed mothers popular in the fifties.

"How many exam rooms does Dr. Cross have?"

"Five. He has an outpatient surgical area and a regular operating room with three rooms for overnight stays. Most of the women who deliver go home after twenty-four hours." Brenda Leigh paused and gestured toward an office. "There's also a midwife. A lot of the women around here choose to give birth at home."

"The trend toward the old days. I read about that."

She frowned at his cynical tone. "Nothing wrong with the old ways, Mr. McCord. Might do this world good to return to traditional values. Cut out all this free sex and divorce and having babies out of wedlock.''

Her comment about unwed mothers irked him. Could this woman be some angel of mercy type whose opinion about babies being given to two-parent homes drives her to kidnap a child and give it to another couple?

''So did you encourage Lindsey to give her baby up for adoption?''

''Heavens, no,'' Brenda Leigh said. ''I've heard she's a great teacher and I knew she wanted the baby. ''

So much for that theory. ''Tell me about the county facility.''

''An ambulance service is available to transfer patients if there's a problem.'' They'd reached one of the patient exam rooms and she halted outside the door, arching her head to study him. ''You sure do have a lot of questions.''

Gavin shrugged, wondering how much to reveal. ''Lindsey's a good friend. I'm concerned about her.''

The woman's lower lip curled in sympathy. ''I know, poor thing. Shame about that baby. Lindsey would have made a good mama, too.''

''Yes, she would have.'' Gavin's chest tightened. But he would have been a lousy father. ''Now tell me about the nursing staff.''

She removed a chart from the door, making notations while she talked. ''We have about ten regulars who swap shifts. Four on duty every night, except when we're full. Then we have to work double shifts.''

A couple of other nurses passed by, one with a medicine tray, the other carrying a food tray. A stoop-shouldered older man pushed a broom in the hallway. He lifted his head to stare at Gavin, but each time Gavin glanced toward him, the man ducked his head back to his chore. He favored his left leg and kept twitching his head to the side. Something seemed a little off about the man.

"How about the night Lindsey gave birth?"

Brenda Leigh shifted. "Everyone except Janet went to County to help out with that factory explosion. We had victims in every available cubicle that evening."

The accident seemed almost too coincidental, Gavin thought, uneasy. He'd have to find out what triggered the explosion. "Lindsey said there were complications with the baby. Why wasn't she transferred?"

"Wasn't time," Brenda Leigh said, her voice low. "Besides they wouldn't have had room for her anyway. Dr. Cross and Janet handled everything."

"This nurse, Janet, do you know where she is?"

She jerked her head back, her eyes sharp. "She's on vacation, far as I know. What do you want with her?"

"I'd like to talk to her about that night."

The old man with the broom raised his head and looked at him again, but he quickly turned away when Gavin caught him. "I thought you were a friend of Lindsey's. You sound more like a policeman to me."

"I'm both. I came here to find out what happened to Lindsey's baby."

The woman made a clicking sound with her teeth. "Her baby died of a heart defect—that's all there was to it. Even doctors can't save 'em all."

His throat felt tight. "Are you aware that Lindsey claims someone tried to kill her, twice? She also thinks her baby might still be alive."

Shock darted across the nurse's plump features. "You're serious?"

"Yes, ma'am."

"And you believe her?"

Did he? "I believe something strange happened that night."

"Mr. McCord, I hate to say this, 'cause I feel sorry for that woman, losing a child and all, but Lindsey held the baby herself after he died. The trauma may have been too much for her. It sounds like she may be delusional."

"I don't know what to think," he said. "But I'm going to find the truth if it's the last thing I ever do."

"You'd be better off seeking psychiatric help for her before she goes over the deep end." She twisted the doorknob and bustled into the room, her earlier friendly demeanor evaporating. Her change in demeanor testified to her anger. Or maybe to the guilt of her lies?

LINDSEY FOLDED her hands around the sheets, trying to forget the fear she'd felt when she'd woken up to the smell of gas and the terror of once again lying in a hospital bed in the same clinic where she'd lost her baby. She stared at the doorway, praying Gavin would show up and take her home.

Praying he'd find their child.

The minutes ticked by weighted in time. Finally Gavin opened the door. He stood in the entryway, looking hesitant and nervous, a shadow of darkness and strength in the filtered light from the doorway.

What was Gavin thinking? Did he believe her? Did he hate her for not telling him earlier or did he feel trapped into helping her?

"Hi, are you feeling better?"

She nodded. "I'm ready to leave."

The toe of his scuffed boot scraped the floor, "Did the doctor release you?"

"No. I was hoping he'd be by soon."

He walked toward her, his face solemn, the taut lines

of his jaw razor sharp with restrained emotion. His dark gaze raked over her, a tiny flicker of need and desire sparking in the depths. Not enough to indicate his feelings for her, but enough to unsettle her already shaky nerves. The same way they had when she'd first met him, when he'd protected her before the trial.

Gavin was wicked but tender. Too tempting to play with. Too private to fully understand. Too damned controlled to ever reveal his real feelings.

If he had any for her at all.

A fine shadow of dark hair broadened his earthy-brown jaw, as if he hadn't shaved again this morning. Framed by thick, long black lashes, his eyes radiated masculinity. The kind a woman couldn't resist.

But she had to. Gavin McCord was dangerous. Like the heat of a fire if you stood too close to the flame. She couldn't allow herself to be trapped into the blazing depths of his fiery eyes like she had months ago.

"Why were you at the house so early this morning?" Lindsey asked.

He shrugged, the fabric of his shirt stretching tight across his broad shoulders. "I couldn't sleep. I was worried." A self-deprecating laugh rumbled from his throat. "Damn good thing."

"Thanks…" The rest of her sentence burned in her raw throat, the words lost.

His jaw tightened again. "I should have been there all along."

She dropped her gaze to her hands, knotting the sheet around her fingers. "I…we can't change the past, Mac."

"It's true though. We both know it."

Lindsey couldn't argue the point so she simply allowed the silence to absorb the tension. Maybe the softly spoken apology would help them move past their mistakes. He had pushed her away when she had needed him most. Not that she wanted him to feel responsible for what had happened, but she couldn't deny she'd needed him during the pregnancy…and then afterwards. But guilt ate at her like a starving animal. She was the mother, the one who'd lost their child. What could *she* have done differently?

His dark eyes probed her with their intensity. "I—"

"Don't." Lindsey refused to listen to false promises. "I told you, Gavin, all I want—"

"I know, is to find our baby."

She nodded, completely lost when she noticed the emotions swirling in his eyes. Grief and guilt, tenderness… and fury. For their baby? For her?

"Why did you come here, Lindsey, to this clinic? You could have driven to Raleigh."

"I live in Maple Hollow." She stiffened, wondering if he was passing judgment on her for her choice of medical facilities. "Most of the women around here use the clinic. My labor came so quickly I couldn't drive myself all the way to Asheville."

He gritted his teeth, obviously understanding the implication—she'd been alone with no one to help her.

"I'm not stupid, Gavin, I know this place is small, but it has a good reputation and it's close," she continued. He sent her a damning expression. Maybe he *was* blaming her, hating her. Just as she blamed herself.

"The whole idea of the clinic is to offer a more home-like experience," she whispered. "The comfortable setting is supposed to be conducive for the mother-child bonding. I wasn't expecting any problems."

"People rarely do," he said more gently than she'd expected. "Do they have emergency equipment? Does the doctor do tests for at-risk deliveries?"

"Yes, I had a sonogram every other month. And if Dr.

Cross suspects a problem, he refers patients to the hospital in Asheville. We had no reason to believe my delivery wouldn't go smoothly.'' She heaved a frustrated sigh. ''The morning I delivered, I'd been in for my regular checkup, and everything was fine. But shortly after I left the clinic, I started having contractions.''

''The nurse who disappeared—did you know her very well?''

''No, but I liked her,'' Lindsey said. ''She had a great bedside manner with the younger patients.''

Gavin frowned, remembering the young girl in the waiting room. ''Are there a lot of young patients?''

''I don't know. Why—''

The door opened and Lindsey faltered as a tall, lanky doctor strode in. ''Dr. Cross, I wasn't sure you'd be here.''

He adjusted the stethoscope dangling around his neck, his eyebrows drawn. ''I know, Avery treated you when you first arrived. But when I heard it was you, I had to see you myself.'' He gave Gavin a quick once-over, then headed straight to Lindsey's side. ''How are you feeling, Lindsey?''

Lindsey sighed. ''Better. It was pretty scary though, waking up to that gas.''

''What did you do, leave on the stove or something?''

Lindsey shook her head. ''No, I don't think so.''

The doctor checked her breathing. ''Sounds clear. And your tests came back normal. I think we can release you.''

''Good,'' Lindsey said softly. ''I can't wait to go home.''

GAVIN WATCHED the exchange, scrutinizing Cross's behavior. He'd expected an old country guy, but Cross appeared well-groomed and fit, probably in his early fifties, slightly salt-and-pepper at the temples, intelligent. Truly concerned about Lindsey. Judging from his tan, probably a golfer. "The sheriff is investigating the gas incident for foul play," Gavin said, watching the doctor for a reaction.

Cross's wide-set eyes flitted from Lindsey to Gavin. "I'm afraid we haven't met, sir."

Gavin introduced himself, studying the man's reaction when Lindsey introduced him as a detective from Raleigh.

But the doctor's expression remained steady. "Does the sheriff have reason to suspect a problem at Miss Payne's house?"

"The fire chief thinks someone cut the gas line in the house. He found some wire cutters outside."

"Oh, my God, Gavin," Lindsey said. "He really thinks someone tried to hurt me."

"It's possible, Linds." He squeezed her hand between his own. "And if they did, I promise we'll find them."

"What possible reason would someone have to hurt Miss Payne?" Cross asked.

"My baby," Lindsey murmured. "I've been asking questions, searching for him."

Dr. Cross appeared stunned. "Have you been taking the sedatives I gave you?"

Gavin rolled his shoulders to suppress his own surprise. Lindsey hadn't mentioned drugs.

"No, I haven't taken the pills at all."

Dr. Cross patted her shoulder sympathetically. "I know losing your baby was difficult, but I thought you were dealing with the grief. You saw Mrs. Odum, the counselor, didn't you?"

"Yes," Lindsey said tightly. "But I've received bizarre phone calls telling me my son is alive." She explained about the card and the autopsy report.

Cross's hand trembled as he tucked his pen in his lab

pocket. "I'm terribly sorry someone is doing this to you, but you and I both know your baby died." He lowered his voice, his tone placating. "I held him, Lindsey. And so did you."

A fine sheen of perspiration broke out on Lindsey's forehead. "I still don't think the baby I buried was mine."

Concern darkened Cross's face. "I know the loss of a newborn is difficult, but try to accept your loss, and move on. You're young, unmarried, you have your whole life ahead of you. You can have another child."

Gavin realized the doctor meant to be helpful, but guilt and remorse and fear clawed at him. He wanted to shake the man, make him say the things Lindsey wanted to hear. The things *he* wanted to hear.

But he was a cop. Becoming volatile would only hinder his investigation. But if he found out the doctor was lying…

He intervened before Lindsey could reply. "Dr. Cross, can I speak with you in your office while Lindsey changes?"

Cross nodded and Lindsey reached for Gavin's hand. "I don't have clothes, Gavin, just my gown."

He squeezed her hand gently and handed her a bag. "I went by your house and picked up some things for you."

Cross gave Lindsey another pitying look as he left the room. Gavin opened the bag and pulled out a pair of jeans and a pale pink sweater. "I'll be back to drive you home. That is, unless you need some help."

She bit down on her lower lip, then shook her head no.

Gavin found the doctor's office and rapped on the open door, then forged in. "I'd like to know what happened with Lindsey's delivery."

The doctor stood behind his desk, angling his body toward the sunlight streaming through the venetian blinds. "I'm not at liberty to discuss my patients—"

"Don't start that confidentiality stuff with me. Lindsey asked me to investigate and that's what I'm doing. We can walk back down there and ask her permission if you want."

Cross frowned, then pulled a file from his drawer. "All right. Maybe you can help Lindsey accept the truth. God knows I've tried." He opened the file and sat down, looking weary as he thumbed through the papers. "When Lindsey came in, she was already dilated nine centimeters. But the baby hadn't dropped.

"Lindsey showed signs of eclampsia. I discovered the baby was breech. The fetus was obviously in distress. Lindsey's contractions were coming one right on top of the other." His face grew more and more agitated. "There were other complications, and we had to do a C-section."

Gavin stood motionless, forcing himself to listen to the details and catalog them as a detective instead of the man who should have been protecting the mother of his child.

"When I delivered the baby, the umbilical cord was wrapped around his neck. He wasn't breathing on his own." He paused, dabbing at his forehead with a handkerchief. "But I unwrapped the cord and gave him some oxygen."

He rifled through more papers. "We administered the Apgar score, put drops in the baby's eyes, all the routine things. Then I let Lindsey hold him for a minute, but she started hemorrhaging, so Janet, my nurse, took the baby while we tended to Lindsey."

"Was Lindsey awake during all this?"

"No, the medicine made her groggy. She slipped in and out of consciousness. Afterward, she was exhausted from the delivery, so we stabilized her and let her sleep." His eyebrows drew into a frown. "The baby died during the night. Apparently he had a congenital heart condition we didn't detect at birth. But even if we had, we couldn't have saved him."

"Lindsey claims Nurse Quinn left town the next day and hasn't been heard from since?"

Cross frowned. "The woman hasn't taken a vacation in years. But she was so upset over losing the baby, she needed some time off. Lindsey's not making something suspicious out of Janet's trip, is she?"

Gavin held up a hand to calm him. "No, but her sudden departure does seem odd. Tell me about the other patient, a woman who was admitted the same night as Lindsey."

Cross closed the file. "There was no other patient. Lindsey must have been confused from the medication, probably heard a couple of the nurses talking. Drugs can play funny tricks on your mind."

"I'm not making up all this," Lindsey argued.

Gavin and the doctor both swung their gazes to the doorway where Lindsey stood, angry and trembling. "And it wasn't the drugs. I heard a woman crying that night. I'm sure she had a baby, too. Maybe she lost it, maybe her baby died instead of mine and someone switched it."

"My God, Lindsey, you don't really believe I'd allow something like that to happen?" With a sweep of his hand, he indicated the wall of baby photographs on the bulletin board behind his desk. "Even though malpractice insurance is sky-high and some doctors are relinquishing their delivery services, I pride myself on caring for women during their pregnancies. I've delivered hundreds of babies over the years. I can't believe you'd even suggest I'd do something so vile." He stood abruptly. "Now,

I need to check on my patients. And Lindsey, I strongly suggest you talk to a counselor.''

Hurt crumpled Lindsey's face. She started to argue, but Gavin took her arm, gently guiding her outside.

''I'm not making this up,'' Lindsey whispered fiercely when they'd left the building and were standing by his car.

''I never said you were.''

She clutched his arms, searching his face. ''Then you believe me?''

The hope in her voice ate at him. ''I don't know what to believe, Linds, but I'm not giving up.''

Gravel crackled behind him, then Gavin heard a strange sound, as if something was scraping the concrete. The janitor from the clinic shuffled toward them, one leg slightly dragging behind him.

Lindsey's face softened. ''Andy?''

''Hey, Miss Lindsey.''

He stared first at Gavin, then at Gavin's hand where he held Lindsey's arm. For some reason, the old guy looked annoyed. No, protective maybe. Even jealous. Gavin dropped his hands to his side.

''You all right, Miss Lindsey?''

Lindsey's soft lips curved into a smile. ''Yes, Andy, this is Gavin McCord. He's a friend of mine from Raleigh.''

''Raleigh?'' The man's face suddenly broke into a smile. ''I got a cousin lives th-there. Right by th-the big mall. He takes me to the c-circus pizza place and we p-play video games.''

Gavin realized he was right about the old man being slightly off. He had to concentrate to string his words together. What did he want?

Lindsey reached for his hand and patted it between hers. "It's good to see you, Andy."

"You was h-hurt?"

"Yes, but I'm fine now," Lindsey said, quickly explaining about the gas leak.

Andy nodded, his mouth twisting sideways. "I sorry about your b-baby."

Lindsey squeezed his hand again. "I know, Andy. He was a boy, you know. I named him Cory."

Gavin's chest swelled with longing at the sound of his son's name. "We came to talk to Dr. Cross about the baby."

Before he could ask if the old man had seen anything, Andy surprised him. "I heard you talking to D-Dr. Cross." His impairment became more pronounced as he tried to explain. "You be right. Somethin' w-weird's going on here."

Lindsey folded her arms around her middle. "What is it, Andy? Did you forget where they keep the juice boxes again?"

Andy's hand shook as he scratched the back of his thinning hair. "No, Ma'am," he said, enunciating each word carefully. "It's somethin' w...orse than that. Somethin' aw...ful." His movements seemed jerky as he leaned toward Lindsey. "I think the d-doctor's lying."

Chapter Six

"What do you mean?" Lindsey ushered Andy onto one of the wrought-iron benches and stroked his back to calm him. "Mr. McCord is a friend of mine. He's going to help me find out the truth about my baby."

"You miss your little boy, don't you?" Andy's expression radiated a childlike innocence.

"Yes." Knowing Andy sometimes lost his train of thought, she prodded him gently, "But you were going to tell me why you think Dr. Cross is lying?"

Andy nodded. "That night you was here, the doc says there wasn't a...nother girl, but that's not t-true. I saw her."

"You saw someone else in delivery?"

"I took her some ice ch-chips."

Lindsey's heart thundered. "What happened to her, Andy? Why doesn't Dr. Cross want me to know about her?"

A faraway look settled in Andy's eyes. "She was real sweet, a y-young girl like Goldilocks."

Gavin gave Lindsey a skeptical look.

"You mean she had blond hair?" Lindsey asked.

Andy nodded again.

"What night was that?" Gavin asked.

Andy's right eye twitched. "Um, last week sometime. M-maybe Friday."

Lindsey bit down on her lip, her hopes sinking. "Andy, my baby was born six weeks ago, not last week."

His hands trembled as he pointed to his face. "I—I don't remember days. B-but I r-remember faces. She had freckles on her n-nose."

"Do you know what happened to her baby?" Lindsey asked.

"She was sad, so I gave her some j-juice to cheer her up." Andy shrugged, his eyes darting around the outside of the building. When he saw one of the nurses appear at the entrance, he seemed to grow more agitated.

"What happened to her baby?"

"I think she g-gave it to someone." He turned innocent eyes to Lindsey. "Y-you didn't g-give your baby to someone, did you, Ms. Lindsey?"

Lindsey cleared her throat. "No, Andy, I didn't."

The nurse waved at Andy and he jumped, shuffling backwards. "I gotta go, I d-don't wanna get fired."

Lindsey's hands felt clammy as she released Andy's and thanked him. She pivoted toward Gavin as Andy awkwardly limped back up the steps to the clinic. "Do you think Andy meant the girl gave her baby up for adoption?"

"It's possible," Gavin said. "But he was confused. He didn't even know what day he saw this girl. He called her Goldilocks."

Lindsey leaned against the bench. Was she so desperate she would believe anything she heard? Sometimes Andy saw a story on the news and it became so real to him he transferred it to his own life. The girl could have been any number of pregnant females who'd delivered over the past year.

"Come on, let's get out of here," Gavin said.

They were in the car pulling away when she finally spoke. "What if Andy saw another girl that night? What if that young girl's baby died, and they'd already promised the child to an adoptive couple so they substituted my baby?"

Gavin's hands tightened around the steering wheel as he pulled onto the main road. "Your theory's possible, Linds, but your friend Andy is obviously mentally impaired. Do you think you can believe what he says?"

"Andy gets confused sometimes, and he has a roundabout way of telling things, but he generally says what he means."

"He could be misinterpreting what he saw." Gavin scrubbed a hand over his face. "Besides, private adoptions are not illegal. There's a gray area where cost is involved, but if Cross is smart, which he seems to be, I'm sure his lawyer has expenses accounted for." He hesitated. "Cross has a good reputation. He'd have to be crazy to kidnap one of his patient's babies and give it to someone else."

"Well, what if the other woman's baby died and she was so distraught she kidnapped mine to replace her own?"

Gavin rolled his shoulders. "That sounds more likely, but if that were the case, don't you think the doctor would know and want to help you?"

He was right; she couldn't think of a reason Cross would cover up such a thing. Lindsey sighed, refusing to give in to defeat. "But what about the phone calls? The card and the autopsy report?"

"I'll send it to Raleigh to have it analyzed. But like Cross pointed out, if he'd switched your baby, there'd be witnesses. Someone would come forward."

"Andy just did. And the person who sent me the note and called me must have witnessed something."

"Anonymously. But we don't know if the note or calls are valid. Besides, Andy simply described a private adoption that could have happened any day, any time. Perhaps the woman handed her baby to a grandparent and he misunderstood the whole situation."

Tears stung Lindsey's eyes. Gavin had a solution for everything, only not the answer she wanted to hear. "What about Janet Quinn? Maybe she skipped town because she knows something but she's afraid to come forward."

He seemed to stew over the possibility. "Let's visit the sheriff and see if he can locate Ms. Quinn. When you talk to her, maybe you'll feel better."

Maybe she'd accept the loss of her baby and go on— the words hung in the air between them while Gavin maneuvered the curvy road toward the center of town. But Lindsey wasn't sure she'd ever accept that her baby was gone.

GAVIN FLINCHED as Lindsey shut down in front of his eyes. She wanted to believe the girl had taken her baby so badly she was grasping at straws. He wanted to reassure her, yet he couldn't give her false hopes. So far, he'd found nothing concrete to substantiate her claims. She'd been medicated during her son's birth. She could have dreamt the bit about the other patient. He'd wanted to talk to the other nurses and see if they corroborated Cross's story, but after angering the doctor, he decided it would be better to solicit the sheriff's help to see if the nurses had been questioned. Besides, according to Lindsey, none of the other staff had been present during her son's birth.

An Eye For An Eye... the threatening note surfaced

from the back of his mind to taunt him. What if...what if someone wanted to get back at him? What better way than to kidnap his own flesh and blood?

But how would anyone know he was the father of Lindsey's child? Especially someone from Raleigh. She hadn't told anyone. Unless they'd followed Lindsey to Maple Hollow, which was far-fetched. Although, something Lindsey had said in his office nagged at his memory, but he couldn't remember the exact wording.

Lindsey pointed to an ancient white, two-story brick building shaded by a live oak. "The sheriff's office is in that building, below city hall."

"I suppose they hold court in the library next door?" Gavin commented as he parked in the lot.

The coral sweater Lindsey wore reflected the same russet brown as her frowning eyes. He'd hit a nerve, a very sensitive one. "So Maple Hollow doesn't have an elaborate law enforcement system. At least they have a sheriff."

"I thought you said he was one step away from retirement."

"True." Lindsey exited the car before he could open her door. "Don't get me wrong, Gavin, I like Sheriff Forbes. But Maple Hollow's never had much crime. The safety factor is one of the reasons I moved here. I thought a homey small town would be a good place to raise a child." She hesitated, grief back in her eyes. "But now something terrible has happened, I don't think he's the man for the job, he's not..."

"He's not as cynical as I am?" he supplied.

Lindsey shrugged and led the way up the sidewalk. "He's trusting. You've seen people do some pretty awful things. Lamar Forbes is plain naive in comparison."

"Being naive isn't such a bad thing." Gavin's gaze

caught hers as he opened the heavy door. "Not seeing the bad in people, in everything—must be a blessing."

She paused and lifted her hand to his face, gently tracing a line on the bruise beneath his eye. Sunlight framed a halo around her golden hair, the fall air mingling with the scent of her shampoo. "But we can't wear blinders, either, can we, Mac?"

He swallowed, barely resisting the urge to take her hand and kiss the palm. "No, we can't."

"That's why I need you to work the case." Lindsey dropped her hand. "If anyone could believe a bizarre story about a baby switch, you can."

She might as well have said she needed his help because he was a heartless SOB. "Right."

Sheriff Lamar Forbes looked less businesslike today, more like a crusty old man with a friendly smile who had one foot resting against a fishing pole and his hand fiddling with a piece of fake fish bait. All his office needed was Aunt Bea to walk in with a picnic basket full of fried chicken and Gavin would be swept back to the sitcom he'd watched as a child. Before he'd grown up and realized problems weren't solved in the span of thirty minutes. No catching real crooks without a gun. No happy endings.

"What can I do for you today, Ms. Lindsey, Mr. McCord?"

Gavin folded his arms. "I hope you can clear up a few things. Did you learn anything more about the gas leak?"

Forbes sorted through his tackle box. "Didn't find any prints. Those pliers do make it look suspicious, but they were just plain work tools, could have come from any discount department store. Might have been a bunch of kids playing around."

Gavin didn't buy that theory for a second. "What about Cross?"

He jammed a hand on his hip, the slight paunch to his belly straining against his uniform. "Even if someone did cut those wires, it wasn't Doc Cross. He's one of the best doctors in these parts. I've told Ms. Lindsey that time and time again. Why, he's birthed more babies than I've been alive in years."

"Have you located Janet Quinn? If Lindsey talked to her, she might feel better."

Forbes's bushy eyebrows knitted together. "'Fraid I can't help you. Jan went on vacation, didn't tell nobody where she was going."

"Lindsey thinks her leaving is odd. Have you checked to see if she really did go on vacation?"

"Don't have no reason to think she didn't. Woman deserves her privacy."

"Does she have family around here? Did she ask someone to pick up her mail, watch her house?"

Forbes paused, a plastic fly in his hand. "Nope. Seems like her people come from the other side of the Parkway."

Gavin was getting nowhere. Could the sheriff be involved? "Would you try a little harder to find her? It would help Lindsey to talk to her."

Forbes studied them both for a long minute, his expression troubled.

"Please, Sheriff," Lindsey said softly. "Janet was in the delivery room with me. I need to see her."

"I'll ask around," Forbes finally agreed. "But she won't say nothing bad about William. She's worked for the doc for years."

"What can you tell us about the adoptions handled at the clinic?" Gavin asked.

A moment of surprise flickered on the sheriff's face,

the age lines around his eyes fanning out. "Occasionally Doc helps an unwed mother find a home for her young'un. But everything is on the up and up. I'm sure you have adoptions in the city."

Gavin nodded. "Who handles the adoptions?"

"Reckon Christopher Little does. He's the only lawyer living in Maple Hollow." Forbes lifted his head, his eyes narrowed. "But if you're hinting that he's doing illegal adoptions, you're barking up the wrong tree. And if Ms. Payne wasn't so distraught over her loss, she'd realize Doc's been trying to help her, too."

"I'm not trying to cause trouble," Lindsey interjected. "But, Sheriff, I really believe my baby is alive."

Forbes ran a hand through the patch of thick gray hair on his head. "But Ms. Payne, I stood right beside you at the memorial service."

Lindsey's face paled, the dark memories sucking the light from her eyes. "Did you find any prints on the card I left or the copy of the autopsy results?"

"No prints," Forbes said. "The autopsy report is a photocopy but it looks legitimate. Your baby died of a congenital heart defect. Doc said there wasn't anything he could have done."

"The blood type on the report didn't match mine or the father's, either," Lindsey said, sounding determined.

Forbes frowned.

"Did Little grow up around here also?" Gavin asked.

"Nope. Believe he came from California. L.A., I think it was. But he's been practicing here for years. Folks think a lot of him." He gathered his fishing supplies. "Now I promised my grandson I'd take him out to Turner's Point. You take care, Ms. Payne. And get some rest."

They both said goodbye and followed Forbes outside. Crisp fall flowers scented the air. Puffy white clouds floated across a clear blue sky. It was a beautiful autumn day, much like the time of year Gavin had met Lindsey. He opened the car door and studied her as she climbed inside. She remained suspiciously silent while he started the engine.

"Are you all right?" Gavin asked.

"I told you he was bosom buddies with the doctor."

Gavin found a soft rock station and adjusted the volume to low. "At least he admitted the gas leak looked suspicious, and he agreed to look for Janet Quinn."

"Right." Lindsey fastened her seat belt. "I just know Janet's going to have some answers."

Gavin cranked the car, hoping she was right. "Let's have a talk with Christopher Little. Maybe the town lawyer can shed a little light on the situation."

Gavin's mind spun to other scenarios. What if someone had kidnapped their child to hurt Lindsey or to get back at him? Perhaps her ex? One of the men he'd arrested? The man whose son had died that awful night when he'd followed him into that alley? He didn't want to voice the frightening thoughts but they would have to discuss the possibilities.

LINDSEY FELT hope blossom for the first time in weeks. If her baby had lived and been adopted, even if by mistake, hopefully the adoptive parents were taking good care of her son until she found him. And she would find him.

But what if there had been another woman...

"Gavin, the more I think about the other girl at the hospital, that she lost her child and kidnapped mine—the more I'm convinced that's what happened. Andy said she was upset. Maybe we can find her."

Gavin tapped the steering wheel in thought. "Maybe,

but I don't know why Cross would cover up a kidnapping. I still want to talk to Little.''

A few minutes later, Christopher Little invited them into his office. Lindsey took a seat on the small loveseat in the corner while Gavin explained the reason for their visit, then began to grill the man. Little clammed up, his slightly pocked face turning bright red with anger.

"I don't like your insinuations," Little said when Gavin broached the subject of his fees. "Occasionally I've assisted families in adoption proceedings but all financial matters are confidential and legitimate. I'd never consider dealing any other way.''

"Did you arrange for an adoption on the night of August the first or any other time that week?''

Little pulled his glasses from his pocket and examined his calendar. "No.''

"How about the weeks prior to that or directly following?''

"I'm not at liberty to discuss my cases," Little said curtly. "People have rights that must be protected.''

"What about Ms. Payne's rights?" Gavin asked. "Were her interests protected the night she gave birth?''

Little thumped a silver pen on the top of his credenza. "I'm sorry for your loss, Ms. Payne, but I don't see what your problems have to do with me. You planned to keep your child, didn't you?''

"Yes." Lindsey's spine straightened. "But I think someone else gave birth that night. Her baby died and she kidnapped my son to replace her baby. Or maybe someone planned to adopt the other baby and when it died, they took mine.''

Little seemed stunned. "And you think I'm involved in something like that? Jesus Christ, I could lose my license." He stood abruptly and waved his hand toward the door, not bothering to let Gavin reply. "Unless you have proof of this ridiculous allegation, I think you'd better leave. I have work to do."

Lindsey stood, her own temper boiling.

Gavin ushered her out the door before she could say anything else. "Why did you leave?" she hissed when they stood in the dimly lit hall. "Can't you get him to show you his records or something? What if he's lying?"

"Making him angrier won't help," Gavin said calmly. "Trust me. You don't want a lawsuit for slander on your hands, Linds. Besides, I'm not sure he's lying. We'll just have to dig a little deeper." He placed his hand at the small of her back and gently pushed her outside. Sunshine warmed her face as they walked to the car, her anger fading as the reality of the day's events tunneled through her mind, the heavy weight of defeat settling on her shoulders. Basically, she had a theory—but they had no proof.

And they weren't any closer to finding her son than they had been this morning.

"Be patient, Lindsey. It's obvious from the gas leak incident that something more is going on here. I've only just begun to investigate."

She searched his face, wondering if he was placating her as the doctor and sheriff had done. But a tenderness softened his dark eyes that suggested he did believe her, that he understood her grief. Because he shared it.

"I want to find the nurse. I have a feeling she disappeared because she knew something. I'll get a subpoena for the doctor's records, too. Try to hang in there, okay?"

"Okay." Gavin's breath brushed her cheek as he leaned close to her. He had a tough exterior that made him appear fearless. Emotionless. But she knew what it was like for him to lose control, to lose himself inside her. She'd also seen his protective instincts kick in the night her ex had tried to kill her. Gavin had deep emotions, feelings he channeled into work instead of sharing with a woman. He had to be hurting now. He'd just been told he'd had a son and that he was missing. Why did he feel he had to shrink-wrap his feelings as if they weren't important?

"So you're not giving up then?" Lindsey asked, knowing full well her heart lay in her eyes.

"No." His fingers wiped away a tear she didn't even realize she'd shed. "You have to trust me, Lindsey. I'll find our son, just give me time."

She hesitated. Did she trust him?

With her son's life, yes.

With her heart, no.

AN HOUR LATER Gavin parked in Lindsey's driveway but he insisted Lindsey stay in the car while he checked her house. He rushed through the rooms, searching for signs of an intruder, even checked the gas line to make certain no one had tampered with it again. Lindsey had obviously felt safe here when she'd first moved to Maple Hollow, had thought this little cabin would be the perfect place to raise their baby. Had she been wrong in her assessment of the town?

"Everything looks okay," he said, as he opened her car door. She nodded, looking wary and drained as she climbed from the car. He'd suggested they stop to eat, but Lindsey had insisted on cooking dinner at home, so he helped her carry bags of groceries to the house. Cooking seemed to relieve her tension, so he didn't argue. In the last three weeks he could count on one hand the number of meals he'd consumed that had been truly edible. And Lindsey made the best country fried steak he'd ever tasted.

Cooking was only one of the little things about her he had missed. Definitely not the most important. The little stolen kisses and tender touches she'd shared with him that one night had gotten under his thick skin in a way the sex hadn't. And the sex had been phenomenal.

"I'm going to make some calls while you start dinner," Gavin said, "that is, unless you need some help."

"Go ahead, I need to stay busy." She gestured toward her bedroom. "You can call from my room if you want. It'll be a little quieter."

And he'd be away from her. Her unspoken message reverberated loud and clear.

He nodded, then stepped into the bedroom and called his partner Simon Durango, but got his voice mail so he left a message. Exhausted, he leaned back and studied the modest furnishings. An antique sleigh bed, a country quilt in blue and yellow, gingham curtains, an oak dresser and chest. Simple but clean, with little touches of Lindsey scattered all through the room. A cross-stitched country sampler. A rag doll. A stool in the shape of a calico cat. Comfortable, homey—a warm haven to raise a child. His gut tightened at the thought. He glanced toward the hallway and the closed door to the nursery and suddenly had the overwhelming urge to pick the lock and go inside.

LINDSEY BREADED the steak and dropped it into the hot oil, then eased a pan of biscuits in the oven. Memories of other nights Gavin had spent protecting her, the nights she'd cooked for him, exploded painfully in her mind. And that last night, the evening they'd made a baby…

She had to forget those times.

Remember the awkward morning after. The times he refused your phone calls. The cold way he sent you out of his life that day at the courthouse.

Lindsey saw Gavin stalk out of the bedroom, stop in the hallway and stare at the nursery door. She'd locked it the morning she'd returned from the hospital and hadn't been able to go back inside since. The counselor had suggested she pack up all the baby things, put them away, out of sight. And she'd told herself she would one day. Only that day hadn't arrived. Was Gavin going to ask her to see the room?

The telephone rang and Lindsey frowned, wondering if it were her anonymous caller. Gavin crossed the short distance from the hallway to the kitchen, his gaze steady as he watched her pick up the receiver.

"Hello."

"Lindsey, darling, are you all right?"

It's my mother, she mouthed to Gavin. Gavin nodded, poured himself some iced tea. "Yes, Mom, I'm okay."

"You didn't call at the usual time last night."

Lindsey winced. Since her mom had lost her vision and moved into the assisted care facility a few months ago, she'd settled into a predictable pattern. Lindsey always called on Tuesday and Thursday nights at seven, on Sundays at six. If she didn't, her mother worried. "Sorry, Mom. I drove to Raleigh yesterday and I was so exhausted when I got back I forgot to check my messages."

"You told Gavin?"

"Yes, he's here now."

Her mother sighed audibly. "Well, thank God. I know how difficult it was for you to accept his help, sweetheart, but I don't think you should suffer through this all alone."

"He's going to help me search for my baby, nothing more, Mother."

Her mother remained quiet for several long seconds. She'd never approved of Lindsey's intentions to raise the baby alone. Finally Lindsey heard a sniffle. "I hope you're right about the baby being alive, honey. I hate to see you get your hopes up for nothing.''

Lindsey bit her tongue, the familiar helplessness building inside again. She didn't want to give her mother false hopes either, so she shifted the conversation to her mother's activities. Gavin found the dishes and set the table, obviously making himself at home.

As she said goodbye to her mother, she tried not to think about how natural it felt for Gavin to be in her house, and how it would feel when he left. Her gaze strayed to the mail and a familiar blue envelope drew her eye—identical to the one that had held the autopsy report. Lindsey tore the envelope open and gasped. A small card with a baby's footprint had been placed inside. Her heart burst into a million pieces—the name beside the tiny blue footprint read Cory Adam Payne.

Chapter Seven

Gavin's stomach knotted as he stared at the tiny blue footprint. For the first time since he'd heard he had a son, the cold reality of his loss hit him—he hadn't been able to share Lindsey's pregnancy, hadn't felt his son kick in her stomach, hadn't seen his little body emerge, hadn't even seen a picture of him. But something about the outline of that small foot, the imprint of five little toes, especially that fourth little crooked one like his own, twisted his insides into a mass of pain. And anger.

He wanted to hold his little boy, feel his baby soft skin, smell that sweet baby powder, tickle his little toes. The footprint might not prove to the sheriff that something sinister had happened with his baby but in his mind, Gavin knew this footprint belonged to his son. The little imperfection had been a long-standing joke, a family characteristic to be teased about in the McCord family, one of the first things his own mother had said she'd looked for when he was born.

With this kind of evidence, evidence so personal in his hand, how could he not know his son was out there? Who the hell had taken him? Were the notes and cards intended to taunt Lindsey or to inform her that her baby was alive?

Lost in his own turmoil, he barely noticed Lindsey stagger, but he grabbed her just as she collapsed into the chair. Her long slender hands were trembling, and those velvety eyes of hers, normally like a beacon of light in the darkness, now glistened with tears of anguish.

"I...I don't understand why someone is doing this, Gavin." She traced her finger over the outline of the baby's foot, then lifted her gaze to meet his. "He's just an innocent little baby, all I wanted was to hold him...to take care of my son."

He knelt beside her and lay his hand on her shoulder, squeezing her gently to reassure her she wasn't alone now. She collapsed into his arms, her soft sobs tearing his heart in two. His own grief almost overwhelmed him, but he soothed her with soft, meaningless words of comfort, promises he hoped he'd be able to keep. His heart clenching, he glanced at the empty bassinet in the den. He might never get to touch that little foot, hold his son, teach him to play ball...

Lindsey surprised him then by turning and wiping at her tears, then tenderly cupping his face with her hands. Her voice resonated, full of strength and determination, "I know you're going to find our baby, Gavin. Whatever wrong there is between us, I'm glad you're here. I have faith you'll bring him home."

He could say nothing, could do nothing but stare into her shining, hope-filled eyes, and draw strength from her words. And slowly, as he allowed her to stroke the tension from his jaw, he began to climb out of the despair that had momentarily trapped him in its dark hole.

They sat for a long time, simply pulling together in the silence. The silence... It was so quiet Gavin shuddered. *He* could almost hear a baby's cry.

He suddenly stood, acutely aware he'd allowed his emotions to rise to the surface and interfere with his detective training. He had to report the card, had to convince the police to put out an APB on that nurse, had to explore every possibility.

As if Lindsey realized the distance he'd placed between them, she stood and silently put the food on the table. Grateful for her understanding, he grabbed the phone and called Forbes. With this latest note added to the knowledge that the gas leak in Lindsey's house hadn't been accidental, the sheriff would have to cooperate. But again, Forbes wasn't in the office so he tried his partner, hoping he'd be in this time.

"Hey, McCord, I was getting ready to call you."

"Good." Gavin relayed the little he'd learned from his conversations with the doctor and lawyer, then explained about Andy and his suspicions. "Would you check out Dr. Cross from the Maple Hollow Clinic?"

"Anyone else?"

"Yeah, Christopher Little, attorney-at-law. I think he's on the up and up but it won't hurt to investigate."

"Right. How's Lindsey holding up?"

"She's amazing," Gavin said, his gaze drawn to the closed doorway in the hall. His baby's room. "Especially under the circumstances."

"Does her story sound feasible?"

Gavin rubbed his chin in thought. "At first, it sounded bizarre but the more I check into things, I'm beginning to wonder. Lindsey claims another woman delivered the same night she gave birth, but the doctor denies the woman even exists. And the nurse who assisted is missing."

"Sounds suspicious. What's the doctor's take?"

"Cross isn't the country bumpkin doctor I expected. He hinted Lindsey was medicated heavily due to complications during the delivery, that she needs to accept her loss and move on. Oh, and someone tampered with the gas line in Lindsey's house last night. She almost died.''

''Jesus, poor Lindsey. Do you think there's a possibility she's right, that the baby is alive?''

Did he? After seeing the footprint... ''Yes.''

Silence descended across the line. ''The baby's your son, isn't he, McCord?''

Gavin had to swallow before he could reply. ''Yeah.''

''Whew.'' Simon heaved a sigh. ''Are you sure?''

''Yes, and I have to find him.'' Gavin explained about the discrepancy with the blood types, the footprint and the baby's crooked toe.

''The print could belong to another baby,'' Simon said.

''Not likely, the toe, it's...'' He paused, his voice cracking. ''It's identical to mine, fourth toe on each foot, it's a McCord trait. But send the copy to the lab to be analyzed anyway.''

''You ready to call in the FBI?''

''Not yet—they'll take over and I want this case myself.''

Simon hesitated, worry evident in his voice when he spoke, ''Look, buddy, you may be too close—''

''I'm staying in,'' Gavin said, cutting off any further argument. ''But you do have a couple of friends who are ex-agents, don't you? Maybe we could use their help.''

''Yeah, Barnes and Jernigan. I'll call them right away.''

''Thanks, Durango. I knew I could count on you.''

''Yeah, well, no big deal. Anyone else you want me to check out?''

''Focus on finding that nurse Janet Quinn. She took a leave of absence the day after Lindsey gave birth.'' Cold nagging worry seeped into Gavin's veins again. ''And check out Jeff Faulkner and Danny Swain. Make sure they're both still locked up tight. Swain threatened revenge at his trial.''

''You think one of them could be involved?''

''I don't know, but I have to consider all angles. Both of them hated my guts. Lindsey was outside the courtroom the day of Swain's sentencing. He could have seen her.'' His mind ticked back to that day, recalling the way he'd pushed Lindsey out of his life when she'd come to reveal her secret. Swain was just the type to get revenge by using someone Gavin lov…cared about. ''Forensics turn up anything on that note?''

''Not yet. I did find out the Faulkners hired a P.I. to watch Lindsey.''

''So the Faulkners might have known about the baby.'' Gavin rubbed the back of his neck. ''Good work, partner. Give me the P.I.'s number. I want to talk to him myself.''

Simon recited the number and Gavin scribbled it in his notepad.

''Faulkner might think the baby is his,'' Simon said.

''Yeah, but Lindsey said he was adamant about not wanting children.''

''Maybe he set up a kidnapping for revenge.''

Or to get rid of the child. Gavin couldn't even acknowledge the possibility. ''Maybe, but he'd need help. And I'm not sure how he'd benefit without letting Lindsey know he had her child. Kidnapping sure as hell wouldn't help him with parole either.''

''I see your point. Any other angles?''

''While you're at it, check and see if Dwight Johnson is still in town. He blames me for his son's death. I keep thinking about that 'eye for an eye' note.''

''You didn't cause the teen to die, McCord. You told the boy to get out of there.''

''Yeah, well, warning him wasn't enough.'' Gavin

paused, willing the memories away. "Just check him out, will you?"

Simon agreed and Gavin added, "Thanks, I'll convince Forbes to issue an APB on the Quinn woman."

"You know we could have the grave exhumed," Simon suggested.

Gavin's throat closed. "I don't think Lindsey would want to go that route yet, but you can work on the court order just in case we need to push it through."

Simon seemed to understand and hung up without arguing. Gavin tried the P.I. the Faulkners had hired, cursing at the voice mail. He left a message, saying it was urgent the man return his call, then hung up.

An image of the cemetery where the Johnson boy lay buried surged through his mind, then the small plot where Lindsey had lain the flowers over his baby's grave. No, he wasn't ready to give up yet, not when he had hopes his son was alive.

LINDSEY STIRRED her fork around in her mashed potatoes and tried to eat but her appetite had vanished. Forcing food down her throat seemed aimless. Gavin didn't have a problem. Of course, she remembered he'd always had a hearty appetite.

"How much did he weigh?" Gavin asked.

Lindsey jerked her head up, his question catching her off guard. "What?"

Gavin fisted his big hand around the tablecloth. "How much did our son weigh?"

Lindsey met his gaze, struck by the intensity in his dark eyes. "Eight pounds, eleven ounces."

His dark eyebrow shot up. "And he was six weeks early?"

"You're a big man, Gavin. The doctor said he would

have been close to eleven pounds if I'd carried him to term.'' Her reply brought another strange tense silence between them.

He glanced toward the spare bedroom. ''Did you decorate that room for him?''

''Yes, I painted it yellow...like the sunshine.'' She closed her eyes, praying he wouldn't ask to see the room. Thankfully, the phone rang, saving her the worry. They both stared at the machine for several seconds before Lindsey finally picked it up. When the sheriff asked for Gavin, she pushed the phone in his hand and began to clear the table.

As she scrubbed the dishes vigorously, Gavin and Sheriff Forbes engaged in a shouting match. Judging from the one-sided conversation, Forbes obviously didn't want to go along with the APB on Janet Quinn. Either the sheriff was hiding something or he simply didn't want the feds infiltrating his safe haven of a little town.

Thank God Gavin had taken action. Knowing she didn't have to fight this battle alone eased some of the burden. As soon as she wiped the counter, she turned to him.

''You finally convinced Forbes to look for Janet?''

He nodded and folded his arms across his chest.

She took the bottle of pills the doctor had given her and shook one into her hand. ''I'm going to lie down.''

''What are you taking?''

''Some vitamins the doctor ordered. I guess I let myself get run down after the delivery.''

''Are you all right, Linds?'' he asked in a low, gravelly voice.

Not trusting her voice to speak, she simply nodded.

His dark gaze roamed over her, and she fought the impulse to run. Not looking at him was almost as difficult as resisting the urge to run into his arms.

"You'll be okay on the sofa?"

"I've slept in worse places."

He meant his assignments, a reminder of the life he lived away from her. The reason she'd gone to him this time. Not for love or because he was the father of her baby, because he was a detective.

"I'll see you in the morning then. And Gavin…"

"Huh?"

"Thanks."

He nodded, his expression tight as she tried to slip by him. He caught her arm, pulling her against him so his breath whispered against her cheek. The scent of his soap and masculine smell invaded her senses, his rock hard body rippling with muscles, full of strength and power, something she desperately needed. The long strands of his hair brushed his collar, his dark gaze troubled, concerned, determined. Full of that dark hunger that had once enticed her into his arms. Into his bed.

But as she stared into his eyes, she saw her son, the dark brown irises, the sharp jawbone, the square face, the small cleft in his chin. Her heart broke all over again. Her baby even shared that little crooked toe, a McCord trait.

In her son, she would have always carried a part of Gavin with her. Now…

"If you need me tonight, you know where I'll be," he said in a husky voice.

She caught her lip with her teeth and slowly pulled away from his grasp. What exactly did he mean? If she had another nightmare? If she wanted comfort? No, she wouldn't fall into that trap again.

Not tonight. Not ever.

"Lindsey?"

"The only thing I need from you is to find our baby." Then she disappeared into the safety of her bedroom and tried not to think about the fact that her words had sparked hurt in his sad, dark eyes.

GAVIN KICKED OFF his boots and tossed his shirt onto the rocking chair in the corner of the room, an image of Lindsey rocking their baby sharp in his mind. Determination filled him and he picked up the phone and tried the P.I. again, breathing a relieved sigh when the man answered.

"Collier Investigative Services. Frank Collier speaking."

"This is Detective Gavin McCord of the Raleigh Police Department."

"Yeah, what can I do for you?"

Gavin immediately explained the situation, stating his interest in the Faulkners and detailing the history of Lindsey's marriage, subsequent divorce and testimony against her ex-husband.

"I'm aware of their relationship, but I don't discuss my clients with anyone," Collier stated baldly.

"You'll either discuss it with me or I'll bring you in on charges of interfering with a kidnapping investigation." Gavin's gut clenched. "Possibly a murder."

"Look, I don't know anything about a kidnapping or murder—"

"Maybe, maybe not, but I know you investigated Miss Payne and followed her to Maple Hollow. I need to know what information you passed on to the Faulkners, exactly what they wanted from you."

"Why do you think the Faulkners—"

"They hated Lindsey for putting their son in jail," Gavin said. "Now, are you going to cooperate or should I haul you in, see about getting that license revoked?"

The man sucked in air sharply, bowing to the threat. "I'll admit that a few months ago, right after the trial,

Mr. Faulkner contacted me and asked me to follow his son's ex-wife. He wanted to keep track of her, make sure she stayed out of his son's life. I was to report back anything I learned on her.''

"And what did this report include?''

"Where she moved, who her friends were, about… about the—''

"About her pregnancy?''

"Well, yeah, I told them she was pregnant. It was pretty obvious after watching her a few months.''

"Were they interested in the baby?''

The man hesitated, his voice cracking, "The old man got upset at first, called her a bunch of names—''

"I get the picture,'' Gavin said, cutting him off. "Then what?''

"They wanted to know about her doctor, about the clinic where she received prenatal care.''

"And you told them?''

"Yes, but Faulkner never mentioned kidnapping or taking the baby. In fact, I got the impression he disliked the woman so much he wouldn't want a grandson by her, even if the baby belonged to his son.''

As if he would have told the man his plans.

"He implied Miss Payne was probably fooling around with a dozen different men so the kid most likely wasn't his son's.''

Gavin clenched his teeth. "Were you near Maple Hollow Clinic the night Lindsey delivered?''

"No. About two months earlier, Faulkner terminated me. Said he had all the information he wanted, sent me the rest of my fee, I haven't heard from him since.''

"You know I can subpoena your phone records—''

"I'm telling you the truth,'' Collier said emphatically. "I swear. The last time I talked to Faulkner was over three months ago. He said he was through with the Payne woman and wanted to forget she'd ever been in their lives."

Gavin gave him another warning, told him he might call back later with more questions and hung up.

Exhausted but troubled, he stretched out on Lindsey's small sofa. So, the Faulkners had known about Lindsey's pregnancy. But the family wasn't convinced the baby was their grandson. He'd thought that they might assume the baby was Jim's and want to raise the child themselves.

From Collier's assessment, the idea seemed off base.

Frustrated, Gavin closed his eyes, knowing he would have to tell Lindsey. In his mind, he saw her cuddling their baby to her breast. He could almost hear the creak of the rocker, the soft sound of her singing in that whispery, loving voice. He could almost imagine their son, a little tow-headed boy with Lindsey's brown eyes, toddling across the room, pushing a toy train.

A collection of pictures sat atop a pine sofa table. One was of her mother, the others a hodgepodge of children she'd obviously taught. Yet there were none of their own child as there should have been.

The loneliness of the past few months played through his head, but he pushed the images away as he did the unbidden images of Lindsey preparing for bed. Sweeping her long silky hair into a ponytail as she scrubbed her face, stripping her clothes and soaking in a hot bubble-bath, lying naked and sleepy beneath the sheets. Her sweet fragrance filling the room, her soft fingertips caressing his bare chest, her delectable lips moving across him…

He bolted upright and jammed his hands through his hair. Now was not the time to indulge in a bout of self-pity or pointless dreams or lust. Nothing had changed since the day he'd sent Lindsey away.

He was still a cop. His job placed him and anyone he cared about in danger. He remembered the terror of being carted off in the night to safe houses, not knowing if his dad would return or if some faceless demon who wanted revenge against his father would attack him in the night.

No child should have to live like that.

Especially his own. He wanted better…he wanted, hell, right now he simply wanted to bring him home to his mother.

The image of the Johnson boy materialized and he shuddered, the familiar guilt welling inside him again like a hundred knives piercing through his skin. Then came the image of the bleak but furious father of the boy, standing over his grave, damning Gavin for interfering, blaming him for his son's death. Gavin had tried to play big brother to the boy and he'd failed. And because he'd hurt Lindsey so badly she'd been afraid to confide in him, he'd also failed to protect his own son.

He sighed and ran a hand over his face, then closed his eyes, praying Simon would have some answers tomorrow. If somehow the Johnson man or that Swain creep had orchestrated a kidnapping to seek revenge on him, he'd find out. And if the other woman in the delivery room had kidnapped his boy—he'd find her.

He contemplated the other possibility—Lindsey's ex.

Tomorrow he'd call first thing and arrange special visitation—he'd confront Faulkner himself, go to the jail and look into his cold-gray eyes and find out the truth. And he wouldn't give up until he brought his baby home and lay him in Lindsey's arms.

Frustrated and suddenly on edge as he remembered that someone had been in Lindsey's house and tampered with the gas line, he paced across to the window. His breath hitching in his chest, he slowly drew the curtain back and stared out the window into the darkness. Was someone out there watching Lindsey? Watching him?

Someone who had their baby?

HE MOVED beneath the canopy of trees off to the side of the mountain house, camouflaging himself in the shadows of the ancient pines. A curtain from one of the front windows slid sideways and he ducked his head behind the tree trunk. What were they up to now? They'd been asking questions all over town, probing and picking at all the hospital staff and that dimwit sheriff. Why couldn't they leave things alone?

The baby was safe. Sleeping like the saints, all nestled in the comfort of his newfound home and in the arms of his new mother. He was changing every day, changing so much the Payne woman wouldn't even recognize him. He'd adjusted to his new home without so much as a whimper. He didn't miss the woman who'd given him birth. Hell, he didn't even know her.

No, the only mother he would ever know was the one who'd bathed him and tucked him in bed earlier that evening. The one who'd already begun to form a bond with him. The one he'd call Mama when he finally learned to talk.

A pine cone hissed beneath his feet as he inched around the side of the tree again, his gaze darting across the lawn as he remembered the wail of the siren the other day. Too bad she'd called in her cop friend. And that the gas leak hadn't killed her.

An owl hooted somewhere in the distance and twigs snapped as deer scampered for food in the woods. God, how he loved the mountains. A perfect place to raise his new son. Yes, he was already thinking of him as *his* son. Amazing how quickly the infant had become a part of their lives. He was a strong man and he might have survived. But *she* wasn't strong. She needed the baby more than Lindsey Payne did. More than his boss.

Suddenly he had the urge to finish the couple off tonight. To rid himself of their nosy poking. The boss would be relieved, too. The curtain slid farther open though, and he knew the cop was watching. He tossed his cigarette onto the ground and crushed it with his boot. No, he'd have to wait until the time was right, when he could catch them off guard. The next time he made his move the job would go off smooth as silk. And he'd damn well cover his tracks.

Because this time he wouldn't fail. And he'd get rid of them forever.

Chapter Eight

The next morning storm clouds brewed, casting the sky in shades of gray and black, mirroring Lindsey's bleak mood. All night she'd felt as if someone were watching her. Shadows had jumped at her from the dark windows, leaves had rustled as if footsteps were approaching. She'd thought she'd heard someone outside her window, tapping against the glass ever so softly, so she'd lain still and quiet, listening for an intruder, grateful Gavin had been in the other room. Now fatigue clawed at her and the dismal sky magnified her exhaustion. But she summoned her courage and reminded herself that Gavin would find some answers.

Maybe she'd be holding her baby in her arms soon.

She puttered around the kitchen, making coffee while Gavin showered, the images of him standing naked with water droplets glistening on his dark chest tormenting. Her house suddenly seemed way too small, the situation too intimate for her already frayed nerves. Sharing a bathroom. Preparing breakfast. Waking to the soft rumble of his slight snoring. Gavin's scent lingered in the hall, his presence filling the tiny kitchen as he emerged from the bathroom.

She tried to avoid his dark gaze but her eyes landed on

his chest and she felt the breath being sucked from her lungs. His shirt hung open, revealing broad shoulders and a muscular chest, bronzed and dotted with damp hair. He hadn't yet bothered to button the top button of his fly so his jeans rode low on those narrow, muscular hips. She remembered the touch of that washboard-flat stomach, the hard muscles and planes of his thighs, the…

The room suddenly seemed stifling. She steered her mind to breakfast, placed a plate of hotcakes and fresh fruit on the table, her hands trembling.

He spoke without preamble. "We need to talk."

Lindsey nodded and sank into a chair, bracing herself for bad news, her earlier reverie forgotten in the wake of his husky, troubled voice.

The oak chair creaked as he slid his big body into the seat beside her. "I've been going over all the possibilities in my head," he said, stabbing a stack of pancakes with his fork. Lindsey watched as he slathered butter on the top, then poured enough syrup for an entire family over the meal.

"My partner's checking out a couple of men who might be suspects."

She raised a brow, waiting for him to explain.

He licked syrup from the tip of his finger, then regarded her through veiled eyes. "One is the guy I testified against the day you came to see me at the courthouse. Name was Swain."

"I don't understand."

"It's a long shot, but he threatened revenge on me. I want to make sure he's locked up tight."

Lindsey nodded. He pushed the hotcakes toward her and she took one, wincing when her stomach rebelled. Still, she forced herself to go through the motions, well aware Gavin would fuss at her if she completely skipped a meal.

"The other man's son died in a crossfire when a bust of mine went down." Gavin chewed thoughtfully, his gaze landing somewhere past her. His expression seemed desolate, as if he were so alone. Lindsey instinctively sensed there was more to his story, that whatever had happened had impacted his life. She toyed with her food, hoping he'd elaborate. He didn't.

"Then there's Faulkner."

Her fork clattered onto her plate. "But I told you I haven't been in contact with him." Her ex-husband's angry face flashed into her mind along with the hateful words he'd muttered when she'd taken the witness stand. "The baby's not even his."

He cradled her hand in his. "I talked to a P.I. last night. Old man Faulkner hired him to follow you after the trial."

Lindsey gasped and Gavin rubbed slow circles around her palm to relax her.

"He told the Faulkners you'd moved here, that you were pregnant. He even told them about the clinic."

Lindsey's face paled. "So…Jim knows I had a baby?"

"And he may think the child is his."

"But the timing—"

"You said the baby was premature."

Lindsey nodded. "Oh, God, what if he…"

Gavin gently squeezed her hands. "The P.I. claimed the Faulkners didn't act as if they wanted the child. They even insinuated that…that the baby might not be their son's. I don't know what your ex thought."

Memories assaulted Lindsey—the horrible night her husband had tried to kill her. The night before the trial when she and Gavin had almost been blown up in that explosion.

Gavin sipped on his coffee. "If Faulkner thought the baby was his, he might have wanted his parents to raise it. If he thought the child was mine, he might want revenge."

"But how would he know about us?"

Gavin shook his head. "That's the glitch. He can't. Which puts us back to square one."

"And he didn't want a baby. He was adamant, almost obsessive, about birth control when we were married. If he changed his mind when he discovered my pregnancy, why wouldn't he contact me?" She stood and paced. "He could have asked for visitation rights, so could his parents. But stooping to kidnapping when he was already in jail? That doesn't make sense. And the Faulkners would never risk prison." *Of course, Jim had tried to kill her. But he'd tried to strangle her in a desperate fit of rage. Kidnapping meant he'd been calculating, cold…ruthless.*

"Maybe he thought you'd convince the court to rule that he didn't have rights to the baby."

Lindsey shook her head, unconvinced.

"I checked with my partner this morning. He said the warden at the pen where Faulkner is confined claimed Faulkner's been on his best behavior, probably trying to get an early parole, so you may be right—he probably wouldn't do anything to jeopardize his chances." Lindsey's hand felt cold and delicate as Gavin pressed it to his thigh. His expression turned grim. "I hate to say this, but I think the only way to find out about Faulkner's reaction to the baby is to confront him. I arranged special visitation for today."

Lindsey tried to temper her reaction but she'd never forget the way her ex-husband's hands had felt clamped around her throat. Jim had begged her not to testify against him for money laundering, but she'd refused. Now she might be forced to beg for her ex-husband's help. She wondered if he would turn her down as forcefully as she had him.

RAIN SLASHED across the windshield, the foggy conditions forcing Gavin to focus on his driving as he guided the Taurus toward the state pen. The grating, monotonous sound of the windshield wipers should have been a welcome reprieve, but the dull blades simply personified the tension in the air. Lindsey had been suspiciously silent since they'd left her mountain cabin, obviously preparing herself for the upcoming confrontation with her ex-husband.

Damn. If there was another way, he'd do it. He didn't want her to have to face the bastard again. But he couldn't make himself believe the man wasn't involved unless he saw his face. Faulkner had this cocky grin that probably melted most women's hearts, this smooth way of talking that enticed listeners into his lies like honey drew flies. But Gavin had seen through him from the first.

Details.

He focused on body language, the little telltale signs. The giveaway for Faulkner—his nostrils flared slightly when he lied. The movement was so small a person would hardly notice, but once Gavin zeroed in on the habit, he'd pegged the man every time, as effective as any lie detector.

"What are we going to say?" Lindsey asked with a shiver. "I thought I'd never see Jim again. I tried to banish his face from my mind."

Gavin's hands tightened to a white-knuckled grip. Maybe this was a mistake. Maybe he should question Faulkner by himself. "You don't have to see him, Linds."

She swung her gaze to him; her chin went up a notch. "Yes, I do have to see him. I'd never forgive myself if I found out he had something to do with Cory's disappearance and I'd been too cowardly to face him."

Gavin released a pent-up breath, reached across the car and squeezed her hand. "You're a strong lady, Linds."

Her soft nervous laugh echoed through the car. "I don't have a choice. I'll do *anything* to get our son back."

He nodded solemnly, watching as she turned to stare out the window. "You asked me what we should say to Faulkner. First, let's feel him out, see how he reacts to us. Just follow my lead, okay?"

Lindsey fingercombed her hair, pushing a strand away from her pale cheek. "Okay, but are you going to tell him the truth...that the baby's yours?"

Gavin's stomach knotted. "I don't know. If Faulkner believes the baby's his and thinks he's been kidnapped, he might help us. If he paid someone to kidnap our baby to hurt you, he'll still protect him."

The implication of the words he'd intentionally omitted slammed into her with blinding clarity. Tears filled her dark brown eyes, the moisture sliding down her cheeks in trails that tore at his heart. "You think he might hurt the baby if he knows you're the father?"

"I don't know what he'd do," Gavin said gruffly, forcing the possibility from his mind. "But I won't take any chances, Linds. Not with our son's safety." He gave her a pain-filled look, knowing he couldn't hide the feelings in his eyes. And for once not caring.

He loved his son.

Maybe he'd never seen him or even known he had existed until it was too late, but he sure as hell loved him. And he didn't care who knew it.

LINDSEY BARELY had time to let his words sink in before they'd veered onto the long drive to the penitentiary. But the minute the fierce possessiveness of Gavin's tone registered, her tears overflowed again.

He slowed the car, paused on the embankment, and gently wiped them away with his thumb. Their gazes locked, his full of regret as he gently brushed his lips across her forehead. Lindsey felt the pull of emotions deep inside. She ached to have him hold her, craved the strength of his arms. At the same time she wanted to console him and reassure him everything would be all right. But a car swerved around them and blew the horn, shattering the moment. Gavin frowned, then turned his attention back to the drive, wound down the mile long road and pulled up to the guard stand.

Police vehicles filled the parking lot, the spaces empty of civilian cars, solidifying the fact that it wasn't visitor's day. Tall wire fences and armed guards surrounded the entire acreage. For the first time since she'd testified against her ex-husband, Lindsey allowed herself to think about the reality of his situation. He probably hated her for putting him here....

When she'd first met Jim, he'd been handsome and confident, an energetic man who'd finished law school at the top of his class, a man to admire. He'd swept her off her feet with his wicked charm and constant flattery. But he'd undergone a metamorphosis during the brief time they'd been married. He'd become controlling and selfish to the point of telling her how to dress, selecting her friends, monitoring her phone calls. Jealousy had become his best friend, her worst enemy. The final straw for her was when he'd insisted she resign her teaching position. She'd balked. His violent temper had forced her to face the true Jim Faulkner—a controlling, manipulative, self-centered man who wanted her as a trophy wife, not a man who truly loved her.

"Lindsey?"

She shook herself back to the moment, faintly aware they'd been parked for several minutes. Either Gavin was collecting himself or he'd simply been giving her time to gain her courage. Thankfully the rain had softened to a light drizzle, but the murky gray of the sky painted a dreary mausoleum atmosphere.

"I'm ready."

He slid out, hurried to her side and opened the door. Lindsey followed up the steps to the yellowed brick structure. She could practically hear the clang of metal doors shutting as they entered, prisoners rasping tin cans across the iron bars. Clichéd, she thought, but her nerves were so wrought, she couldn't conjure up any images that hadn't originated from television or movies.

Once inside, she instantly felt the coldness of confinement closing around her. Guards ushered them through a set of heavy double doors and security. Finally a guard escorted them into an empty room with a few long, cafeteria-style tables and hard vinyl chairs. The near-bare room smelled of fresh paint, sweat and cigarettes. She gripped the edge of the chair, suddenly wondering how her ex-husband would react to her visit. Would he be surprised? Angry? Shocked to see her?

Gavin stroked the indentation of her spine. "I know this is hard, Linds. But remember, he can't hurt you. I'm right here."

She nodded slowly, but the door squeaked open and they jerked apart. The moment her ex-husband recognized her, hatred sparked in his eyes. Then that familiar cocky grin slid on his face as he swaggered toward her. His hands were cuffed, his golfer's tan long since faded. His eyes bore through her. Steely cold gray, the color once she'd thought so unique, the color she'd grown to despise. His brown hair was a little longer, not as neat, certainly not styled with the expensive mousse he preferred. Gray tinged the edges and age lines had created grooves beside his eyes. Jim Faulkner was such a vain man, he must hate the change.

The guard, a beefy man with leatherlike skin and a tattoo of a lizard on his forearm, kept a hand on his arm as shoved her ex-husband into a chair.

"Watch what you say and do," the guard stated flatly.

Jim smirked. "Did you miss me, baby?"

She shook her head and dropped her gaze to the number on his generic prison uniform. He immediately stiffened. Then Gavin emerged beside her and Jim actually rose in his seat, the heat from his eyes firing daggers at Gavin.

"What the hell are you doing here?" Venom laced his voice as he stood, his arms dangling down in front of him, his hands balled into fists. The guard stepped forward in warning, but Gavin shook his head, signaling he had things under control.

The two men faced each other, almost toe-to-toe. Gavin's impressive stature dwarfed her ex. The tension between the two men stretched taut and thick. "We have to talk, Faulkner."

His sour gaze scanned the room. "You have my undivided attention."

Gavin pulled out a chair for her and another for himself and she willingly sank into it.

"What's wrong, baby? You're skin and bones. Single life not as great as you thought it would be?"

Lindsey couldn't miss the sarcasm in his voice. "I'm sure it's better than this place," she said quietly.

His sharp gaze cut to Gavin, then back to her. "Is that why you came here? Worried about me?"

"Dream on," Gavin muttered gruffly.

Her ex reached for her, but Lindsey pressed her back as far into the chair as possible, unwilling to allow him to touch her.

"I've never seen you at a loss for words. You sure didn't have any trouble speaking your mind in court."

How could she ever have been blinded by this man's charm? "We came because I needed to talk to you."

Her ex leaned back in the chair, his expression almost amused. "Talk away, honey. I've missed the sound of your sexy voice."

"I'll do the talking," Gavin said.

Faulkner stood. "Then I'm out of here." He motioned to the guard. "I'm ready to—"

"No, Jim, wait."

Faulkner hesitated, his lips twisting into a smug smile. "All right. But he has to stay out of it." He sat back down, a swarmy look on his face. "So, honey, what can I do for you?"

Lindsey's lips pinched together in a frown. "I had a baby about six weeks ago. But the doctor said he died."

"Then again, you already know that, didn't you, Faulkner?" Gavin asked.

Faulkner shot Gavin a lethal look and let his gaze slide over Lindsey suggestively. "I know a lot of things about my little ex, don't I sweetheart?"

Tears instantly burned Lindsey's eyes, but she blinked them away furiously, determined not to let her ex intimidate her. "I think my son is alive and I want to know what you had to do with his disappearance."

"What I had to do with our baby?" Faulkner puffed up his chest. "Why, darling, I planted the seed. Or have you forgotten that night?'' He reached out to trace a finger over her hand but Lindsey pulled her hand away in revulsion.

''And you didn't have the decency to even let me know you were pregnant. You were a naughty girl, Lindsey. You sent the father of your baby to jail. What did you plan to tell our little boy when he got old enough to ask about me?''

''You never wanted a child so what difference does it make?'' Lindsey clenched her hands together. ''I just wanted to raise the baby in peace. But then...''

''Then the little tyke died,'' Faulkner said in a deep voice. His grin faded, a moment of almost-remorse darkening his features. ''I really was sorry to hear about that, babe. But if you want, we can try again, you could request conjugal visits—''

''Shut up,'' Gavin snapped. ''What did you have to do with the baby's disappearance?''

Faulkner frowned. ''I thought the baby died right after birth.''

''We have reason to believe he's alive, that he was kidnapped,'' Gavin said.

Faulkner's cold eyes stared at them unblinking. ''And you think I kidnapped my own son—from prison?''

Lindsey swallowed, fighting her emotions. ''Someone's been sending me notes. They mailed me his...footprint,'' she murmured brokenly. ''Did you hire someone to take him to hurt me?''

''You're crazy,'' Faulkner growled in contempt.

''You had someone following Lindsey during the trial, that's how you found her at the safe house. They tried to kill her, so she couldn't testify against you,'' Gavin said. ''And your parents hired a P.I. to follow her when she moved to Raleigh. They kept you informed. Were they the ones who set everything up?''

"This is all bullshit.'' Faulkner stood, knocking his chair over in his haste. The guard grabbed his arm but her ex-husband jerked it away. Gavin held out a hand in warning and nodded toward the guard. "First, you put me in jail, now you come here and accuse me of something else,'' Faulkner snarled. "What the hell are you doing, trying to screw up my chances of parole?''

"If you had something to do with this baby's disappearance, you won't ever see parole,'' Gavin said.

"I know you hate me, Jim,'' Lindsey said. "But if you know where my son is, you have to tell me. Please don't do this to me. I know he's alive. I can't explain it, but I can hear him crying for me at night.''

He stared at her long and hard, a muscle ticking in his jaw. "I did know about the baby. But think about it, Lindsey. My parents could have taken you to court, sued for custody, and, with their connections, would have gotten it. So, you see, you're off base here.''

Lindsey's mind reeled. She couldn't tell if he was sincere or not. He'd lied to her so convincingly all those other times.

"You wanted revenge,'' Gavin said. "And you're heartless enough to do something like this, just to hurt Lindsey.''

"I'm not as heartless as you think.'' He turned to Lindsey. "Let me know if you find out the baby's alive. And if you get a ransom note, call me. I might be able to talk my folks into paying it.''

In exchange for visitation rights? Lindsey wondered.

Faulkner gestured to the guard, turned and walked through the heavy concrete doors without even looking back.

A few minutes later, Lindsey's legs wobbled as she and Gavin exited the prison. As soon as she climbed into the car, she sagged against the seat, her emotions flying into a tailspin of guilt and frustration and concern.

If her ex hadn't kidnapped her baby, who had? And if her baby had been kidnapped and the kidnapper wanted a ransom, why hadn't they already contacted her with demands?

GAVIN TWISTED sideways in the front seat of the car, instinctively pulling Lindsey into his arms. Had he put her through seeing her ex for nothing?

"You think he's telling the truth?"

Lindsey clutched the front of his denim shirt with her fingers, pressing her face into the comfort of his arms. "Yes. I...I don't know."

He nodded, then set his chin on top of her head, and stroked her back. Trouble was, he thought Faulkner was telling the truth, too. His nostrils hadn't flared once.

"I know seeing Faulkner was difficult, but I still think we had to confront him."

She remained silent, motionless, except for the small quiver of her body. The soft wispy strands of her hair tickled his jaw, reminding him of the night they'd slept together. He felt her chest heave against his and knew she was fighting for control. He hugged her closer, his hand rubbing the back of her spine, roving up to her neck, then sliding into her hair. The scent of that lavender body wash she loved mingled with her own sweet female scent, resurrecting a need that had gone too long unfulfilled. He pressed a tender kiss into her hair and felt her breasts swell, her nipples straining against the thin cotton of her blouse.

One of the side doors swung open and he spied a group

of prisoners being led outside. He gently eased her from his arms, rerouting his mind and libido to the present.

He tipped Lindsey's face up, offering her a benign smile. "You okay?"

She smiled, that gut wrenching brave smile she'd wielded like a coat of armor during the trial.

His heart rolled in his chest. "We'd better get out of here before someone spots us."

She glanced out the window, saw the prisoners and nodded, suddenly withdrawing and sliding back to her seat. He started the car, shifted into gear and eased down the drive. A few minutes later, he settled the radio station on a soft rock station to fill the silence. When his cell phone rang, he readjusted the volume so he could hear.

"McCord here."

"Gavin, it's Simon. I have some news."

"Yeah?"

"Word is Johnson's still pretty hostile. His wife had a nervous breakdown after they buried the boy."

Gavin stewed over the information, wondering if there could be a connection.

"And Danny Swain, seemed he held an ice-pick grudge against you while he'd been in the slammer. Mouthed off about what he planned to do to you after he finished his sentence."

"I'm not surprised."

"It gets worse."

His partner's tone sounded so bleak, he braced himself for the worst, his gut tightening. "He's out, right?"

"As of three weeks ago. Bought a bus ticket to Raleigh."

Gavin muttered a curse. "Anything else?"

Simon sighed. '''Fraid so. His cellmate said he kept a newspaper photo taped to his wall.''

''Yeah. Of who?''

''You and Lindsey Payne.''

Chapter Nine

Although an icy chill had seeped into her body, Lindsey struggled to control her panicked reaction when Gavin explained his partner's findings. Horrid as it sounded, she'd rather her former husband have kidnapped the baby than some strange criminal who wanted revenge on Gavin. Or her.

"But if that man you arrested kidnapped my baby, why hasn't he contacted us for some sort of ransom? How would he even know you and I had been together?"

"Good question. I only wish I knew the answer." Gavin turned into downtown Raleigh, maneuvering through traffic with ease, his face a mask of frustration.

Lindsey bit down on her lip. "Oh, my god, the letter."

"What letter?"

"The one I told you I'd written about the baby. I took it to the courthouse that day. When you told me to go away, I tossed it in the trash on the way out."

Alarm sprang in Gavin's eyes. "So Swain could have found it."

"But if he kidnapped Cory, why wouldn't he have contacted you by now?"

Gavin averted his gaze, wondering about the note, *An*

Eye For An Eye… "I don't know. He's a long shot. I want to talk to Faulkner's folks."

"What?"

"Even if your ex didn't arrange to kidnap the baby, there's a possibility his parents did. They hired the P.I. And they made no bones about how they felt about you at the trial."

Lindsey nodded, remembering the elderly couple's animosity. "They thought I should have supported my husband, no matter what."

Gavin reached over and covered her hand with his. "You did the right thing, Lindsey. Faulkner had to be stopped."

"But you said the Faulkners thought the baby might not be Jim's?"

"That's what they *told* the P.I., maybe to throw him off. Whether or not they believed it, we can't be certain. We have to question them, see their reactions when we confront them the way we did Jim."

Lindsey's fingers tightened around his palm. "What if I brought this on myself? What if our son is in danger because I turned against Jim?"

"Don't do that, Linds."

"What?"

"Don't blame yourself. None of this is your fault."

Lindsey lay her head back and tried to rest. Maybe there was something else she could do.

"Gavin, one of my teacher friends has a sister who's an anchor for the local noonday news on channel eleven."

"And?"

"Maybe she'd let me go on air and make a plea for help. You know, do one of those human interest pieces where I could tell my story, beg people to call in with information."

Gavin's jaw tightened. "I don't know, Linds. Sometimes public pleas draw prank calls that can be misleading. We haven't brought in the FBI yet."

"Maybe it's time we did. The more exposure the better." Lindsey began rehearsing her plea in her head. "Gavin, please, I have to do something. Maybe someone has seen something, knows something that can help us. Or maybe Janet or that girl will see me and call in. We have to try every possible way to find our baby."

He gave her a grim look and he handed her the cell phone.

"You're right. Go ahead and call. And see if you can set up the interview for today."

A FEW MINUTES later Gavin veered his car down Bristow Drive to the gated country club/polo community of Saddlebrook, the elitist neighborhood where the Faulkners resided. His mind, however, had checked out miles back down the road with Lindsey's question. If Danny Swain had kidnapped his baby, why hadn't the man let Gavin know? Gavin had been unable to answer her, unable to speak his worst fear. Maybe he *had* let Gavin know. Maybe Swain had sent the note—*An Eye For An Eye...*

Had he been hoping Lindsey's ex would have the answer and he wouldn't have to explore the other possibilities? Of course, the more probable explanation was that the other woman Lindsey claimed to have delivered the same night as she had kidnapped her baby. Dealing with a distraught grieving mother seemed much less threatening than dealing with Swain—a cold-blooded killer.

His head spinning, he maneuvered into the entrance to Saddlebrook, faintly aware Lindsey had retreated into her shell again. Probably bracing herself for her encounter with the mother-in-law from hell.

The security guard checked his ID, his eyes narrowing in disgust at Gavin's car. "Is there a problem?" He scanned his clipboard. "I haven't been notified—"

"No trouble. I'm conducting an investigation and simply need to ask the Faulkners a few routine questions."

The guard nodded reluctantly, then allowed them through.

From the freshly manicured lawns and colorful gardens to the spacious five-acre estate lots, wealth obviously abounded. His small sedan looked sorely out of place compared to the Mercedeses, Jaguars, and other foreign sportscars gracing the cobblestone driveways. Lindsey had once lived this lifestyle with Faulkner.

He couldn't imagine. He had no idea what kind of house she and Faulkner had shared, but judging from the man's expensive taste, he would never have brought her home to anything less than a mansion. Far from the dive he lived in himself. Not that it mattered—

"It looks like nothing's changed here," Lindsey commented dryly. "Still as stuffy looking as always."

He relaxed slightly, why he didn't know. Lindsey and he still lived different kinds of lives.

Lindsey fiddled with a loose thread on her pale pink blouse. "I wonder if we should have called."

"No. I want the advantage of surprise on our side."

"They might not be home."

"I'll chance it." He pulled into the ostentatious circular drive, glanced briefly at the pond by the gazebo where gardeners tended to the variety of roses climbing the white latticework, then to the monstrosity of a stucco house.

"I never liked this house," Lindsey murmured as they climbed from the car. "Unfortunately Jim's goal was to outdo his parents and own an even larger one."

He stared at her in disbelief. "Did you?"

Lindsey laughed. "No, but I'm sure money drove him to make some of his underhanded deals."

Gavin nodded. He'd seen greed do that to people before. They walked in silence to the door and rang the bell. Seconds later a bald-headed butler escorted them into a study the size of Gavin's entire apartment. Polished marble floors sparkled like crystal, ornate Oriental artwork decorated the butter-yellow halls and the dark leather furniture and Persian rug in the study could have paid for…his son's college education.

The man gave Lindsey a look of pure disdain. "I thought we'd surely seen the end of you."

Lindsey flinched. "I'm sorry you feel that way, Walt. But please tell the Faulkners we're here."

"I don't believe they'll want to talk to you."

Gavin frowned. Walt's loyalties obviously lay with the people who wrote his paychecks. "It doesn't matter whether they want to talk to us or not. This is not a social call. And if they refuse, I can take them down to the station."

Walt gasped, squaring his shoulders as if insulted. "That won't be necessary."

"As a matter of fact, maybe you can answer a few questions about the Faulkners and their interest in Miss Payne."

"I don't discuss my employers," Walt stated curtly. "Especially where it concerns Miss Payne, not after what she did to this family."

"I only did what I thought was right," Lindsey said.

Walt glared at her. "You destroyed this family by sending little Jim to prison. How can that possibly be right?"

"He hurt a lot of innocent people, Walt."

Walt finally admitted he'd worked for the Faulkners for fifteen years, but he refused to offer any more information, other than to solicit a glass of water for Lindsey and verify that Mrs. Faulkner was indeed home.

Seconds later, Yvonne Faulkner, dressed in a shocking red silk pantsuit with emeralds gleaming off her earlobes, wrist and neck, strode in, appearing confident but annoyed. Until she saw Lindsey. Her expression immediately transformed to one of pure hatred.

Bright red nails thumbed through her short, artificially auburn waves. ''I can't believe you'd actually have the gall to visit me.''

''I can't quite believe it myself, Yvonne,'' Lindsey said softly.

The bitter woman bristled. ''You may no longer call me by my first name. That privilege is reserved for family members.''

Lindsey squared her shoulders and stood her ground.

He decided to forget small talk. ''Is your husband here? We'd like to speak with both of you.''

Mrs. Faulkner poured herself a scotch and sipped it. ''No, he's away on business. I suggest you state yours as quickly as possible before I throw you out.'' She gave them a haughty stare. ''That is, if you actually have business. If you simply came to harass me, you may leave now.''

God, the woman was cold. Remembering how equally callous she'd acted the day Lindsey had testified, Gavin refused to give her further recovery time from the shock of seeing Lindsey. He immediately launched into the reason for their visit.

''Yes, we knew you were pregnant,'' Mrs. Faulkner said. ''At first we suspected the baby might not be Jim's but that P.I. said he didn't see you with anyone else. I suppose no one else would have you after what you did to my son.''

"Just tell us what happened," Gavin said curtly.

"Then we waited. We hoped you would at least have the decency to tell Jim, but you didn't, did you?"

Lindsey said nothing in defense, she simply sat and stared at the angry woman.

"So, you told your son about the pregnancy?" Gavin asked.

"He had a right to know he was going to be a father."

"And this private investigator kept watching Lindsey during the pregnancy?"

"We simply wanted to make certain she didn't take the baby and flee somewhere so my son would never see him."

"You knew when the baby was born?" Gavin asked.

"We were informed. Maybe if we had been there, our grandson wouldn't have died."

As if they blamed Lindsey.

Gavin fisted his hands on the chair. The woman had no way of knowing the baby was *his*, that he should have been there, protecting, taking care of Lindsey and his child.

"And if my baby had lived?" Lindsey asked. "What did you plan to do?"

"We would have sued for custody," Mrs. Faulkner said without hesitating. "In some cases, money talks, you know."

The ice cubes in Lindsey's glass clinked as she tried to steady her hands. "I suppose it does."

"You could have paid someone to fake the baby's death, then kill Lindsey—"

"You're out of your mind coming in here with such accusations!" Mrs. Faulkner's eyes burned with contempt. "My husband and I have an upstanding reputation in the community, at least we did until this woman spoiled it. Do you think we'd risk prison to get our grandson when we could have achieved the same results in court?''

It didn't seem likely, Gavin admitted silently.

"Now, I think you two had better leave." She stood, waving her hand like a queen dismissing her charges.

But Gavin wasn't finished. "We believe Lindsey's baby is alive, Mrs. Faulkner." He crossed the room to stand in front of her, then stared at her heavily made-up face. "If you know something about the baby's whereabouts, I suggest you tell us now. Kidnapping is a very serious charge. You don't want to wind up like your son, spending the rest of your life in a jail cell." He made an exaggerated point of letting his gaze scrutinize the room. "The accommodations aren't nearly as opulent."

Mrs. Faulkner's painted lips parted in shock. Anger quickly replaced it. "I asked you to leave. Now get out and don't come back."

In one fluid motion, she sauntered from the room, leaving the cloying scent of her expensive perfume and her hatred of Lindsey lingering in the air.

"ARE YOU SURE you're up for this?" Gavin asked Lindsey two hours later at the local TV station.

"I'm fine, Gavin, stop worrying."

Gavin accepted a cup of coffee from the stage manager but Lindsey declined, afraid the caffeine would upset her queasy stomach. She'd been feeling slightly dizzy and a little nauseated all morning but she assumed stress had caused her physical symptoms.

"We could come back tomorrow," Gavin offered.

"No, I want to do the interview today." She laid her hand on Gavin's arm, aware his muscle automatically flexed beneath her palm. Even through his denim shirt, she felt the heat and tension radiating from his body. Part of her wanted to bury herself in that heat, in his strong arms and body, but the self-preservation part of her warned her to keep her distance. The moments with Gavin were precious, but they wouldn't last. "Every day we wait is one more day until we find our son."

Gavin's forced smile did nothing to alleviate her anxiety. She realized he was walking a fine line between being positive and not raising false hopes but she was determined to be optimistic. They would find her baby.

Then she would bring her son home and be his mother.

Beyond that—what would happen between her and Gavin—well, she couldn't think that far ahead.

"You know there may be repercussions in Maple Hollow. The sheriff isn't going to like the fact that you went public. The doctor may even bring a lawsuit."

"I don't care," Lindsey said firmly. "I'm not giving up. And I'm not letting them convince me I'm crazy or railroad me with some lawsuit."

Gavin started to reply but Terry Blake, the friend of Lindsey's schoolteacher buddy and anchorwoman for noonday news, approached them, tucking the small wireless mike into her lapel. She paused and took Lindsey's hands, squeezing gently. "I'm so sorry you've been through this, Lindsey. When April called, I felt terrible for you."

"I appreciate you letting me appear on the show, especially at the last minute," Lindsey said. "You can't imagine how much this means to me."

The tall redhead nodded, gesturing toward the desk and chairs, "Once the station manager talked with the other detective, Mr. McCord's friend, he felt your situation warranted our help. You'll only have about three or four minutes so give as much information as possible. We're live, but we'll rerun the interview several times."

Lindsey agreed, reciting in her head the short-and-to-the-point speech she and Gavin had sketched out in the car on the way over.

"And don't worry about giving your address, in fact, you shouldn't do that," Terry continued. "We're directing callers to phone the police station. If any calls come through here, they'll be forwarded."

"We'll tape all the calls and save them for possible evidence," Gavin added.

It was something he'd arranged in the car on the way over. Simon's ex-FBI agent friends had agreed to meet them at Lindsey's after the broadcast. All calls would be forwarded to her home phone. Thank heaven for Gavin's connections.

Suddenly the stage lit up and camera men swung into action. Terry ushered Lindsey to one of the chairs.

Terry turned a brilliant but compassionate smile to the camera then introduced Lindsey, explaining that a baby's disappearance was dire and asking people to pay attention.

Lindsey folded her hands in her lap to keep from fidgeting and briefly paraphrased her situation. Emotions thickened her voice as soon as she began. "I'm appealing to all of you. My baby is missing. I heard another woman crying in the clinic where I gave birth that night. Whoever you are, if you can hear me, I feel for you. I honestly do. If you lost your baby that night and didn't think you could go on, I understand why you might take my son." She paused, fighting for composure. "But what you've done isn't right. You've taken a child from its rightful mother, a mother who wants and loves her baby. I'm begging you, please bring my baby home to me."

Terry made a sympathetic sound. "But you aren't sure this woman has your child, is that correct, Ms. Payne?"

Lindsey nodded. "No, I'm not certain. If not, *whoever*

you are, for whatever reason you kidnapped my baby, please let me know what you want. I'll do anything you say, but please bring my son back home.'' Her voice broke and she dabbed at her eyes with a tissue.

"Thank you, Ms. Payne. Listeners, if you have information regarding this baby, please phone 555-616-3434 and ask for Detective McCord. I'll be saying a prayer myself for the infant's recovery." Once again, Terry recited the baby's birth date, weight and reiterated the phone number for the police, then the number flashed onto the screen.

A few minutes later she staggered outside and inhaled the scent of fresh rain permeating the air. Water droplets clung to the sunparched sidewalks mirroring the tears clinging to her eyelashes. The entire staff had been so supportive and compassionate they had restored her faith in goodwill.

"You did great." Gavin hugged her, his eyes full of emotions. Turmoil, hope and that undeniable loneliness that radiated through the dark irises of his eyes, and drew her whole body into a knot of need. And want.

He cupped her face with his big hands, stroking the sides of her jaw with his callused thumbs, his calm betrayed only by the slight quiver of his breath brushing against her cheek. "God, I'm so proud of you, Linds. You're the strongest woman I've ever known."

Lindsey licked her suddenly dry lips and brought her hand up to rest over his. A few dark hairs dusting the tops of his hands and his skin felt warm and slightly rough, reminding her of the strength of his masculinity. She ached to pull him into her arms, to reassure him she would always be there for him.

But he didn't want to hear that.

And she couldn't be a fool for him twice. So she simply

squeezed his hand. "Thanks for being here and taking over the investigation, Mac."

A muscle ticked in his jaw. "You know I want to find our baby, too. This isn't just a job to me, Linds."

Her heart thumped off-beat at his tone. He slanted his head sideways, lowered his mouth and covered hers, consuming her with the urgency of his demanding kiss. Unable to hold back the groan that rose from deep in her throat, she clung to his arms, her head spinning. He delved deeper, reaching all the way inside her with his hunger as if to extract her very soul.

But the sound of traffic intruded. When Gavin finally pulled away, she felt his withdrawal like an earthquake stealing the solid ground beneath her feet. A strange expression crossed his face as he stared down the street.

"What's wrong?"

"Nothing. I…I thought I saw somebody I knew." His voice sounded whiskey-rough. "I'll go get the car."

She started to argue but realized he needed a moment to get his libido under control. And so did she. Good heavens, she'd almost asked him to make love to her in the middle of the busy street. He hurried toward the parking lot, coasting through traffic as he crossed the street, and she hugged her arms around herself. Gavin was the only one who could take away her chill. But when he deserted her, she would be colder than ever. More alone.

She couldn't kid herself. He would leave again.

A horn honked and she glanced up as he inched his car toward the parking attendant's booth. A tall woman wearing a scarf pushed a baby stroller past the meter. Lindsey's heart clenched at the sight. Then the woman stopped and turned to stare at her and pain rippled through her chest. She seemed to be staring directly at Lindsey. Something about the way she was looking at her... Who was she? Could the baby be her son?

Lindsey had to find out. Had to see for herself.

She stepped to the curb to cross the busy intersection and the woman jerked, then started pushing the stroller faster, hurrying away from Lindsey in the opposite direction. Lindsey rushed forward just as the no-walking sign lit up. She couldn't wait. She was losing the woman. Losing her baby. No, not again. She had to run.

She dodged the cars and honking horns and ran faster. Seconds later, she caught up with the woman and reached for her arm. The woman spun around, looking wild-eyed and frightened, then launched herself in front of the baby carriage.

Chapter Ten

Lindsey rocked back on her heels at the sight of the baby girl, wrapped in a fluffy pink blanket.

"Why are you following me?" the woman hissed. "What do you want?"

Shocked at her own actions, Lindsey stared at her, shivers racking her body. "I'm sorry, I thought—"

"Get away from me or I'm calling the police."

"I thought you were someone else. I...I didn't mean to scare you." Lindsey's last words caught on a sob and she turned and fled back the other way.

What had she done? She'd accosted some poor innocent woman and her baby on the street. She must be losing her mind....

GAVIN'S HEART completely stopped when he saw the scene play out in front of him.

Poor Lindsey. The day had been too much and she'd finally buckled under the pressure. He rolled the car to a stop beside the street, climbed out and walked slowly over to her. She stood trembling, her eyes dazed.

He pulled her into his arms and held her, his own eyes filling with moisture. "Shh, honey, it's okay. Let's go home now."

Lindsey simply nodded against his chest, her sobs quiet but so heartwrenching his own throat clogged with tears. He hugged her to him, soothing her with quiet words as he settled her into the car. Unable to stand the tormented look on her face, he shifted into gear, pulled across the road and parked. Then he turned to her and dragged her into his arms, desperate to offer her comfort.

"Oh, Gavin, I…I scared that poor woman. I thought that was our baby…."

Her words broke and he rocked her back and forth, leaning his face into her hair, whispering soft words of comfort while she wept. "It's okay, Linds. It's been an awful day, just let it all out."

"I just wanted to hold him, I wanted it so bad…" She clung to him, limp and trembling, soaking his shirt. The anguish in her voice, in her whole body seeped into him and he ached deep in his soul. But he continued to hold her, to press loving kisses on her cheek, in her hair, wanting to give her his strength, his determination. Finally, when she seemed spent, she lay her head in his lap and closed her eyes. He gently stroked her hair along the sides of her face as he started the car, not surprised when she fell into a deep, exhausted sleep on the ride home.

Unable to shake the worry nagging at him, he brushed at the tears that, in spite of all his willpower, trickled from the corners of his own eyes and rolled down his cheeks. They were no closer to finding their son than they had been that morning. Statistics rattled through his head, twisting his nerve endings into a massive knot of anxiety—ninety-five percent of kidnapped babies were recovered shortly after being snatched. It had already been six weeks since their baby was born. Since he'd disappeared.

With every day that passed, the chances of finding their son grew slimmer.

THE DAY HAD taken more of a toll on Lindsey than she'd expected. She slept most of the way home, barely cognizant of the fact that it had rained the better part of the trip. She was going crazy.

She'd totally lost herself back there with that woman and the guilt was enormous, but she had to collect herself. She couldn't start depending on Gavin.

The scent of wet grass and fall leaves assaulted her as she dragged herself from the car and walked up to her front porch. Dusk fell in radiant orange and yellow streaks, the sky turning a pinkish hue as the sun slid below the horizon. The night would soon descend upon them, plagued with nightmares and darkness. Another night without her baby.

Gavin massaged the tightness from her neck as she unlocked the door and she tried not to think about how wonderful the simple tender ministrations felt. The sound of a car spitting gravel took them both off guard and they pivoted to see a dark sedan park in the drive, the sheriff on its tail.

"Looks like trouble," Gavin muttered.

"I'm sure Sheriff Forbes is miffed we went on TV," Lindsey said. "Who are those men?"

"Probably my partner's friends, the ex-FBI agents he told me about."

"How can you tell?"

He laughed softly. "The suits. The car. You learn to pick 'em out in a crowd."

"I'll put on some coffee."

"Probably a good idea. They're going to set up the surveillance equipment to monitor incoming calls."

Sheriff Forbes lumbered up the steps after the two ex-FBI agents, his fat cheeks ruddy. Gavin greeted them, then invited them inside before the sheriff could start in with his complaints. Lindsey filled the coffee pot and set out several mugs.

"I'm Rob Barnes and this is Detective Jernigan," the younger of the two former agents said, shaking both Lindsey and Gavin's hands. Barnes was fit and trim and handsome in a preppy sort of way, probably in his late thirties. The taller man's age fell in the fifty-plus range. Jernigan's tie hung askew, his round glasses had been cracked.

"You're a friend of Simon's?" Barnes asked.

Gavin nodded.

"Sorry to hear about your baby, Miss Payne."

Lindsey smiled tightly and offered the men coffee. Rob Barnes took his black while Jernigan overflowed his with sugar and creamer.

"This is Sheriff Forbes," Gavin said. "He's been investigating the gas leak I told you about."

The sheriff's bushy eyebrows climbed his forehead. "I was a little out of the loop today," Forbes admitted, with a warning glance at Gavin. "Mind filling me in on when you decided to go public?"

"I insisted we go on the air today," Lindsey said. "I thought it was time we broaden the search for my baby."

"The more people looking for him, the better our chances are of finding him," Gavin added.

"Miss Payne, do you have a baby picture we could post?" Jernigan asked. "I want to get this into the National Center for Missing and Exploited Children as soon as possible."

"No…no picture," Lindsey said quietly.

Barnes frowned. "So basically all we have is the baby's length and weight at birth?"

"That's right," Gavin said. "Although Lindsey received an autopsy report and footprint. I've already sent them to be analyzed."

Barnes hesitated, but finally nodded in agreement. "Let's set up the surveillance equipment."

"I want all calls transferred here," Gavin said.

Jernigan nodded. "We'll handle things, McCord."

Gavin jerked the phone line from the man's hands. "I started this—"

"You're not objective and you know it." Barnes placed a hand on Gavin's arm to calm him. "Let us take the show from here. Your partner filled us in on the details. If this is indeed a kidnapping—"

"We're talking about my baby," Gavin cut in. "I don't intend to sit on my ass and twiddle my thumbs while you guys work the case."

The sheriff coughed in shock. "*Your* baby?"

Gavin hesitated, realizing he'd revealed his secret. "Yes, *my* baby." He approached Forbes, menace written on his features. "But no one, I mean *no one,* is supposed to know that, do you understand me?"

Forbes's hand shook but he nodded amicably.

Lindsey relayed the story about her ex-husband, Gavin's part in protecting her when she was a witness, their visit to the jail.

"Now don't you think something strange is going on?" Gavin asked.

The sheriff shifted sideways, folding his arms. "Maybe, but I still don't think Doc is involved. He's a good man."

"You are going to cooperate with us?" Barnes asked, indicating the surveillance equipment. "Share any information you might receive on a local level?"

Forbes nodded.

Jernigan slurped his coffee. "I still think you should pull yourself off the case, McCord."

Gavin squared his shoulders. "No way. Whoever kidnapped my son might be trying to get revenge on me."

"Any suspects?" Barnes asked.

Gavin filled them in on Swain, the prisoner who'd threatened revenge on him, then explained the possibilities related to Lindsey's ex and his parents. He still wondered about Johnson… "Any news on Janet Quinn, the nurse who disappeared?" Gavin asked.

Forbes shook his head, along with the agents. Lindsey reminded herself to think positive. She had Gavin and the former FBI agents working on her side now. Something had to happen to break the case. She poured her cold coffee down the drain and stared at the tiny little rattle in the bassinet. Unable to resist, she picked up the pale yellow baby blanket and pressed her cheek against the downy softness. Her baby needed her.

Yes, something had to happen soon. It simply had to.

AN HOUR LATER, Gavin breathed a sigh of relief when the ex-agents and sheriff finally departed. Lindsey looked exhausted. She'd thrown together a stroganoff dish while he'd checked the equipment with the agents and coerced Jernigan into letting him monitor the incoming calls for the night. They'd replayed a few calls that had come in shortly after the TV show. Several false leads had surfaced already, a couple of pranks. Unfortunately nothing helpful.

The agents had wanted to stay the night. Gavin knew they were only doing their jobs, but Lindsey's place felt cramped enough with the two of them. They didn't need two uptight former FBI agents to add to the mounting tension. He guessed Barnes wasn't so bad, except he hadn't liked the way he'd looked at Lindsey. As if he'd noticed she was a woman and he'd be glad to comfort her.

Gavin scrubbed his hand over his tired eyes and sighed.

God, he couldn't believe the direction of his thoughts. He actually sounded jealous. Not that he had any claims on Lindsey…except she had carried his child.

Cory would always tie the two of them together.

He'd always sympathized with people who'd lost children, but he'd never understood the gutwrenching emotions that could steal a person's sanity. Now he *knew*.

Focus on finding your son. Do your job. You can't afford to let your emotions get involved.

They ate in silence, both too exhausted to rehash the day's events. At least he ate. Lindsey simply pushed her food around with her fork to give the semblance of actually eating. She wasn't fooling him, though. When the phone rang, she hurried to answer it, and he followed her to the den, easing up the receiver to the other line to listen.

"Lindsey, this is JoAnn. I saw the news today. Are you all right?"

Lindsey leaned against the sofa. "Yeah, thanks for calling, Jo."

So this woman was the Jo she'd called from his apartment, not Joe a man. He slowly lowered the second phone to give her some privacy and decided to clear the table. Her soft voice cracked as she confided the day's events to her friend.

"Thanks for calling, Jo. Good luck with the kids tomorrow." She murmured something low and discernible. "Don't worry, I'll let you know when we find him."

When we find him.

The hope in her voice tore through him. He couldn't disappoint her.

As soon as she hung up, the phone rang again. "Mom, oh, hey. Thanks for praying for us, I can feel your wishes all the way to my heart."

He smiled at the affectionate tone she used, his chest

tightening as he heard her describing their day. He wandered outside on the porch to give her some privacy, scanning the yard and woods for anything suspicious. A few minutes later, he glanced through the window and saw her sway slightly as she hung up the phone.

He rushed in and caught her. "You need to eat something."

She shook her head. "I can't. My stomach's been upset all day."

"You're under a lot of stress, you're probably exhausted." He helped her settle back on the sofa and brought her a footstool, then slipped off her sandals. "Do you need a doctor?"

"No, I'm just a little queasy. I'm sure it's simply nerves. I'll be all right after I rest."

"Stress can do strange things to the body." He found her bottle of vitamins on the windowsill, shook out two pills, filled a glass with water and brought them to her. "At least take these. If you don't, you're going to wind up back in the hospital." She downed them, then murmured a weak thank-you as she sipped the water.

He lowered himself beside her and gently brushed her cheek with his hand, his voice low and tender. "You want to keep up your strength, Lindsey. When the baby comes home you'll need it."

The first smile he'd seen all day graced her face. But even as she smiled, tears filled her eyes. "We will find him won't we, Mac?"

He curved his arm around her and hugged her to his chest. "I won't give up until we do."

She nodded against his chest, draping her arm across his stomach and curling into him. He brushed the soft strands of her hair, gently stroking the ends and massaging the tense muscles at the base of her neck. His mind replayed the day she'd asked him to find their son, the way she'd discounted the night they'd spent together as if it had meant nothing. Did she have feelings for him at all?

Her gaze lifted slightly and swung to the phone. "I thought we'd hear something before now."

He shrugged. "Don't give up yet."

She nodded again, and let her head rest against him. They sat together for what seemed like hours as he held her and comforted her. She slid her arms around his waist and kneaded the muscles in his back. The air hummed around them with unspoken tension. His lips touched her hair. He inhaled the sweet fragrance of her shampoo and his senses swirled into a maelstrom of desire. Desire that reached beyond the physical.

Desire that could never be slaked by anyone but Lindsey.

Her breath whispered against his shirt as she traced her fingers over his stomach and drew tiny circles over his abdomen. He inhaled sharply, every nerve ending in his body responding to her provocative but innocent touch. Then she lifted her head, her chin resting on his chest as she gazed into his eyes.

He wanted her.

Wanted to bury himself inside her and let her soothe away all the pain. Replace the icy loneliness in his soul with her gentle warmth. Wanted to tear away the distrust and hurt and ache in her eyes and fill her with his strength. Push into her and bring her to such mindless ecstasy the sadness would be wiped from her face. And he'd finally see her smile. At least temporarily.

Their breaths mingled as he lowered his mouth and sipped at her lips. She opened for him, the yearning in the way she inched her hands up to cup his face almost his undoing. He gripped her with his hands, forcing himself not to jerk her in his lap and ravage her the way he so desperately needed. Forced himself to take only what she offered. But the heat in her body sank into him, bit at his chill, melted his resolve and before he realized what had happened, he was hungrily devouring her. Kissing her like he might die any second. Pulling at her clothes and cupping her breasts.

She groaned in return, her response as fiery as his own, her body molding to his as they slid deeper into the cushions. His body hardened as his mouth consumed her, his tongue sought the inner recesses of her mouth with a ferocious hunger that she matched in return. She reached for the buttons on his shirt and one popped just as another sound penetrated the air around them.

The phone.

They jumped apart, wild-eyed and breathing hard. He gasped and tried to calm himself, hating the fear and guilt he suddenly saw in her eyes as she reached for the handset.

He grabbed the other line and Lindsey quickly straightened her blouse, yanking it back into place as she pressed the receiver to her ear. "Hello?"

She hesitated, then raised a brow at Gavin in question when no one replied.

He gestured for her to speak again.

"Hello, is anyone there?"

A low raspy voice sounded over the line. "Miss Payne?"

"Yes."

"Are you the woman they showed on the news today talking about your missing baby?"

Lindsey gulped. "Yes, that's right." Her knuckles whitened as her fingers tightened around the phone. "Do you know something about my baby?"

"I...I'm not sure."

"Anything you can tell me will help. Do you know who kidnapped him, where he is?"

Gavin placed a comforting hand on her back, massaging the tension in Lindsey's shoulders, trying to nod encouragement so she wouldn't spook the caller.

"I don't know anything for sure. But..." the voice trailed off, warbling slightly. "You wanted to know about some girl who had a baby that same night you did?"

"Yes, I mentioned the name of the clinic. It's in Maple Hollow."

The voice on the other end cleared his throat. "Yeah, well, I think I know the girl you're looking for."

Chapter Eleven

"Where is she now?"

"She's a student over here at Brevard college."

Lindsey recognized the place. Brevard was a small Methodist college about twenty-five miles from Asheville. "Do you know her name, where I could find her?"

The young man hesitated. "I think it's Candy Sue. Don't know her last name. I've seen her around campus. People been talking, you know, saying she was pregnant but she hadn't told anyone. Been wearing these big tent-like dresses, kept to herself."

A seed of hope sprouted, but frustration pulled at Lindsey. "What else can you tell us? Can you describe her, give me her address?"

A clicking sound punctuated the air as if he'd flicked a cigarette lighter. "Don't know where she lives. She's got black hair though, freckles, short girl, wears some of them funky round glasses. Hangs out near the library most of the time."

"You said she had the baby. Have you seen him?"

"No. Heard she gave the kid away."

A tremor rolled through Lindsey. If this girl hadn't kidnapped Lindsey's baby, where was he? And what had happened to the girl's child? Had she lost her baby and stolen Lindsey's to replace it? Could this boy be involved?

"Can you give us your name, maybe meet us on campus?"

"Look, lady I'm just a student here. I don't want any trouble."

"You're not in trouble, we just want you to meet us and point her out?"

As if the caller realized they might be tracing him, he claimed that was all the information he could offer and abruptly hung up. Lindsey stared at the phone in silence, barely aware when Gavin removed the receiver from her hand and checked to see if the tracer had picked up a location. The caller had used a pay phone from the school cafeteria. It could have been one of a hundred students calling.

"I don't understand." She searched Gavin's face for answers. "I thought maybe the woman was so distraught over losing her own child she'd kidnapped our son, but now…"

Gavin rubbed her hands. "Now we have a place to start looking." He tipped her chin up and lay his hand against her cheek. "Don't think beyond that, Linds. This is a start."

"But—"

He pressed his finger over her lips, silencing her. The intensity of his look reminded her of what they'd been doing before the phone call. Hunger and need still glimmered in his dark brown eyes, but the moment for lovemaking had passed. Regret had obviously taken center stage to his emotions. "It's been a long day, Linds. Let's get some sleep. Tomorrow we're going to Brevard."

GAVIN TRIED to stifle the surge of excitement over finally getting a small lead in the case. He'd chased a lot of dead trails in his life and prayed this wasn't one of them. But the man's call had stamped a seal of possible validity on Lindsey's argument about the other woman. And if they found the woman, he'd go straight to that cockamamie doctor's office and beat the truth out of him.

The shower kicked on and he fought images of Lindsey standing naked beneath the spray of warm water, her sexy body dotted with moisture and bubbles, her skin slick and wet and warm...waiting for his touch. God, how he wanted to join her, to wash the soapy, soft skin of her back, to tickle the underside of her perfect breasts with his fingertips, to drive her wild with pleasure.

But if they'd followed through on the ravenous lovemaking they'd begun earlier, would he be able to walk away from her again?

His head told him yes; his heart vetoed the probability.

But he would have to walk away.

Feeling anxious, he paced the homey cottage, pausing to study the small white bassinet. The pale yellow blanket dotted with bunny rabbits. The little blue teddy bear crouched inside. His gaze roamed to the nursery and he stalked toward it, aching to go inside. This was his son's room. He had a right to see it.

But he paused, his hand clutching the cold doorknob. A feeling of regret and longing swept through him so deep that his whole body began to shake. He could go inside, could pick the lock and finally look at the room Lindsey had prepared for their son's arrival. Moisture suddenly filled his eyes, pricking at his eyelids like a thousand needles trying to jab through his skin.

But he would be invading her privacy.

When Lindsey was ready to share the nursery, she'd show it to him. And when they solved the mystery surrounding his son's disappearance, they would open the door together. He rubbed his thumb over the train whistle in his pocket. When he found his son, he wanted to give him the special trinket so if he ever got lost again, he could blow on the whistle and Gavin would be able to find him.

THE NEXT DAY Gavin left Agent Barnes in charge of manning the phones at Lindsey's. Lindsey and Gavin drove to the Brevard campus, scrutinizing students as they walked to the dean's office.

"Should we look around first?" Lindsey asked.

"No, we don't want to alert the students we're here and take a chance on scaring her off."

A squatty looking gray-haired man greeted them, introduced himself as Dean Evans and invited them into his office. Gavin quickly explained the situation.

"Yes, I saw the news clip. I'm so sorry for your problems, Miss Payne."

"We received an anonymous call last night saying the young woman we're looking for is one of your students. We'd like to talk to her."

The older man regarded him with concern, then turned to Lindsey. "Do you think this young lady kidnapped your child?"

"I honestly don't know. She may be an innocent in all this, but it would help if I spoke with her. Her name is Candy Sue."

"We don't have a last name, but if you could check your computer—"

"I know Candy Sue," the dean said. He smiled when Gavin looked surprised. "This is a small campus, Mr. McCord. We take an active roll in all the students' lives."

"Then you know of her situation."

"Somewhat. And I can assure you she's not a kidnapper."

"Will you take us to her?"

Once again, the man studied him, but seemed to realize he should cooperate and motioned for them to follow. "We'll see if she's in the dorm. I'd like the chaplain to be present when you talk to her."

"No problem," Gavin and Lindsey both replied.

A few minutes later they met the chaplain and followed the men across campus to a medium-size dorm. When they reached the hall where Candy Sue lived, they found another girl inside.

"This is Jeanie, Candy Sue's roommate," the dean explained.

The chaplain took Jeanie aside and explained the situation.

Jeanie eyed them both, chewing on her lip. "She's due back any minute. She had an early class."

"I don't see any baby paraphernalia," Gavin whispered to Lindsey.

Lindsey nodded, glancing at the colorful posters on the wall, the scattered shoes, typical teenage CDs and books and clothes. A photograph of a thin girl sat on the metal desk. Scraggly hair, a plain pale face, freckles on her nose, she looked barely old enough to drive—could the innocent face in the picture actually have committed a crime?

"You knew she was pregnant?" Gavin asked.

Jeannie nodded.

"Do you know what happened with her baby?"

"I'll answer that."

"Candy Sue." Jeanie raced toward her friend but Candy Sue shrugged off her concern. A thin redheaded young boy wearing clunky glasses stood beside her, looking protective.

"I...I'm Candy Sue. I saw you on TV last night." The young woman actually held out a trembling hand to shake Lindsey's. Lindsey accepted the gesture and indicated a wooden desk chair. "Can we sit down and talk?"

The girl nodded and sank onto the bed, but Gavin kept his gaze trained on her, determined to scrutinize her every movement to see if she was lying.

"You're the boy who called us?" Lindsey asked.

He shook his head. "No, I'm Bobby. I don't know who called."

So they didn't know they were coming. "Then I'm glad you'll talk to me, Candy Sue," Lindsey said softly.

A Planet Hollywood T-shirt and baggy pair of denim shorts hung on the girl's skinny frame while pale thin white legs stretched below. She clutched the books to her as a shield, looking frail and scared to death. The boy moved behind her, one hand braced on her shoulder while the chaplain and dean hovered nearby.

"Look, Candy, we're not here to hurt you or accuse you of anything, but I think something terrible happened the night I gave birth and I'm trying to put the pieces together." Lindsey explained about the odd circumstances surrounding her baby.

Tears slowly slipped down the girl's cheeks. "I...I don't know what happened with your baby." She lowered her head, her voice a thready whisper, "But my baby didn't make it."

"You gave birth to a little boy, too?" Gavin asked.

The girl nodded, then began to sob. "He was stillborn. He had a heart problem, and the doctor said there was nothing he could do."

Except for the stillborn part, the story was exactly the same one the doctor had told Lindsey, right down to the heart condition. "Then you disappeared."

"I had a memorial service for him, then came back to school." Misery wrenched the girl's words. "That nice doctor at the clinic helped me arrange things."

"Did you plan to keep the baby?" Gavin asked.

Candy Sue nodded. "I thought about adoption but…" She looked up and squeezed Bobby's hand. "Bobby was going to help me raise him. Then he…he didn't make it."

She started to cry softly and Lindsey drew her into her arms and consoled her. "Shh, it's all right. You shouldn't go through this alone. Have you told your folks?"

The young girl shrank back in horror. "No, I couldn't. Please, promise me you won't tell them. My daddy will kill me."

Lindsey's troubled gaze flew to Gavin as if to ask, what next? Should they search her place, talk to her parents?

He didn't think there was any need. He had a gut feeling Candy Sue was telling the truth. The girl looked too fragile and miserable to be lying. And she was definitely afraid of her father. No, first, he would get a copy of the autopsy report for Candy Sue's child. Instincts warned him it would be identical to the one Lindsey had received. But if Candy Sue planned to keep her baby, then Cross and the lawyer hadn't switched Lindsey's son to replace Candy Sue's for an adoption. So what happened next? And why had Cross lied? He'd get a search warrant for Cross's office and files, but that would take some time. He'd confront the doctor first, make him tell the truth.

"Candy Sue, you heard Lindsey's story," Gavin said in a low voice. "I hate to suggest this, but would you mind taking a blood test? We simply want to clarify the results of the autopsy report."

Candy wiped her eyes and agreed, then followed them to the car, clinging to her friend Bobby as she went. Gavin took Lindsey's hand, adrenaline pumping. Soon they would have enough to nail Cross and force him to talk, and he couldn't wait to do it.

TWO HOURS later, after Candy had submitted to lab work and they'd dropped her off at the chaplain's office, Lindsey and Gavin returned to Maple Hollow. Lindsey tried to summon her nerve as they pulled into the hospital parking lot. Gavin had muttered obscenities about Cross all the way from Brevard to Maple Hollow. He'd also had his partner check Candy Sue's phone records, and true to her word, she hadn't been in contact with anyone off campus. Just to be cautious, he'd run a check on Bobby and his roommate and they'd spoken with the dean before they left, but the dean verified they were good boys, both visible on campus, certainly not capable of plotting a kidnapping scheme and hiding out a baby.

Lindsey felt shell-shocked and numb. She'd hoped the young woman had her son. At least she could have understood her reasons for kidnapping her baby. She could have even sympathized. But now, other possibilities nagged at her.

The doctor had definitely lied to her.

But why? Why would he tell her she'd been his only patient that night? Why would he allow someone to take her baby?

None of it made sense.

Unless that horrible man Gavin had arrested had stolen her baby for revenge. Maybe he'd threatened the doctor and forced him to cover for him. So far, neither she nor Gavin had been able to voice that fear.

Gavin tore into the hospital, a man desperate for answers. Lindsey had never seen him so furious, so out of control. Seconds later, Gavin slammed a fist on the nurses' station. The receptionist jumped, a look of alarm spreading on her face at Gavin's menacing presence. "We want to see Dr. Cross—*now*."

"He... I'm not sure he's in." The young redhead bounced from her seat and darted toward the back corridor. Gavin followed, Lindsey trailed right behind him. Two nurses hurled themselves out of his way as he stalked past them, fear evident in their shocked expressions. The receptionist grabbed the nurse's arm, her voice a panicked whisper. "Brenda Leigh, get the doc."

The heavyset nurse who'd been so kind to Lindsey during her stay worried her lip with her teeth as she held up a warning hand to Gavin. "Stop there, Mr. McCord or I'll call security. Dr. Cross is with a patient—"

"I don't care, I want to see him right now."

"He's in the middle of an exam," Brenda Leigh said. Gavin reached for the door, but Lindsey caught his hand.

"Wait, Gavin, that woman doesn't deserve for us to walk in on her."

Her calm statement seemed to shake him back to his senses. He nodded, but spoke curtly to the nurse, "Let him know we're here. And he'd better not slip out the back door."

Brenda Leigh's eyes narrowed as she rushed inside the room. Moments later, she appeared with the doctor by her side. He gestured toward his office and led the way. Gavin shut the door as soon as they entered, placing himself between the door and the physician.

"You'd better have a good explanation for lying to us, Cross, because right now I'm contemplating arresting you for at least a dozen different offenses."

"What?" Cross's hand went to his heart in shock. "How dare you come here and—"

"Cut the bull!" Gavin glared at the man's quivering

form. "I'm not playing games here, Cross. We know you lied—we found the girl who delivered her baby the same day as Lindsey."

Lindsey studied Cross's face, sickened that she'd ever trusted him. "Her name is Candy Sue."

"She also claims she lost her son that night." Gavin's voice rose to a thunderous level, "So either you had two deliveries go wrong that night, two babies who died identical deaths or you're covering up something." He paused, watching the vein in Cross's forehead pulse. "And my bet is on the latter."

Cross stammered a denial. "She's confused, she must have meant another night. I did deliver a young girl's baby that week but it was the day before."

Gavin jerked the doctor's collar and shook him. "We're not buying it, doc. You said Lindsey was confused, you blamed the medicine before and we both know you lied. Where is her baby?"

Cross's head wavered back and forth. "I told you, her baby didn't make it. The other girl was in the day before."

Gavin growled an obscenity. "I'm bringing the feds down on you. You won't even remember you had a practice when I get through. Now tell me what happened to my son."

"Your son?" the doctor squeaked.

Gavin hesitated, his voice steely. "Yes, Cross. *My* son."

Cross wavered for a moment as if he was going to spill his guts, then sank his nails into the wood grain of his desk. "I...I don't know," Cross said shakily. "I tried to save him, his heart was too weak..."

"No," Lindsey bellowed. "That's not true. Why won't you stop lying?"

Gavin balled his hand into a fist and shoved it into Cross's face. "You'd better start talking, Cross, before—"

The door swung open and Sheriff Forbes burst in. "What's going on William?"

"He stormed in here threatening me," Cross said in a whiny voice. "The man's crazy."

Forbes slowly closed the distance between the door and Gavin, flicking his thumb in a gesture for him to release the doctor. "Come on, William, let's go down to the station and talk."

Gavin released the doctor's jacket with such force he toppled back and hit the wall.

A FEW HOURS later, Lindsey and Gavin returned to her place, Lindsey's head throbbing. Gavin had spent an hour grilling the doctor but he hadn't budged. When his lawyer, Little, had arrived, Cross's teeth had clenched tighter than a cemented wall of bricks, ending the interrogation. On the way home, Gavin had called his partner and asked him to get a search warrant for Cross's office.

Could they all be involved in her son's disappearance— the doctor, the lawyer and sheriff? But why?

"He'll give it up sooner or later," Gavin said in a rough, tired voice.

Lindsey mumbled an agreement and massaged her temple. "I have to lie down."

"Would you like something to eat?"

"No, no food."

"At least take your vitamins, Linds. You haven't eaten much at all the past few days."

She downed the vitamins with a glass of water and saltines. The look of concern on Gavin's face nearly brought her to tears but she refused the weakness. "I just need to rest, okay?"

He gently kissed her forehead, then pulled her to him for a long moment, stroking her back. "We're going to find him, Linds. I promise."

"I know." She lifted her gaze to his and saw the hope and worry and...love?

For their son, yes.

For her...no, she couldn't allow herself to climb on that roller coaster tonight.

As if he realized she was at the end of her emotional and physical rope, he guided her to the bedroom. She had no energy to fight him, not when it felt so wonderful to have someone care for her, if only for a few brief moments.

Her breath hitched in her throat as he gently unbuttoned her blouse and pulled away the fabric, his fingertips grazing the sensitive swell of her breasts. Her nipples puckered, strained against the satin fabric of her pale, pink bra. His throat constricted, his hands sweeping down her side, feathering light touches over her delicate midriff.

She shivered, drawn by his dark hungry stare. His gaze fastened to her face as he knelt and undid the buckles of her sandals, slipping off her shoes and massaging each foot with firm hands. Legs trembling, she leaned against him and closed her eyes, savoring the feel of his fingers kneading her tense muscles. His gentle ministrations soothed the anxiety from her nerves, seduced her into feeling alive again for the first time in months. How right, how wonderful it felt to be here like this with him, to shed the barriers between them and seek solace with one another in the quiet of the night. He caressed her calves, massaging, working up her inner thighs and she moaned, idly sliding her fingers into his thick dark hair. Higher, softer, more... Just when she might have given in to the passion sparking to life, his hand moved back to her foot, traced along the underside, and he released her foot and rose, his gaze once again imploring her with silent questions.

She had no answers. Only the silence that hummed between them. The desire they shared, and the pain and secrets that lay between them.

Finally he turned and fumbled through her drawer and found a dark green nightshirt. He helped her put it on, the dark brown of his irises turning smoky black in the dim light of her bedroom. Moonlight streaked his dark brown hair with honeyed tones, bathed the room in a surreal light. She slid her skirt down her hips and he picked her up in his arms and carried her to bed. When he eased back the covers and lay her on the crisp yellow sheets, she cradled her arm around his neck and inhaled his strong masculine scent. Woodsy and earthy, just like him. Solid, stable, a rock of corded muscle that felt like a wall of security to her. A tendril of his dark hair had fallen over his face and she brushed it back, itching to thread her fingers through the thick, overly long strands. Their gazes locked. Hearts collided for a second. Inhibitions, reservations floated away on some nameless cloud of doubt.

"Will you hold me for a while, Mac?" Lindsey asked softly.

He arched a dark eyebrow and she smiled, remembering that night so long ago when they'd forgotten all the reasons they shouldn't be together and had just taken. Taken and given all through that long lonely night.

She wished they could do it again.

But then there was Cory. And all those lonely months afterwards…

"You know I want you, Linds."

His whiskey-rough voice rolled over her like a warm

tide. But another dizzy spell assaulted her and she pressed her fingers to her head.

"I know. But—"

"Shh, you don't have to explain." He brushed his lips across her cheek and slipped down on the bed beside her. Without another word, he pulled her into his embrace, showered her with gentle kisses and rubbed the aching part of her lower back until she fell asleep.

GAVIN LAY in a pained position, his body hard and aching for the woman beside him. For a moment, just a brief moment, he'd almost given in. Almost taken Lindsey up on the need he'd seen so vibrant and alive in her eyes. But she wasn't feeling well and he couldn't take from her again without knowing that he had something to give in return.

She groaned and rolled over and her body seemed so fragile in his arms, worry hit him. She'd been under such stress lately, hadn't been eating, or resting—was she really all right?

Suddenly she fought off the covers, a tortured moan escaping her as she bolted up and sprang off the bed. He jackknifed to a sitting position, his pulse racing as she staggered into the bathroom. He ran after her, his stomach clenching as he heard her heaving violently. He hurriedly wet a washcloth and pressed it to her forehead but she slumped over the toilet, her head lolling sideways. Then her body went limp and she lost consciousness.

Chapter Twelve

Lindsey flailed sideways but Gavin grabbed her before she could collapse on the cold, hard tile. He quickly called an ambulance, then held her, rocking her gently while he waited. At least she was breathing but her pulse was weak, her pupils dilated, and her skin felt cold and clammy.

Was she simply dehydrated? Going into shock?

His own heart pounded, aching and tight. He stroked her hair, whispering soothing words, praying she'd be all right. Sirens sounded in the distance, pummeling closer, beating through his tightly reined control. He wrapped a blanket around her, scooped her into his arms and carried her to the den, pacing in front of the window, finally breathing again himself when he saw the blinding lights. The ambulance zoomed down the drive and screeched to a stop, siren wailing. He flung open the door.

"Hurry, she's unconscious!"

As soon as he lay her on the gurney, the paramedics went to work. One EMT took her vitals while another started an IV. The middle-age stocky one glanced at him. "Are you her husband?"

"No, a friend."

"What happened?"

"She's been under a lot of stress, hasn't been eating

much. Right before she went to bed, she said she hadn't been feeling well all day. Complained of nausea.'' He lay a hand over her damp forehead, willing her to open her eyes. ''She slept for a short while, then woke up violently ill. I found her in the bathroom, sick, then she passed out.''

''Sounds like food poisoning—''

''She hasn't eaten enough to get food poisoning.''

''Is she taking any medication? Drinking alcohol?''

''No, no alcohol. And no medication that I'm aware of, except…except she's been taking vitamins the doctor ordered.'' And they'd been prescribed by Cross. His heart thundered in his chest. What if the vitamins were tainted? He suddenly felt ill himself. He'd actually encouraged her to take them earlier.

''Get the bottle,'' the EMT ordered.

Gavin leapt from the ambulance and raced inside. By the time he returned, they had her settled in the back of the ambulance, and were ready to roll.

''The clinic—''

''No, take her to the county hospital.''

The younger paramedic frowned. ''Sir, the clinic's closer and the staff is competent.''

Hell, someone on the staff might have tried to kill her. ''No, I'm a detective. I want her at the county hospital.''

''Is there a relative we can call?''

''No, no relative.''

The EMT nodded at his demand and set the ambulance into motion. Gavin climbed in beside Lindsey, took her hand in his, planted a tender kiss on her palm, then bowed his head as the vehicle spun down the drive. He didn't care what the paramedic thought. He'd act irrational too if he thought the woman he loved was going to die.

And that he'd handed her the pill that might possibly end her life.

Two hours later, Gavin paced the waiting room, sipping muddy cold coffee from a foam cup, cursing the circumstances and his own stupidity. Lindsey had to make it. He needed her, his son needed her.

Why hadn't he figured out where his son was? What could he be missing in the investigation?

His boots squeaked as he made the rounds of the small, pale green room. An elderly couple sat huddled together, comforting one another and holding hands, obviously pulling together in some medical crisis of their own. The way he and Lindsey had pulled together in this crisis. Would they be together in old age to comfort one another like this couple?

For the first time in his life, he wanted that…that bond with a woman, a permanent connection to last through time. Maybe Cory would be that bond. No, his love would be. All his former reservations beat a sickening rhythm in his head. If Lindsey could forgive him. If he could forget he'd put them in danger…

A doctor approached, and he paused and tossed his nearly full cup in the trash.

"Is there someone here from the Mendelson family?"

The white-haired couple stood, clutching one another, their bony frames bracing for whatever news the doctor had to relay. Whispered heads bent, listened, nodded. Seconds later, the couple released a joyous exultation and began to hug one another. He hoped his story had a happy ending like theirs.

Shadows fell across the room and he turned to see his buddy Simon approaching. "I came as soon as I heard."

Gavin clapped him on the arm. "Thanks, man. I still don't know anything."

Simon thrust a fresh cup of coffee in his hand, gesturing at the Dunkin' Donuts logo. "I figured the hospital sludge was almost as bad as the precinct's."

Gavin chuckled and accepted the cup, keeping one eye on the door. "I hope you found something."

Simon twisted the corner of his mustache with his fingers, a gesture Gavin recognized as nerves. "First off, I'll have that search warrant for Cross's office soon. And I talked to the warden at the state pen. Said Faulkner hasn't had any visitors recently. Not even his folks."

Gavin gritted his teeth. He'd wanted to find something to link Faulkner. If he wanted revenge, Faulkner had found the perfect way to hurt Lindsey. But then why try to kill her? A man like Faulkner would glean more satisfaction by tormenting her.

"Any news on Johnson or Swain?"

Simon rubbed his hands together. "Johnson took his wife up to the mountains. Seems they have a cabin up there. So far no sign of a baby with them though, although some kids' furniture was spotted through the window. We're still tailing them."

"How about Swain?"

"One of our men saw him in Raleigh the same day you and Lindsey did the TV interview."

Gavin exhaled shakily. "I thought I saw him outside the station."

"I've got an APB out on him. We'll pick him up for questioning when we find him."

Geez, if Swain had his son...

"There's more," Simon added in a grave voice.

Gavin prepared himself for the worst.

"Turns out Swain had a sister named Wanda. She lived

in Maple Hollow, worked as a fill-in nurse at that clinic where Lindsey delivered. We're looking for her now.''

Too much of a coincidence. Maybe the sister had his son.

A gray-haired doctor appeared in the doorway, adjusted his bifocals, his long face drawn and serious. ''Mr. McCord?''

''Yes.''

''I'm Dr. Albright, the attending physician for Lindsey Payne.''

He squeezed his coffee cup so hard hot coffee sloshed over on his hands but he ignored the burning sensation. ''How is she?''

''We've stabilized her. Are you family?''

She was the closest thing to family he'd had in a long time. He shook his head. ''Her mother is in a nursing home. I can contact her—''

''No, that's not necessary. I wouldn't want to upset her.'' He gestured toward the row of maroon vinyl seats. Gavin followed him while Simon indicated he'd phone Barnes and see if any more phone calls had come through. Gavin sat down and braced his arms on his legs watching as Dr. Albright referred to his clipboard.

''We ran a series of tests and discovered Miss Payne has a thyroid imbalance. She's actually hypothyroid, a condition almost the opposite of hyperthyroid. The paramedics claimed you weren't aware she was taking any medications, but we found traces of a drug called methmizole in her system.''

''As far as I know she hasn't taken anything but those vitamins. I want them analyzed.''

''They've been sent to the lab already.''

''So what did this drug do? There wasn't any permanent damage, was there?''

"I don't believe so." The doctor studied him over his glasses. "It's true Miss Payne recently lost a baby?"

Gavin explained the situation and the stress Lindsey had been under.

"Hmm. Many women suffer naturally from post-partum depression, which in turn can affect their thyroid, creating a hypothyroid condition."

"And?"

"Under the circumstances, I can imagine Miss Payne might have suffered from some depression." His gray eyebrows knitted into a frown. "All the more reason her doctor wouldn't prescribe a drug which would worsen the condition. The side affects of methmizole alone are troublesome and can include heart problems, confusion, depression, loss of appetite."

"She hasn't been eating or sleeping. I just assumed her loss of appetite was due to stress."

"Probably was partially. Exactly the reason a competent doctor wouldn't have prescribed methmizole for her. It can increase depression, and it certainly doesn't help the patient cope."

Gavin's hands tightened once more around the foam cup, nearly squashing it in his hands. He couldn't shake the feeling that the doctor had prescribed the pills hoping they would confuse Lindsey so no one would believe her story. "Lindsey is a strong woman, Doctor, but she's been through a lot lately. You can treat her, can't you?"

The doctor tapped his pencil on the clipboard. "Yes. We've already started her on thyroid replacement therapy. She should feel better soon and be able to leave the hospital in a couple of days."

Relief filled Gavin. "Thanks. You'll let me know as soon as you get the test results on those pills?"

"Certainly." The doctor made another notation on the chart, then excused himself.

William Cross was going to be in a lot of trouble when the results came through, Gavin thought. And he would make sure the man paid for every lie he'd told. And for almost killing Lindsey.

LINDSEY TRIED to move but her limbs felt languid and heavy, and her head swam with a dull throb. She fought the pain and forced herself to open her eyes. Bright light assaulted her. Strange odors filled her nostrils. Some kind of cleaning supply. No, the smells weren't cleaning supplies. They were hospital smells—ammonia and alcohol.

Tubes traced a path from her arm to an IV and a soft bleeping sound punctuated the silence around her. An oxygen machine, no, some kind of heart monitor. What was wrong with her? Had she been involved in an accident?

The memory of the incident in her bathroom slowly drifted into focus, Gavin beside her, mopping her face, lifting her, carrying her…where? An ambulance. The sounds had bombarded her subconscious but she hadn't had the energy to respond. Where was Gavin now?

"I'm here, Linds."

The sound of his voice, rough with worry, soothed her frazzled nerves. She turned her head to face him, a weak smile spreading on her mouth when she saw his handsome face, those wide-set dark eyes probing through her, full of concern. His mouth was pressed in a taut line. She wanted to reach up and trace his lips until he smiled. Only she didn't have the energy to lift her hand.

"You're going to be okay, sweetheart."

It was the first time he'd called her the endearment and she struggled not to let the tears that sprang to her eyes overflow. He must have seen them anyway.

"Are you in pain? Do you need anything?"

She licked her dry lips. "No, I just feel weak."

He brought a cup of water to her lips and bent the straw so she could drink. Lindsey greedily inhaled the water, wondering if she'd ever quench her thirst. But he pulled the cup away after several sips. "That's probably enough to start off with. You've been pretty ill. You don't want to overdo it."

"What happened? I remember getting sick but was it—"

"Not the flu or food poisoning," he said sharply. "Apparently you have a thyroid imbalance."

She frowned. "But I've never had one before."

"Dr. Albright, the doctor treating you, said post-partum depression can sometimes trigger it." He hesitated, wondering how much to reveal. They were in this together, though, and she'd come to him. He owed her honesty. "He thinks you were given some kind of medicine that suppressed the function of your thyroid. You haven't been taking anything I'm not aware of, have you?"

She frowned, puzzled. "No, just those vitamins."

He nodded and reached for her hand, threading her limp fingers with his. "They're being analyzed right now."

He saw the moment the implication set in. "But Dr. Cross gave me those right after Cory was born."

He couldn't keep the fury from his voice. "I know." Gently he lifted a loose tendril of hair from her forehead and brushed it back, savoring the sight of her beautiful heart-shaped face. Those exquisite brown eyes, that porcelain face so full of kindness and love. Their gazes locked, the current of awareness skittering between them, silently binding them.

Emotions battled within him. He wanted to tell her how much she meant to him, how much he loved her. He wanted to hold her forever, wrap his arms around her and make her his woman until eternity, stand before a judge and have her take his name, put his baby in her arms and another one in her belly.

But he didn't deserve her, not after the horrible way he'd deserted her. Not after all he'd put her through these last few months. So he settled for simply staring at her, reminding himself she was alive, smiling and offering him hope when he'd thought a few hours earlier that life might not go on.

The doctor knocked once, then bounded in, interrupting the moment. "Hi there, how's my patient feeling?"

"Better," Lindsey said in a low voice. "I'm just really weak."

Dr. Albright smiled. "It'll take a few days to regain your strength. Be patient, dear, you were pretty sick."

Gavin immediately understood Lindsey's look of impatience—she didn't have time to be sick. Time kept ticking away, every second without their son a precious moment lost.

Finally he folded his stocky arms, his face grim. "I don't know if Mr. McCord filled you in on my diagnosis?"

"Yes."

He nodded curtly, shooting Gavin a questioning look.

"Go ahead, we both want the truth," Gavin said.

"The tests results showed the vitamins you were taking were not actually vitamins. They were laced with a drug called methmizole." He explained the effects, basically reiterating the conversation he'd shared with Gavin.

"I'm not sure if the pharmacist made some kind of mistake or the doctor misdiagnosed your case when he prescribed this drug, but I'm obligated to report the incident," Dr. Albright said.

Gavin explained his background, the circumstances of Lindsey's situation. "I'm calling my partner right now. I want them to question Cross immediately."

And this time they wouldn't release Cross until they had the truth.

As SOON AS Lindsey fell asleep, Gavin kissed her good-bye, then left a guard at her door, and headed toward Maple Hollow Clinic. He wanted to see Cross in handcuffs. And he wanted a chance to sneak into the man's files before he could cover anything up or delete them.

If Cross hadn't already done so.

Exhaustion clawed at him but he ignored his aching muscles and drove like a crazy man, taking a detour through a mountain road he'd discovered while investigating another case. Mountain cabins sprang up, interspersed between the rolling hills and farmland. Could Johnson's cabin be close by?

A place to hide an infant?

Once the idea took root, he couldn't release it. He phoned Simon to pinpoint a location. After he examined Cross's files, he'd personally check out Johnson.

When Gavin finally reached the clinic, his anger had magnified to a full-fledged fury. He stormed into the clinic, for the second time that week clearing halls with his intimidating presence.

"Dr. Cross isn't here," Brenda Leigh said in a nervous whisper.

"Has he been here at all today?"

The redheaded receptionist shook her head, dropping papers in her haste to answer him. "No."

"It's his day off," Brenda Leigh explained. "Sometimes he likes to go fishing up in the mountains."

Gavin stifled a curse, praying the ex-FBI agents would

locate him. He tried to convince Brenda Leigh to let him into the doctor's office but she firmly refused.

Gavin left, then slipped around to the side entrance and searched for Andy, the mentally impaired orderly he and Lindsey had talked with the first day he'd arrived. He didn't have time to wait for the search warrant. He needed to get into the doctor's files right away. Finally he spotted him, restocking the juice cart in the kitchen.

The man seemed spooked for a moment, but Gavin quickly calmed him by reminding him he was a friend of Lindsey's.

"I need your help, Andy," he said. "Miss Lindsey's in the hospital."

His right eye twitched. "Is…is she all right?"

"She will be, but I need to examine some of Dr. Cross's files. We're still looking for her baby."

"H-her baby? I thought sh-she lost it."

Gavin lowered his voice to a conspiratorial whisper. "That's what they told her, Andy. But you were right. Dr. Cross was lying. We found the other young woman who delivered the same day as Lindsey."

His eyes widened like saucers. "She had Miss Lindsey's son?"

"No, she didn't. But she confirmed that Dr. Cross is lying. If I could look into his files for a minute, I might find something to help Ms. Lindsey."

"B-but I'm not s-sposed to let people in."

Gavin patted his arm. "I know, but Dr. Cross wasn't supposed to lie. This is important, Andy. You may be able to help Miss Lindsey find her son."

Finally the mentally impaired man agreed. He craned his neck into the hall, motioning when the area was clear, then showed Gavin into the office and locked the door behind them. Gavin immediately rushed to the computer and began trying to hack through the system.

At first glance, the clinic's files seemed to be in order although he could have hidden costs or padded bills. He didn't find any large payments indicating foul play. Andy limped over to the bulletin board, studying the baby pictures on the wall.

Gavin typed in the word adoptions, but a password protected the files and he didn't have time to hack through it. On a hunch, he scrolled for at-risk deliveries, women seeking fertility treatment. A list of three women over the past two years. Delores Beechum, Kim Scotsdale, Janice Hopkins. Maybe one of them had become so desperate to have a baby they'd bought Lindsey's. But why would Cross have agreed?

He quickly scanned each of their files. The Beechum woman had finally conceived, the Scotsdale woman had moved to Georgia two months ago, and the Hopkins woman had adopted a baby in January. A dead end there.

On a hunch, he searched for any women who might have lost babies other than Candy Sue but came up empty. So an adoption gone awry hadn't been the motive.

Andy coughed and Gavin saw him smiling at the photos, obviously enchanted with the infant pictures. Unfortunately, Gavin found zilch concerning Lindsey, except for a copy of the autopsy report she had shown him. He did, however, find a file on Candy Sue, confirming her story. The autopsy report was identical to the one Lindsey had received. With his impeccable reputation, Cross hadn't banked on anyone questioning his files.

Pretty damn smart. But frustrating as hell.

He tried a different file and stared at the screen in shock. It was a description of Lindsey's delivery, of the complications, a report on his baby's statistics. Payne

Baby—boy. Eight pounds eleven ounces. Twenty-one inches long. Apgar score—eight. The copy of the footprint—the baby's little crooked toe.

All the information detailed a healthy baby—no indication of a heart condition. There was also no reference to what had happened following the birth. Damn.

He printed the information, then quickly checked the employee's files, specifically looking for anything on Swain's sister and the missing nurse Quinn. Records showed a pretty slow turnover. Wanda Swain had worked at the clinic on the weekends but she'd married and transferred to a hospital in Seattle before Lindsey delivered. Too far for her to have dropped in to help her brother take the baby.

Then he found notations on Janet Quinn. A remarkable record, glowing comments—but she'd suddenly resigned. No forwarding address. So, the doctor had lied about this, too—the Quinn woman hadn't taken a vacation, she had quit.

Andy mumbled something and he glanced up and saw him studying the photos again. "Three-thirty-four, Samson baby girl. Five-eighty-one, Grogan baby boy…"

Gavin froze, an idea occurring to him. "Andy, are all those photos numbered?"

The man turned with a huge grin. "Yeah, they come from Doc's p-picture file."

"His picture file?"

Andy's head bobbed up and down. "I like to look at the pictures of the b-babies."

"Cross keeps a photo of every baby he delivers?"

Andy nodded again and pointed to the computer. "I seen it in there one time."

"Can you show me how to access it?"

"I don't know n-nothing about computers. It was th-there when I came in one day."

Gavin bit down on his lip and began to scan the program again, finally locating the file. Another click and a dozen photos filled the screen, each numbered and dated. He scrolled the system until he found the date of Lindsey's delivery. His son's birth.

His heart clenched at the picture that suddenly appeared on the screen. His baby boy. A tiny round face, a button nose, square chin, patches of fine, dark hair. Emotions overwhelmed him. As much as Lindsey had talked about their son, he hadn't seemed real until this moment.

Suddenly Andy was shaking his shoulder. "I...th-think someone's coming."

Gavin hit the Print button, tapping his foot while he waited. Finally the machine spit out the paper and he grabbed the printed picture and stuffed it in his shirt. He'd get it to Simon and have him put it through the database, flash it on every TV screen in the United States. They would find his son. And he'd have the grave exhumed to make certain his child wasn't inside. His cell phone chirped and he heard footsteps at the door to the office.

Andy's face registered panic. "Get me out of here."

Gavin silenced his phone with a flick of his thumb, catching Simon's number and making a mental note to return the call. Andy ushered him through a side door, then a narrow hallway leading outside.

"Thanks, Andy," he said when he'd made it to his car.

"Y-you're welcome. T-take care of Miss Lindsey."

"I will." He patted Andy's arm. "You were a big help, Andy. I'll have Lindsey bring her baby to see you once we find him."

Andy's smile lit up his eyes. "I...I like babies."

"I know. And I'm glad you do." Gavin said goodbye,

climbed in his car, phoned his partner and reported his findings.

"Check out Wanda Swain, now it's Wanda Bridges— she's at the university hospital in Seattle. And I'm faxing you a picture I want on every TV news show possible. Send it through the FBI's database, too."

"What picture?"

"A picture of my son."

Simon cleared his throat. "Will do. We finally found that address for Johnson and his wife."

Gavin cranked his engine and headed toward a copy shop to fax the photo, then he'd go on to the mountains. And on his way, he'd call Lindsey and tell her about the photo.

"SWING LOW, SWEET CHARIOT, coming for to carry me home."

He watched in awe as once again his new little son turned big brown eyes up to her face. The baby's cries wilted at the sound of her soft voice, soothing, humming out famous lines of lullabies from times gone by. Good times. Family times.

No one knew how she had suffered. How difficult it had been for her to conceive in the first place. The fertility treatments. The miscarriages. The painful disappointment over losing another pregnancy.

But soon this little one would grow and fill the house with love and laughter. A boisterous boy wielding sticks and stones and toy trucks. Climbing trees and scraping knees.

He'd buy him a toy train set for Christmas and watch his eyes light up as the engine chugged and clanked around the Christmas tree. Life would once again be filled with the musical sound of children. And she would be so happy, baking cookies and pies and teasing the kids with her funny stories. She would be vibrant and alive. Just as she'd once been when their other son had been the apple of her eye.

She'd already begun to change, he could see the tiny differences in her—all because of their new little son. No, he couldn't let the Payne woman take him back now. And he wouldn't let the boss have him, either.

He paced the old wooden porch, the weathered steps creaking as he shifted his weight back and forth and stared at the night sky. The sounds of the forest slivered around him, the brisk, cool mountain air clean and intoxicating. That damn detective and the Payne woman just wouldn't stop their snooping.

They had to die.

Chapter Thirteen

"You found a picture of our baby?" Lindsey's pulse clamored in her throat.

"Yes, in Cross's files," Gavin said, excitement filling his voice. "He keeps a photo of every child he delivers. It's amazing. Your friend, Andy, gave me the idea to check when he was looking at the pictures on Cross's walls."

Lindsey twisted the phone cord in her hands. "What does he look like, Mac?"

"He's beautiful," Gavin said a little gruffly. "He...he has dark hair like mine and this button nose and..."

Lindsey smiled at the emotions in Gavin's voice. "He looks like you, doesn't he?"

"I don't know. It's hard to tell, he's sleeping so I can't see his eyes and he's all wrapped up in this blue blanket, but his little fists are sticking out and he looks tough and strong, like a little fighter."

Lindsey closed her eyes and lay her head back, trying to imagine her infant's face as Gavin described the photo. Wondering how much he had already changed. "He does look like you, Mac. He has your strong chin. And your mouth...I remember now."

"We'll find him, Linds," Gavin said in a low voice,

"I swear to you I won't stop until I bring him home and put him back in your arms."

Tears trickled from Lindsey's eyes at the fierce determination in Gavin's voice. No wonder she loved this man so much. "I know, Mac. I have faith in you."

He hesitated for a moment, then cleared his throat. "I sent the picture to Simon. They'll probably run it on the news tonight and it's gone into the FBI database so hopefully we'll get some real leads."

"Are you on your way now? I want to see the picture."

"I'll be there as soon as I can. I have one stop to make before I can get there."

"Be careful, Mac."

"I will." He hesitated again, his voice husky. "Take care of yourself, Linds. I'll see you soon."

And maybe soon he'd be bringing her baby back to her.

Lindsey heard the silent promise and swallowed back more tears. When Gavin said goodbye, she dialed her mother to tell her about the picture.

A CHILL crept over Gavin as he passed Graveyard Falls and slowly wound around the Blue Ridge Parkway. The mere name of the falls gave him the creeps but certainly didn't deter the tourists, only intrigued them to flock to the site and probe for morbid stories related to its origin. Sightseers parked along the curb, drifting toward the guardrail to photograph the majestic view, some lingering to walk the historic trails, others monitoring their little ones so they didn't fall down the steep incline. A little boy wearing a baseball cap and overalls clung to his mother's hand as they stooped to examine a turtle creeping along the side of the road. An image of his own son exploring the small animal flashed into Gavin's mind. His stomach knotted.

Was he getting close to finding him? Would he be able to carry his son back to the hospital and place him in Lindsey's arms today? On the heels of his excitement, sprang turmoil. Would he be able to walk away when he did?

The narrow, secluded drive leading to the Johnson's cabin seemed to go on forever. Heavy underbrush and weeds marred the dirt path, gravel spewing beneath the tires. Seconds later, a small log cabin came into view, the front porch partially sagging and weathered, an ancient ringer-type washer leaning against the splintered door-frame.

Definitely a hideaway. For Johnson and who else?

He pulled the car to a stop several hundred feet from the front, scanning the place for signs of life. A baby stroller maybe?

A dented white van jutted out from under a makeshift carport built of wood covered with a green plastic tarp. No plates. Tension knifed through his tight muscles as he eased the car up the embankment and parked behind the van, blocking its way out. Opening and closing his door without making noise proved to be a challenge. He spotchecked the van for a carseat but found nothing.

As he climbed the steps he spotted a brown and white flop-eared mutt sprawled on the third step. The mangy animal lifted his head, checked him out, then flopped back down with a low growl. Gavin leaned over to pet him, muttering a calming word just as the screen door screeched open.

Dwight Johnson, wearing faded jeans and a flannel shirt, his thinning brown hair swept back to cover his bald spot, appeared in the doorway shouldering a rifle. "What the hell are you doing here?"

"I came to talk to you and your wife—"

"We don't want to talk to you." He raised the rifle and aimed it at Gavin's chest, his bony arms amazingly steady. "Now go on your way, Mr. McCord. You've already caused us enough heartache."

The bitterness in the man's voice ate at Gavin. Had he actually thought the man's anger might have abated?

"Mr. Johnson, please listen for a moment. You can't imagine how sorry I am about what happened to Rodney."

"Sorry don't bring him back, does it?"

Gavin scrubbed a hand over his neck. "No, but I really was trying to help him." Gavin inched up the steps. He could hear the man's wife singing softly, some kind of lullaby. "I'd like to speak to your wife. Please let me come in and talk to her. I want to tell her how sorry I am."

The gun wobbled as Johnson brushed a gnat away from his beard. "I don't want you to upset her. She's just now starting to act like herself."

"Maybe there's something I can tell her about Rodney that will make her feel better."

The old man frowned, stewed over Gavin's intimidating size for a minute, then nudged open the door. "You've got five minutes. And don't go badmouthing my boy."

Gavin nodded as the old man allowed him inside the dark cabin. The smell of dank wet wood and cigarettes was almost stifling and he had to blink to focus in the dim lighting. Exposed beams, a homemade afghan spread on a faded brown couch, an antique cradle, although it appeared unused. A high chair sat in the corner of the kitchen area, a few plastic toys scattered on the braided rug. A baby had definitely been here.

He tempered his shocked reaction when he saw the thin woman sitting in an oak rocker in front of a stone fireplace, rocking back and forth, humming a lullaby, her arms cradling something swathed in a blanket.

The air collected in his throat in a painful surge.

Was she holding his child?

"Mrs. Johnson?"

She turned, her eyes widening when she spotted him, a little girl pressed to her chest.

Disappointment ballooned in his chest.

"Shh," she whispered. "I just got Cindy to sleep. She's had a bad cold."

He nodded. "Whose little girl?"

"This lady I met at the counseling center. I'm baby-sitting her children while she works." She gestured toward the den where a small boy played with a stack of wooden blocks. "I enjoy keeping the two of them. And I feel like I'm helping her. She's a single mother and can't afford to miss work."

"Sounds like the arrangement is good for both of you."

A tiny smile curved her mouth as she stroked the little girl's back. "They can't ever take Rodney's place, but it feels good to have little ones around again. The place has been so quiet lately."

"I can understand that," he said, thinking about the empty bassinet at Lindsey's house. He surveyed the tiny cabin, wondering if it was possible they had his baby hidden in a back room. But a quick glance through the open doors indicated the rooms were empty. And Johnson wouldn't let him in if he was holding the baby here.

His apology came slow and steady. "I'm so sorry about Rodney, Mrs. Johnson. I really cared about your son and wanted to help him. I had no idea Rodney was going to follow me to that alley." He paused and cleared his throat. "I'd do anything to change that day, Ma'am, to bring him back to you."

Her glazed, anguished eyes haunted him.

"You had no business making him think you was going to help him, then letting him get killed," Mr. Johnson said.

Gavin's stomach clenched as guilt resurfaced. This man lived to blame him. It was probably useless to try to explain, but the sight of the woman cradling the child reminded him of Lindsey and his own son.

"I sincerely wanted to help him, Mr. and Mrs. Johnson, otherwise I wouldn't have joined the Big Brother program. Rodney was a good boy at heart. He had a lot of courage."

A small flicker of emotion crossed Mrs. Johnson's face. She reached for his hand and actually cradled it in her own. "He was a good boy, my Rodney, wasn't he?"

"Yes, Ma'am, he was."

"He was the light of my eyes." She smiled sadly. "You know, Mr. McCord, nothing is as important as your family. You don't realize that sometimes until they're gone."

Gavin thought of his own son. Of Lindsey and how important they had both become, and realized she was right. "He was taken too soon, Mrs. Johnson. I'm truly sorry. If I could change things, I would."

She pressed her hand to her chest. "He's not gone. I have him right here in my heart and I always will."

Emotions thickened Gavin's voice, "Yes, Ma'am, you do. Nobody can take that away from you."

As no one could take his love for his own son away from him. But he'd like the chance to hold him just one time and tell him how he felt.

She began to rock again, the soft words of her melody wafting in his subconscious as he said goodbye and walked back to the car. The man watched him leave, his expression full of bitterness. As he drove away, he could still hear the words to the song she'd been singing, "Swing low, sweet chariot, coming for to carry me home."

LINDSEY SLEPT most of the day, waking occasionally to find her room empty, save the beautiful vase of red roses the florist had delivered from Gavin.

She stared out the hospital window, watching the night lights flicker in the dark sky, signifying another day had passed. Another day without her child. Was he safe? Cold? Hungry? Was he being taken care of? Was her baby changing, growing? Would she even recognize him when she did find him?

A nurse wheeled a young mother onto the covered portico of the hospital, the woman cradling a tiny infant in her arms. The father took great pains lifting the baby and tucking her into a car seat, then helped the mother in the front seat of the car. Judging from the pink blanket and balloons, they'd had a baby girl. Had things been different, had Gavin loved her, the cozy family scene could have been them. A low sob welled in her throat, but she pushed it back down to the grinding pit in her stomach, determined to remain positive.

"Lindsey?" JoAnn tiptoed through the doorway, looking worried and shaken as she placed a basket of cookies on the nightstand. "I've been worried about you."

"I'm okay," Lindsey said softly, reaching up and hugging her friend. "Thanks for the cookies."

"You look pale. Are you all right?"

Lindsey forced a smile. "Actually I'm already feeling better. Whatever Dr. Albright gave me must be working."

JoAnn pulled the hard vinyl chair up beside the bed. "Tell me what happened?"

Lindsey explained about her thyroid imbalance, trying to gloss over the harshness of the truth, but JoAnn's expression turned to shock. "I can't believe all this has happened to you. It's like something out of a horror show."

"I know." Lindsey patted her hand. "I just want to find my baby, Jo."

"I want that, too. Everyone from school says to tell you hi. They're all praying for you, Linds."

"Thanks. Tell them I hope I'll be back soon." Lindsey squeezed her friend's hand and told her about the photo Gavin had found. "Maybe I'll be able to bring my baby by for everyone to see."

She and JoAnn gushed over the possibilities for a few minutes, recounting the times they'd joked about changing diapers and midnight feedings before Lindsey's delivery.

"We could dress him in all the little outfits you received at your baby shower and take pictures," JoAnn suggested with a big smile.

Lindsey was so caught up in the fanciful imagery she didn't realize Gavin had arrived. He cleared his throat, waiting in the doorway as if he didn't want to intrude. Lindsey immediately introduced him.

"Hi, JoAnn." Gavin smiled, although his expression seemed strained and Lindsey realized how difficult the last few days had been on him.

JoAnn stood. "I'd better go."

"No, please stay, Jo."

"I'm sure the two of you have a lot to discuss." JoAnn squeezed Lindsey's hand between her own. "Take care and call if you need me, all right?"

"I will." Lindsey hugged her friend. "Thanks again for visiting."

As soon as JoAnn left, Gavin settled his long body into

the chair, then pulled out a folded photocopy and handed it to her. "Here's our son."

Lindsey's hand trembled as she took the paper, her heart squeezing at the picture of her baby. "Oh, God, Mac, he's so beautiful."

Gavin moved over to sit beside her, gently tracing his thumb down her cheek. "Yeah, he is. Thank you for having him, Linds."

Lindsey looked into Gavin's eyes and saw all the tenderness and love she'd ever wanted. He might not be able to voice the words, but she knew seeing the picture of his son had moved him deeply. She memorized each feature of her son's face, the tiny dark eyebrows, the pug nose, his creamy skin, the way his little mouth was pinched together in sleep, the little patches of baby-fine hair.

Gavin's phone chirped and Lindsey tried to control her emotions while Gavin conferred with his partner. Finally, he hung up, looking slightly relieved. "That was Simon. The autopsy report you received was identical to the one for Candy Sue's baby and her blood type matched."

"Then…then our baby is alive."

"I know he's out there." Lindsey automatically reached for Gavin and he pulled her into his arms, hugging her tightly.

"You've never given up." Gavin cupped her face in his hands and kissed her gently.

Lindsey stroked his jaw. "And I'm not going to."

"Neither am I."

"I do feel bad for Candy Sue, though."

Gavin nodded, sympathy in his eyes. "I know. But she's young. Maybe when the time's right, when she's finished with school…" He let the sentence trail off.

"I didn't care if the time was right for me, Gavin. I wanted our son."

He slid down on the bed beside her, careful of her IV. Using his thumb, he traced a gentle path over her cheek to brush away a tear. "I know, and you're going to make a great mother, Lindsey. Our baby will be lucky to have you raise him."

Lindsey smiled and kissed his cheek, her body tingling when he lowered his mouth and took hers. The kiss was sweet and gentle and full of tenderness. They lay together for several minutes, simply holding one another, clinging to their newfound hope while they stared at the picture of their son.

AFTER THEY'D watched the news and seen the photo air, Gavin had fallen asleep beside Lindsey. He immediately woke at 4:00 a.m. when his cell phone rang.

"No word on Cross yet, but we have an address on the Quinn woman," Barnes said.

"I'll get right on it." He scribbled the address, his gaze zeroing in on the picture of his son, then Lindsey. She was sleeping soundly, her hand tucked beneath her head like a child's. As soon as the doctor released her, they'd find the nurse.

Finally Lindsey stirred, her sleepy eyes registering surprise to find him still sitting beside her bed. "I thought you'd go home for the night."

He smiled, rubbing a hand over his rough early-morning stubble. "I figured I might as well stick around, give you a ride home if the doctor says it's okay."

She pushed a strand of hair from her face and tried to sit up. Thankfully her cheeks had regained some color and the hollow look in her eyes had filled with life again.

She reached for some water. "Did you hear anything?"

He nodded. "I have an address on the Quinn woman."

"Then let's go." She pushed the covers aside and

swung her legs over the edge of the bed. He caught a glimpse of her shapely slender thigh and stifled a groan.

"I told you, you're not going unless Dr. Albright says you're healthy enough to leave." He pointed to the IV pole. "Besides, he has to unhook your IV."

Her pretty eyebrow shot up. "You could remove it."

The corner of his mouth quirked into a smile. "No way, I hate needles."

She smiled and jabbed his chest. "Then go find the doctor."

A half hour later, a nurse wheeled Lindsey to the front door. Dr. Albright hadn't been pleased about releasing her so soon, but Gavin had promised to make her rest and eat. When they'd explained the circumstances, he'd agreed that the best medicine for Lindsey was to find her baby. By seven-thirty they'd both showered and were back in the car on the way to Wilmington to see Janet Quinn.

HE TURNED OFF the television set, praying she didn't see it as she strolled into the kitchen with the baby tucked beneath her arm. The boss wasn't going to be happy about this latest development. Within seconds, the phone rang. He answered, already knowing who it would be.

"Did you see the news?"

"Yes. I can't believe it."

"How did they get that picture?"

"That damn cop probably dug it up."

A long sigh hissed over the line. "First, we find out the baby belongs to that detective, now this. We have to change our plans."

A nerve tightened in his neck and he reached for a

cigarette, knowing he'd agree to whatever the boss said. But in the end it wouldn't matter—because he had his own agenda and the baby was going to be his, no matter what.

Chapter Fourteen

Lindsey awakened as Gavin pulled into the complex where Janet Quinn had been spotted. She stretched, faintly aware of Gavin's breath fanning against her cheek. "Are you sure you're up for this? You can always wait in the car."

"No, I'm going."

He smiled and unfastened his seat belt. She didn't wait on him to open the door, but leapt out herself. The large complex consisted of upscale condos reminiscent of Charleston row houses with separate entrances and private backyards for the owners. The swimming pool and tennis court community featured a clubhouse and restaurant. The expensive cars parked in the lot definitely indicated the club catered to the upper class.

"Simon said Miss Quinn has been staying with a friend from nursing school."

"I wonder if she intended to return to Maple Hollow."

"I don't think so. In Cross's files, I found a notation that she'd resigned." Gavin rang the bell and Lindsey's nerves jumped in her stomach.

"She's been working the night shift at the local hospital so I hoped we'd catch her coming home."

Finally the door creaked open, the chain still intact. An

attractive brunette peeked through the narrow opening. "Who are you?"

"We came to see Janet," Lindsey said.

The young woman frowned. "Janet who?"

Gavin pushed at the door. "Look, miss, we know Janet Quinn is staying here." He flashed his badge. "Miss Payne and I need to talk to her."

"Let them in."

Lindsey froze at the tremulous voice on the other side of the heavy wooden door.

The door closed, the chain glided across the metal lock, then the brunette opened the door, watching them warily as they entered. "I'm Renee Rosenthall. You'd better behave or I'm calling security."

"We're not here to hurt anyone," Gavin assured her. "But we do have some questions for Miss Quinn."

A middle-aged auburn-haired woman appeared, huddled inside a thick terry cloth jogging suit, her pudgy face void of makeup, her blue eyes shifting away from Lindsey. "I...I knew you'd find me...eventually."

Lindsey clasped her hand. "Janet, why did you leave?"

Janet raised a shaky hand to her temple, her voice heavy with defeat. "Let's go in the den and sit down. I guess it's time I told the whole story."

"I'll make some coffee." Her friend retreated to the kitchen as they settled themselves on the plush burgundy furniture. Lindsey noticed the glass and chrome coffee table, ornate art, expensive vases. Cold. Formal. Definitely not a homey place.

Not the kind of place to raise a child in. Then again, her baby wasn't here. She knew that immediately.

She only prayed Janet had answers.

The silver tray filled with coffee and condiments rattled as Renee bustled in. They accepted the refreshments, giv-

ing the anxious nurse time to compose herself. Janet
grabbed a pack of cigarettes from a glass table, smacked
them against her hand, took one and lit it with trembling
fingers. Her fingernails had been chewed down to nubs.

"I hope you don't mind. It calms me." A nervous
laugh escaped her. "Believe it or not, I'd given up smok-
ing until a few weeks ago."

"What happened a few weeks ago?" Gavin asked.

Janet's gaze cut to Lindsey. "She knows. So do you,
that's the reason you're here."

"Tell me about my baby," Lindsey said softly.

The woman blew a smoke ring, tapping the ashes into
a swan-shaped glass ashtray. "Your son is alive."

Lindsey swallowed painfully. "You sent me the note?
And the autopsy report?"

Janet nodded, staring off into space. "Dr. Cross had
been acting strangely for weeks. I've never seen him like
that. All tense and nervous, jumping and snapping at
everyone. I even suggested he get a physical." She
laughed again, a hollow sound as cold and brittle as the
china coffee cups. "He'd been receiving weird phone
calls, then he'd hang up and go irate, leave the office, not
return for hours."

"Why was he so upset?" Gavin asked.

Janet shook her head and took a long draw of her cigarette. "I don't know. But that night..." She looked at
Lindsey with sympathy in her eyes. "No, let me back-
track. That morning another young woman came in—"

"Candy Sue?" Lindsey asked.

"Yes. It was awful. We tried to save the infant, but her
baby was stillborn. Afterwards, Doc closed himself in his
office with the phone for a while, wouldn't take any calls,
didn't want any interruptions. Even had me reschedule all
of his regular appointments. Except for you."

"I had my weekly check-up that day."

"Yes, and he made it a point to examine you. I thought that was odd since Mrs. Beechum was a high-risk delivery but he switched her appointment." She paused as if to allow them time to absorb the information. "Doc left right after you did, in a big hurry. But he came back later."

"Was something odd about his return?" Gavin asked.

"He wasn't supposed to be on duty that night." Her dead-eyed stare made the hairs on the back of Lindsey's neck prickle. "Anyway, it was as if he *knew* you'd be back in to deliver. And you did."

"But I hadn't even started dilating that morning."

"I know, I saw your chart. We both figured you had a few more weeks to go."

"But I started having contractions almost immediately after I left the clinic."

The nurse stared at her long and hard. "I know, I wondered…"

"Wondered what?" Gavin asked.

"If Dr. Cross might have done something to force you into premature labor. He could have made a tiny tear in the amniotic sac so your water would leak."

Lindsey gasped. "Then I came in and had problems."

Janet crushed her cigarette in the ashtray, stood and stared out the picturesque window. Lindsey saw the well-kept, small rock garden but had a feeling Janet wasn't seeing it. She was lost in memories of that night. When she spoke again, her voice sounded low, distant. "I took your son to the nursery after the delivery. He was fine. But I had to leave to check on Candy Sue. She was so upset, she needed me." Her gaze rose to Lindsey's, sorrow and regret deepening her voice.

"The next thing I knew, Dr. Cross told me there was trouble, that your baby didn't make it. He ordered me to break the news to you. And when I asked to see your baby, he refused.'' She turned then and Lindsey saw the horror on the woman's face. ''He wasn't like the Doc I knew. It was as if he was a stranger.''

''But you suspected he was lying?''

''I didn't know what to think,'' Janet said in an agitated voice. ''I...Andy said he saw a man at the back, he thought Doc gave him your baby.''

So the mentally challenged orderly really had seen something.

Janet rubbed her hands up and down her arms as if to ward off a chill. ''Problem is, I don't know why he'd do such a thing. You have to believe me, Dr. Cross is one of the finest doctors I've ever worked with. He always prided himself on taking care of his patients....'' Her voice broke. ''That's why his behavior seemed so odd and scary.''

Lindsey's fingernails dug into the palms of her hands. ''You don't know who he gave my baby to?''

Janet shook her head. ''No, but I planned to find out. Only, when I went home that night, a man was waiting for me in my apartment. He...he had a gun.''

''Did you see his face or recognize him?''

Janet teared up. ''No, he was wearing a mask, he...he threatened to kill me. I know I should have called the police, but he said he'd slit my throat....'' She turned to Lindsey, her tortured expression begging for forgiveness. ''I was terrified. And he said if I told anyone about your baby, he'd kill my parents, they're both in their seventies...'' As if the burden had been too much, the nurse buried her face in her hands and burst into tears.

Lindsey rose and closed the distance between them, placing her hands gently on Janet's arms. ''Janet, you were scared, shh, it's okay. I understand.'' Lindsey pulled her into her arms and hugged her. "You don't know what it means to me to know my son is alive."

Gavin cleared his throat. "Is there anything else you can tell us?"

The woman shook her head and wiped at her eyes. "No, just that I'm sorry, I...I hope you find your little boy. And I hope Dr. Cross tells you the truth this time."

Lindsey hesitated at the door. "I don't understand though, Janet. I was so upset I let Dr. Cross handle things, but if Candy Sue buried her baby and Dr. Cross gave my son to someone else, then whose child did I bury?"

Gavin lay a comforting hand on Lindsey's shoulder. "My guess is—the grave's empty. Right, Janet?"

Janet choked up, then simply nodded in reply.

SEVERAL MINUTES later, Gavin and Lindsey said goodbye. Gavin radioed for a patrol car to watch over Janet and her friend until they found the person who'd threatened her. Lindsey was obviously shaken from learning about the empty grave and he had called Simon to give him the definite go-ahead on the exhumation for verification. He and Lindsey were walking to the car, contemplating their next move when a loud noise suddenly exploded behind them. Glass shattered on a nearby car, jagged slivers pelting the sidewalk and flying around them. Lindsey screamed. Gavin grabbed her and dove into the bushes just as the second shot whistled through the air.

Chapter Fifteen

Lindsey screamed again as another bullet zoomed above her head. Was Gavin hurt?

No, no blood, no visible wounds. He knelt, yanked a gun from the waist of his jeans and fired. She clutched his arm as he braced himself in front of her, the bushes clawing at her skin as he pushed her to safety. A motor rumbled. Tires screeched on the pavement. She peeked through the leaves and spotted a black sedan peel from the parking lot, exhaust fumes infiltrating the air behind it.

Gavin tore through the bushes and started to fire again but a group of young kids roller-bladed around the corner. When they spotted Gavin with his gun, they raced the other way. He stuffed his gun beneath his shirt, then backed toward Lindsey, keeping his gaze on the car speeding out of sight as he phoned in the incident. Several garage doors slid down, barricading the inhabitants into their safe nests.

Gavin turned to Lindsey. "Are you all right?"

Lindsey nodded. "Who was it?"

"I don't know. I couldn't see. No license either." He plucked a leaf from his shirt. "I called in the make of the car. Maybe the police will track 'em down."

Minutes later, a black-and-white rolled into the parking lot and Gavin waved for him to stop. A hulking uniformed officer with no neck met them on the sidewalk. "You call in a shooting?"

Gavin explained about the incident.

"We got a sighting on North and Main. Two patrol cars are in pursuit."

Gavin pointed toward Janet's condo. "Come on, Officer. We'd better let Miss Quinn know her hideout isn't safe anymore."

A tremor ran through Lindsey. Janet had been living in terror ever since she'd discovered Lindsey's baby had been kidnapped. But she'd still managed to send Lindsey messages to alert her to search for her son. If it weren't for Janet, she wouldn't even know her baby was alive.

And now she and Gavin had led the kidnapper right to Janet's door.

GAVIN HATED the look of terror in Janet Quinn's eyes when he'd told her about the shooting. She'd heard the gunshots, had known she'd been exposed before he'd even rung the doorbell. But worse, he hated the guilt so obvious in Lindsey's troubled eyes.

She had no reason to feel guilty. She was the victim here—she and their innocent little son. Yet how finely the lines blurred when a decent person had to shoulder the responsibility and reality of another person's crime.

As he'd been doing with the Johnson boy.

Mrs. Johnson's words rose to taunt him—nothing is as important as family. You don't realize how much they mean to you until they're gone.

More important to him than his work?

He'd lost Lindsey and his son once—could he stand to lose them again?

When they left the complex, he pulled Lindsey's hand in his own and settled it over his thigh, needing to feel her warmth, needing to reassure himself she was safe and alive beside him. "Janet will be all right, Linds. The police will keep her safe until we figure out what's going on."

Lindsey sighed wearily, her foot tapping a steady beat on the floor mat. "I can't help but feel this is my fault."

"Don't, Linds. You're the victim here. Janet was involved because she worked at the clinic—she just happened to be at the wrong place at the wrong time." He shook his head, dislodging bitter memories of the Johnson boy. "Believe me, it happens all the time. Focus on the information she gave us. We know Cross was definitely involved and our baby survived. We're going to find him."

"I don't understand why a respected physician would jeopardize his reputation by kidnapping our baby?"

"Money maybe. Or fear." Various scenarios raced through Gavin's mind, at least two he didn't want to even voice to Lindsey. "Maybe the doctor had some secret in his past he didn't want exposed."

"You mean someone blackmailed him?"

"It's possible."

"But who would do such a thing?"

"I don't know, but I'm damn well going to find out." Dwight Johnson maybe—no, he'd discounted him after his visit. Danny Swain? Jim Faulkner or his parents? One of them could have hired someone to investigate the doctor's past. And hadn't he recently learned Danny Swain's sister had once worked at the clinic? Swain had just been in Raleigh, too. Could his sister have blackmailed the doctor to help her brother?

Lindsey lapsed into silence, obviously pondering the

possibilities while he phoned Simon. He didn't waste time with preliminaries. "Have you found Cross?"

Simon hesitated. "Afraid so."

Gavin's pulse accelerated. "What's wrong?"

"He finally came home, but now he's holed up in his office and refuses to come out."

"The police are there?"

"That local sheriff and Jernigan. It doesn't look good, either. His wife says he keeps a gun in his desk."

Great. He only hoped the doctor didn't kill himself before he could come clean.

"We'll be right there." He started to hang up but Simon caught him first.

"Wait, man. A couple more things. That explosion at the factory. It turned out it was set off by faulty wiring in a machine."

"So it wasn't a diversion?"

"No. And you may want to go by Lindsey's. Barnes said an envelope arrived for her earlier."

"Something suspicious?"

"Maybe. He thinks you should take a look at it."

Gavin agreed, then hung up and pressed the accelerator, spinning the car into high speed. He really wanted to talk to Cross. He had a feeling the sooner he saw the doctor, the sooner he would find his little boy.

Hopefully, the kidnapper had seen the photo on TV and they'd forced him into making a move. And maybe this letter was a note from the kidnapper telling them what he wanted in exchange for Gavin's son.

LINDSEY'S HAND trembled as she opened the crisp white envelope. It was nothing like the one Janet had sent. This envelope had been addressed with letters cut from a magazine, the letters glued on in a haphazard manner. Gavin's normally unflappable face paled as he stared at the message.

Gavin and Agent Barnes hovered nearby, watching intently. Soft white tissue paper crinkled as she unfolded it. A tiny lock of her baby's hair had been placed inside, taped to a small computer printed note—*If you want to see your baby again, you'd better cooperate. Call off the feds. Wait for further instructions.*

Lindsey reached out to touch the baby soft hair but Barnes caught her hand.

"We'll have the note and hair analyzed," Barnes said in a no-nonsense voice that grated on Lindsey's nerves.

She stabbed a finger at the agent. "You have to go, Mr. Barnes. You have to leave now."

Gavin and Barnes exchanged worried looks, obviously deciding she was an irrational female.

"I'm not irrational. I'm doing the same thing any mother would do to protect her child. This is my baby, damn it! How can everyone act so calm?"

Gavin reached for her. "Lindsey—"

Barnes waved a calming hand, but stepped out of touching distance. "Miss Payne, calm down, please."

"She's right," Gavin agreed.

Barnes frowned. "McCord, you know procedure, statistics—"

"I don't give a damn about procedure or statistics." Gavin exhaled, then lowered his voice, his tone still lethal. "You'll need to make it look like you left," Gavin said. "In case someone's watching."

Lindsey spun to face him. "No, they might *know,* he has to really leave, go back to Raleigh!"

Gavin stroked Lindsey's arms, gently forcing her to meet

his gaze. "Linds, listen. We'll make it look good, I promise. But we need all the help we can get right now—"

"But what if they *know* and they do something to our baby? Do you want to be responsible for him being hurt?"

The air in Gavin's lungs constricted painfully. The guilt overwhelming. Could he take that chance?

Lindsey fisted her hands by her side, the fear palpable. Seconds passed, each one tormenting as they waited. When she spoke, though, her voice held regret. "I'm sorry, Mac, I'm so sorry, I shouldn't have said that. I know you're only trying to help."

"We'll find him. I promise." He wrapped her into his arms, whispering soothing words, letting her fiery courage and warmth seep into him. He prayed he was right, that he wasn't making another bad judgment call as he had with Johnson's son.

"I'm sorry...you've been so good, Gavin, you came—"

"I came because I want to find our son." He gently lifted her face with his hands and she studied the tightness of his throat muscles as he swallowed. Her eyes ached from the blinding tears fighting to escape. His were luminous and dark, worried, frightened. Sad. "I love him, too, Linds. Trust me? Please."

His husky heartfelt plea hacked away her last argument. She finally nodded, composing herself. Even if he didn't love her, he loved their baby. Maybe he'd want to keep in touch once they found him. "Okay, what do we do? Wait until we receive their demands?"

Gavin released her, obviously reigning in his emotions as he turned into the efficient die-hard detective. "You stay here and wait for a message. Barnes will monitor every call so he'll know when the kidnapper phones with his demands."

Barnes headed to the door. "I'll set up an undercover team, a cable crew or something in the neighborhood that won't draw suspicion."

Gavin pulled Lindsey into the crook of his arm. "I hate to leave you here alone, Linds. But I need to see Cross."

"I'll be fine, Mac."

"Do you want to call a friend to come sit with you?"

Lindsey considered the idea. Normally she wouldn't hesitate to call JoAnn. "No, I don't want to put anyone else in danger."

He nodded. "Stay inside and keep the doors locked. If someone calls, remember Barnes will be close by. I'll be back as soon as possible."

Lindsey nodded, surprised when Gavin lowered his mouth and kissed her. Not a chaste, quick kiss, but a kiss full of hunger and need and hope. She ached for more, but he pulled away and rushed out the door.

Adrenaline surging through Lindsey, she paced the room, anxious for the phone to ring, the kitchen clock ticking like a time bomb in her mind. Finally she would find out what the kidnapper wanted in exchange for her son. Then she'd have her baby back safe and sound, at home where he belonged.

Only then she'd face another problem—once she had her baby back in her arms, would Mac walk out of their lives for good?

GAVIN COULD still taste the luscious sweetness of Lindsey's kiss as he drove to Cross's house. Lindsey's passion had stoked the embers of his hunger for her. But more than the physical need for her, the memory of her tough perseverance through this ordeal would haunt him forever. If she hadn't insisted their son was alive, hadn't fought against all the conspiring elements, he would have never known he had a son, much less had the chance to hold him.

His cell phone rang, and Simon's voice reverberated on the other end. "Cross is still holed up in his office. We haven't made any headway. He won't talk to his wife, the cops, no one. Even worse—he asked his wife to call their priest."

"Damn." He hung up, veered onto the shoulder of the road, pulled his siren from the floor and whipped it on top of the car. A minivan full of children waved at the blue light as he passed. A tow-headed little boy, four or five years old. His gut clenched. One day he might take his own son for a ride in the squad car. Would Cory like that? Or would he be afraid of all the bad guys he dealt with?

His tires squealed as he turned off the parkway and launched down a side road. Not bothering to brake for the stop sign, he peeled into the ritzy neighborhood and parked sideways on a neighbor's lawn, amongst a dozen other cars. Gore and violence drew curious onlookers like a drought drew fire. As soon as he jumped from his car, a gunshot splintered the air.

The officers surrounding the house drew their weapons, aimed, prepared to fire. He tore through the curious spectators, ignoring a reporter who shoved a microphone at him when he yielded his badge for the on-duty officer to approve his entry. Simon approached, his lean face bleak. "The shot came from inside his office."

Gavin muttered a curse. "Get me in there, Durango. I have to talk to him before it's too late."

TICK TOCK. Tick tock. The clock's noisy insistence on counting away the minutes could be used as a slow form of torture in police interrogations, Lindsey decided thirty minutes later when she'd worn a path in her kitchen floor with her pacing. She had to gain control. Stay calm.

She'd make herself some tea. Hot chamomile tea with lemon and honey. She'd turn on the radio. Distract herself before she went completely out of her mind. But first, she picked up the phone to call her mother.

"Yes, Mom, they showed the picture on TV. I wish you could have seen it."

"Describe him to me, sweetheart. I'll close my eyes and see him in my mind."

Lindsey traced a finger over the baby picture, describing her son's face in detail.

"He sounds like quite a little man."

"He looks like Gavin, Mom."

Her mother spoke softly, "Then he's a tough one. He's going to survive."

Lindsey smiled, her love for her mother growing with her own sense of motherhood. "Mom, I'd better go in case another call comes in. But I'll keep you posted."

"All right, honey, I've got everyone here praying for you. And I'm keeping these old wrinkled fingers crossed."

Lindsey laughed, nearly choking with emotion. "I love you, Mom."

Still jittery after she hung up, she filled the teakettle with water and set it on the stove, then flipped the radio to a slow rock station. A news report cut into the latest hit from Jewel.

"This late breaking news: Renowned OB-GYN Dr. William Cross, who has delivered thousands of babies in Maple Hollow over the last twenty years, has been holed up in his home office threatening suicide for the last hour. We just received a report saying a gunshot was heard from the inside of the house."

Lindsey's breath exploded from her chest. She sank onto the kitchen chair, shaking. What if it was too late? What if Mac didn't get to talk to the doctor?

No, she couldn't think like that.

"Pamela Underwood, reporting live from Cross's home, says that police are now trying to get into Dr. Cross's office to see if he is still alive. We'll return to our regular programming, but will keep you updated on the latest developments."

Lindsey sat in shock, weighing the implications.

The teakettle whistled.

Someone pounded on the door.

She nearly jumped out of her skin.

Finally, she took a deep breath and raced to the door, wondering if Gavin had returned or if it might be Agent Barnes. She unlocked the door, keeping the chain intact. "Who's there?"

The door suddenly exploded, the latch dangling, wood splintering. A huge bearded man with tattoos on his arms and a feral gleam in his gray eyes bolted inside the room and jerked her by the arm. Lindsey tried to scream but her voice died in her throat when the beefy man waved a shiny switchblade in her face.

Chapter Sixteen

With Dr. Cross's wife's permission, Gavin broke down the doctor's office door, then scrambled across the polished mahogany floor to find Cross slumped in a pool of blood over his cherry desk. Ironic that the only thing stained on the near-perfect surface was a piece of paper folded into a perfect square. Probably a suicide note. Ironic, too, that behind him scads of family pictures, baby photos and awards boasting of the man's exemplary career lined the gleaming, dark-paneled walls.

Gavin checked his pulse and found it weak and thready. The bullet had been a clean shot through his chest. Damn, he might not make it to the hospital. He pulled out a handkerchief, secured the man's gun, then waved the paramedics in, hoping Cross would live long enough to tell them who had Lindsey's baby. Praying the note held the answers, he carefully lifted it by one corner and flipped it open. Cross had scrawled two pitiful words on the bloody page, ''I'm sorry.''

Damn.

Cross's wife burst into hysterics. Other officers rushed in to secure the crime scene and EMTs immediately set to work, checking Cross's vitals, applying pressure, hauling him onto the gurney. Minutes later, Cross groaned and opened his eyes.

Gavin shouldered his way into the man's vision, leaving Simon to handle the officers who'd arrived on the scene first and were acting territorial.

"All right, Cross, this is it. Level with me."

Cross's eyes drifted shut, then slowly opened again. He struggled but finally found his voice. Weak as it was, Gavin had to kneel to hear him.

"You were right. Miss Payne's baby is alive. I…I lied."

"I know, we talked to Janet Quinn. Where's Lindsey's son?"

A tear rolled down the side of the man's weathered face into the gray hair at his temples. His wife stood crying softly by his side. "A few weeks before Lindsey was due, this man called, he threatened me."

"What man?"

"I don't know. He never gave me a name, just phoned me at the office. Said he had all kinds of information on Miss Payne, claimed she was unstable, had a drug problem, was unfit to be a mother."

"You'd been treating her. You knew that wasn't true."

"They had more." Remorse and sorrow filled the doctor's voice when he gazed at his wife. "They had stuff on me, things they'd made up, all lies. Files saying I'd mistreated patients, had caused two babies' deaths the year before. They would have ruined my career."

"If the stories were lies, you could have proven it in court," Gavin said in a hard voice.

Cross's eyes fluttered as he tried to cope with the pain, his breathing raspy. "They had pictures of me with other women, my patients…but they weren't real—"

"Oh, William," his wife murmured. "I would never have believed anything bad of you."

A steady stream of tears tracked his cheeks now. "The scandal would have ruined us, ruined our lives, all we've worked for." Cross's gaze flickered to the family portrait on the wall. "Our own children, they would have had to deal with gossip, with lies about their father...."

Cross broke into a tortured cough. His wife lay her head on his arm and cried. Time was slipping away. He could see it in the pallor of Cross's skin and the way his breathing had turned shallow. The EMTs called in his condition, preparing to transport him.

"Who threatened you? Who kidnapped Lindsey's baby?"

"A man...he and his wife...lost their son..."

Cross coughed again, then his eyes fluttered shut, his body convulsed and his sentence trailed off as he slipped into a coma.

LINDSEY STARED at the sharp blade of the knife as it jutted toward her face. Although her insides quivered with fear, she tried her best to sound calm. "Who...who are you? What do you want?"

The man's thick neck pulsed as a growl erupted from his deep voice. "I want you to call that cop boyfriend of yours off my butt."

"I don't understand—"

"Listen, Sugar, and listen good." He pushed his face in hers, so close she could see the pores in his ruddy skin, could smell the strong scent of sweat and beer. "I did my time. I don't need no two-bit cop hulking after me now I got released. You understand?"

Lindsey nodded, wincing at the tight grip he kept on her arm. "I...who do I tell him—"

His dark beady eyes silenced her. "Danny Swain." He growled, then released her so hard she staggered backwards and hit the edge of the sofa table, sending pictures crashing to the floor.

Gavin burst through the door, his face a mask of barely controlled rage as his gaze found Lindsey. "Touch her again and you die, Swain."

The huge man turned on Gavin, his fists flying in the air. But Gavin snapped his gun from the waistband of his jeans and aimed it at Swain's chest.

"Go ahead, give me a reason," Gavin said through clenched teeth. "As if I don't have enough of one already."

"I don't know what the hell you're talking about," Swain bellowed. "I got released, been trying to make a fresh start, then find some cop on my tail. I knew it had to be you."

"You earned a tail when you kidnapped Miss Payne's baby."

Lindsey slowly picked herself up, watching the beefy man's reaction. "Do you know where my baby is?" Lindsey asked.

His eyes blazed a dirty trail over her body. "Lady, I don't know anything about a kid."

"I don't believe you," Gavin snapped.

Swain folded his massive arms across his chest. "Leave me the hell alone, McCord."

Gavin pressed the tip of his gun to Swain's chest. "Tell me where the baby is."

Lindsey saw the first sign of fear flicker in Swain's face when his ruddy complexion turned white. "I told you I don't know—"

Gavin clicked the safety off his gun and Swain tensed, his bushy eyebrows shooting upward. "You sent me the message *An Eye For An Eye,* then you kidnapped my son.''

Swain raised his hands, waving him to calm down. ''I sent the message to shake you up, but I didn't take no kid.''

Gavin pushed the gun at Swain's chest. ''You'd—''

''Move away, McCord, I'll take it from here.'' Agent Barnes appeared in the doorway, nursing a knot on his head, but appearing calm. ''I'll call the locals to take him. Assaulting a man and woman with a weapon definitely violates your parole, buddy.''

Gavin's hand tightened on the weapon. ''I'm not through with him.''

Barnes slowly moved toward Gavin, finally resting a calming hand on his shoulder. ''You gonna beat the answers out of him?''

''If I have to.''

A shudder coursed through Lindsey. ''Please, Mr. Swain, if you know where my baby is, tell me.''

The man refused to look at her, simply muttered in a harsh voice, ''I told you I don't know nothing about your kid.''

Gavin stood ramrod straight, the anger pounding through him.

''You don't talk, I'll see to it you serve your full sentence and then some.''

Barnes handcuffed Swain and pushed him out the door. ''Don't worry, McCord. We'll get to the truth.''

Gavin fisted and unfisted his free hand, then stared at his gun for several seconds before recapping the safety and placing it on the table. Lindsey's legs trembled as she walked toward Gavin.

''Are you all right, Linds?''

''Yes. Are you?''

Gavin nodded, then dragged her into his arms, his heart hammering. She curled a hand on his chest, soaking up his heat and the strength in his big-steely arms. He soothed her with gentle kisses and stroked her hair until her shakes dissipated. Only then did Lindsey feel the fine tremors in his tightly controlled muscles.

He cupped her face with his hands, searching her eyes. Protectiveness, concern, desire, fear, anger all darkened his eyes.

"What did he say before I got here?"

"The same thing he told you—to quit tailing him."

A muscle ticked in Gavin's jaw. "Did he hurt you?"

"No."

His gaze dropped to the red bruises on her wrist, then flew back to her eyes, rage darkening his features. "He did hurt you."

"He threatened me, that's all." Lindsey glanced toward the door. "Where was that Agent Barnes earlier?"

"Swain must have seen him in the truck. He knocked him out, but obviously he's okay."

"If Swain had our baby, why wouldn't he have made his demands?"

"I don't know. Maybe he's playing some kind of sick game."

"Or maybe he doesn't have our baby."

"Right." Gavin pressed against her, his expression closed.

Lindsey closed her eyes and sighed tiredly. "What happened with Dr. Cross? I heard about the shooting on the radio...."

"He confessed."

"He told you where our son is?"

"I'm afraid not, Linds. He slipped into a coma before he could give us a name."

Chapter Seventeen

Gavin clung to Lindsey, his breathing ragged in the silence that followed. Her disappointment scraped him raw. And he couldn't stop quaking from the realization that Danny Swain had had his hands on Lindsey, the only woman he'd ever loved.

The man could have crushed her fragile body with his bare hands.

If he'd lost her... God, he couldn't allow himself to think about losing her. At least not yet. Not until they found their son.

But then he would have to leave.

Or would he? *Family is the most important thing in the world. Sometimes you don't realize it until they're gone.*

His old fears rose to haunt him. He'd put Lindsey in danger, just as his own family had been in danger so many times from his dad's job. And now, Swain had barreled into Lindsey's life and threatened her, right in her home. Sure, this time she was all right. But what about the next maniac he angered? Would he use Lindsey to get to him? Would he hurt her?

No, he couldn't put Lindsey through that kind of life. She deserved better. And so did his son.

He pulled away. Crossed the room. Resisted the urge

for a stiff scotch. Grabbed a cold soda from the refrigerator, popped the top and took a long sip. If the caller phoned with demands, he wanted steady hands and eyes. Given the chance to shoot, he intended to nail the sucker in one round.

"So, what now?" Lindsey asked quietly, sounding resigned.

He curled his fingers around the can.

"We wait for demands. Meanwhile Barnes will break Swain. Maybe Simon will turn up something I missed. He was examining Cross's files when I left."

She nodded, stooping to pick up a shattered picture frame. He knelt to help her, their hands touching as they both reached for it. Gavin's breath felt trapped when he realized Lindsey had framed the photocopy of their son's picture.

"I'll get another frame." Her fingers trembled as she lovingly traced them over the cherublike face and hurried to the bedroom. No doubt in his mind she'd love his son unconditionally.

As had his own mom before the alcohol had changed her. Then she'd dished out affection so sparingly he could barely remember it. The train ride to D.C. wormed itself into his mind. His mom and him rushing out of town because of another threat. Bunking in one of the small compartments, taking an adventure, visiting the Lincoln Memorial, the Smithsonian. The memory was one of the few good ones he had, the reason he'd always loved trains.

But after that his mother had started drinking and had gone downhill fast. The days and nights had rolled into one big black void for her. And for him.

Eventually he'd ended up in juvenile. He'd decided his father had chosen his job over him and decided to punish him. Then his dad had died in a freak car accident. Ironic—after all his mother's worrying, his father's death hadn't been in the line of duty. If Walter Perkins hadn't arrested him and taken him under his wing in that Big Brother program, he would probably have wound up courting the other side of the law. In jail with guys like Swain and Faulkner. The very reason he'd tried to be a Big Brother to Dwight Johnson's boy.

No, he wouldn't make a good parent.

But he didn't want his son to think he didn't want him, either. To think he'd purposely chosen his job over him. *Family is the most important thing…*

The sound of shattered glass being swept into a pile brought his attention back to Lindsey. She'd swept up most of the debris, repositioned the photographs on the sofa table, and placed their son's picture in the center.

"Why don't I make us some dinner?" Gavin suggested.

Lindsey emptied the glass into the trash. "I'm not really hungry."

"You aren't feeling ill again, are you?"

"No, it's just—"

"You're eating."

Lindsey didn't argue. She gestured toward the kitchen. "Okay, there's a couple of steaks in there if you want to grill them. I have some salad and bread to go with it."

"I can handle that."

She rubbed her hands up and down her arms, reminding him of the filthy man who'd been pushing her around a few minutes earlier.

"I think I'll go take a bath."

He nodded, trying to focus on the image of her immersing herself in a sea of bubbles instead of Swain pushing her to the floor. She left the room without even looking at him. He set to work preparing the simple meal and prayed the phone would ring and end their torturous waiting.

LINDSEY'S BATH momentarily washed away the stench of Danny Swain's hands on her, but nothing could alleviate the tension in the house. She stared at the phone during dinner, willing it to ring, but the machine remained painfully quiet. Just like the rest of her home. Except for that confounded clock on the wall. Different birds chirped the hour with their individual sound; something she'd thought adorable when she'd first seen the clock at the nature store. She'd imagined telling Cory about each kind of bird, hearing him imitate the fluted sounds of the red robin, then the sparrow.

Now, the clock only reminded her of all she had lost, carving each excruciating hour without her baby into her memory with its barrage of sounds.

She would buy a new clock. A quiet clock that didn't remind her of the long hours of waiting she'd endured. The long hours without her baby.

The tension between she and Gavin had doubled since he'd returned from Cross's. She only wished she understood the reason. But he wouldn't talk. Had simply retreated into his brooding, dark shell.

Well, let him brood.

She scraped the dishes, unlocked the nursery door and slipped into the baby's room while he phoned his partner. Her heart bled at the sight of the beautiful white crib, the white rocking chair with the blue gingham cushion, the tiny diapers stacked on the changing table, the wallpaper border...

What was she doing in here? Trying to tear her own heart out?

Blinking back tears, she quickly slipped from the room and locked it, then turned to see Gavin watching her from the den. His gaze cut to the room and back. Her hand tightened on the doorknob.

"Did Simon find out anything new?"

He shook his head.

Suddenly weary, she said good-night and headed to her bedroom. Loneliness welled inside her, almost cutting off the oxygen to her lungs as she slipped on a soft blue nightgown and climbed into the big sleigh bed. She pulled up the blue-and-yellow comforter, craving its soothing warmth as she buried her face into her pillow, letting the tears fall. Tears for the baby she longed to hold in her arms.

Tears for the man she had hoped would someday live there with them.

GAVIN FORCED himself to stretch out on the sofa, well aware he wouldn't sleep. Not with his mind on the phone call that hadn't yet come. Not with Lindsey lying in the next room. Not knowing how much he needed her tonight.

He considered the information Simon had given him. Apparently Swain's sister had worked at the clinic, but only briefly. She'd left long before Lindsey had delivered. A dead end there. And he was inclined to dismiss Johnson from the list. But Swain?

An Eye For An Eye... The note taunted his subconscious. Was the message a threat or a declaration of a crime already committed—*A son for a son?* Or had Swain been telling the truth?

He checked the phone. Sometime during the night, the kidnapper would phone with demands. Hopefully, tomorrow he would find his son, give him back to Lindsey and step out of their lives to keep them safe. Maybe one day he'd be able to explain to his little boy the reason he'd left, make him understand he loved him.

His body ached, physically hurt for Lindsey's touch. But his soul needed her even more. Needed one night to hold her in his arms before they said goodbye.

Knowing this might be his last chance, he rose from the sofa, tiptoed to her bedroom, and pushed the door open. Moonlight spilled like a halo around her golden hair which fanned across the pale pillowcase. Shadows played and fell across the room, her lithe, beautiful body draped in a pale yellow sheet. The soft whisper of her breathing told him she was asleep. He didn't want to bother her.

But he had to hold her. Just for a little while.

He slipped off his shoes and socks, shucked his jeans and shirt and crawled into the bed beside her.

She smelled like fresh flowers and rain. He closed his eyes, savoring the erotic scents. Her back faced him, the soft fabric of her gown gliding across his bare chest as he slid his arm around her waist and cradled her spoon style. Her bottom fit perfectly against his groin, her long soft hair tickled his chin. She moaned and snuggled farther into his warmth. He couldn't resist. He brushed a kiss into her hair and whispered the three words he thought he'd never say to a woman. "I love you, Lindsey."

LINDSEY LAY perfectly still, her mind spinning with the realization that Gavin had just climbed into her bed and whispered his love in the dark.

He thought she was asleep.

She let him believe that for a few minutes, knowing his admission had been a private confession, not meant for her ears. Then his hand slipped around her waist, gently stroking her abdomen, his leg brushed hers so she felt the coarse hair on his thighs against her legs, his breath whispered behind her ear. All the tension and love and hunger she'd had bottled away for months sprang to life with an intensity she couldn't ignore. Vonda Shepard's song about love and breaking your heart flowed through her mind, but she knew there was no turning back. Her heart had always been his to break, since that night they had lain together, body and souls merging into one, hearts embracing love in the most intimate form. She had to have that love one more time, even if it was given only in the darkness of night, with whispered words she was never meant to hear.

Her hand slid down to stroke the top of his, her leg entwined with his muscular one, her bottom nestled farther against his sex. He moaned, the soft purr of his lips on the nape of her neck sending a thousand delicious sensations skittering up her spine. She gently glided her foot up and down his thick calf, warmth pooling in her abdomen as his firm muscle flexed beneath her touch. His hand skimmed up to stroke the underside of her breast, circling slow, cupping, kneading her curves, then traced a path of ecstasy in her every pore when he stroked her nipple to a hard peak of desire. One by one he slowly unbuttoned the small buttons of her nightshirt and parted the silk fabric, his hands hot as they found her bare skin. She continued to stroke his legs with her foot, reaching behind her to rub his waist, his hips, to feel his hard, firm body pressing into her with more urgency.

His lips tasted her neck, the inside of her ear, his tongue teased her earlobe, her cheek. With a growl, he rose slightly, tilting her face around so he could find her sweet lips. Lindsey groaned and parted her lips, savoring his tongue as he plunged his warmth into her mouth. They danced a slow heat, awakening need and hunger left buried for long lonely months, until every cell in her body screamed for release. She suckled his lips, clutched at his bottom, drove herself against his throbbing heat. Their bodies rocked together, mimicking the joining of lost souls.

But she needed more, needed his clothes completely off, needed to feel his heavy weight within her.

''Oh, Mac.'' She turned into his arms and saw the fire glistening in his dark eyes. Sweat dotted his bronzed chest, the black hair on his chest curly and thick, and so enticing she sank her hands into it, stroking his nipples and hungrily meeting his kiss.

''I want you so much, Linds,'' Gavin whispered. ''I've wanted you all these months.''

''I'm all yours, Mac.'' She tunneled her hands through his hair. ''Make love to me.''

''I wish I could make promises, but I—''

''Shh.'' Lindsey silenced him with a kiss. ''Just love me tonight, Mac. That's all I want. Make me forget all the bad things that have happened, make me feel alive again.''

He nibbled her neck tenderly, threading his fingers through the long strands of her hair, stroking them away from her face. Lindsey lowered her mouth and took his nipple between her teeth, teasing and torturing him with hungry kisses. He cupped her chin, bringing her face back to his, stroking her mouth with his tongue just as he wanted to plunge himself inside her. His hot breath scorched her neck as he skimmed the nightgown from her body. Her panties came next, then he wedged his thigh between her legs. His hands were everywhere, on her breasts, twisting and loving her nipples, gliding down across her thighs, parting her legs, teasing her heat.

She grasped the edge of his boxers and pulled at them, aching to hold his sex in her hands, smiling when the pulsing evidence of his arousal twitched and jutted toward her. He moaned and rocked his body into hers, slipping a finger inside her and kissing her at the same moment, deep, deeper as if he could fill her with his soul. Lindsey arched toward him, clutched his hips and dug her nails into his back as he rose above her. He paused and took her chin in his hand, tipped her face up to gaze into her eyes, dropped a kiss on each of her closed eyelids. "Open your eyes, Linds. I want you to watch me inside you."

A chill of excitement skittered through every nerve ending in her body as she did as he asked. He suddenly reached for his jeans and she whimpered, afraid he was going to pull away. Instead he grabbed a small foil packet and ripped it open with his teeth.

The protection they'd forgotten the first time they made love.

She was relieved he'd remembered this time. "Let me do this," she whispered.

He grinned and actually pressed himself into her hand. She slowly took the condom from him and molded it to his hard shaft, enjoying the tortured look he gave her as she rubbed and stroked him. Finally, he grabbed her hand and pulled it up to his face, pressing her palm to his cheek. He smelled of musk and heat and sex. His powerful body poised above her, the muscles of his arms strained as he tried not to crush her. His huge sex pushed against her feminine folds and she ached for completion, so she lifted her hips, whimpering when the tip of his erection played at her heat, then retreated. She saw the devil in his eyes, smiling wickedly, enjoying the torture, and she reached down again and took his hard sex in her hand, stroking it from the base to the tip until she felt his hips convulse. His smile faded, his control snapped.

He took her hard and fast, pulling her hips up to meet

his thrusts as he drove inside her, drew out, then drove even deeper. Lindsey moaned and clawed at his arms, struggling to hold back, to prolong the sweet pleasure but the waves of euphoria rippled over her in a hundred different colors as their bodies danced together. She saw the moment his own release began; his face contorted with both pain and pleasure, and his gaze never once left hers as he moaned and rode the crest with her.

THEY MADE LOVE all through the night. But sometime during the early hours of the morning, Lindsey felt him slipping away from her. Maybe it was the intensity of his lovemaking, maybe it was the way he rolled away and faced the wall the last time. She tried to sleep but his on-again, off-again attitude had done a number on her already frayed nerves.

"Gavin?"

"Hmm?"

"What's going to happen now?"

He sighed, then rolled to his back and stared at the ceiling. She nuzzled up to his side, but he stiffened and anger suddenly churned within her. Lindsey jerked the sheet around her bare chest and leaned against the headboard.

"I can't stand this waiting, this not knowing. One minute you're comforting me, the next you're throwing up these walls—"

Gavin swung around. "Look, I'm trying to help, but I don't want to give you any false hopes."

"False hopes?" She picked up the pillow and crushed it between her hands. "As in a happily-ever-after ending for us? Well, don't worry, I didn't expect you to offer me forever."

"I didn't mean to hurt you, Linds."

"I know you only came because I begged you to help find our baby."

Gavin slid off the bed and stalked across the room. Lindsey tried to ignore the fact that he was completely naked. Hard and naked. "I never pretended to be husband or father material. I told you that up front. For God's sake, I grew up in a cop family. I know what it's like to be the son of a policeman." He grabbed his jeans and yanked them on, then paced back and forth, the words coming fast and furious. "I know what it's like to be carted off to safe houses, to be afraid some maniac my dad put in jail would come after me. I saw the terror on my mother's face more than once. She finally got sick of it and skipped out. I swore I'd never have a family and put them through that."

"You're afraid of putting your loved ones in danger— that's the reason you don't want a family?"

"It's a good reason, don't you think?" He swung his hands in the air. "Jesus, you're living that nightmare right now. Someone tried to kill you. They kidnapped our son. How can you not *hate* me for putting you through this? Our baby might have been kidnapped to get revenge on *me.*"

"I don't hate you, Mac." Lindsey's voice sounded strong. "And I don't blame you for something some crazy person has done."

"Well, maybe you should. If you hadn't gotten involved with me, none of this would have happened. You'd probably have met some nice man by now and be married with his baby."

"Is that what you want, Mac?"

"Hell, no." He paused to stare at her, slicing his hands through the air angrily. "It doesn't matter what I want."

"Of course it matters what you want. How can you even say that?"

"Because I have that kind of job. I'm a cop."

"And your job is more important—"

"No. Family is. But my job, it's what I do. It's a part of me."

Just as her teaching was a part of her. She could never ask him to give up his work. People needed him. But she needed him, too, and so did their baby.

"So you don't ever want a family or a wife or a home?" she asked quietly.

His hands fisted by his side. "The only thing that matters is that you and our son are safe."

"We would be safe with you."

"No, you wouldn't." He resumed pacing. "Believe me, I tried playing father before and failed."

Lindsey struggled to reach for her robe, spotted Gavin's shirt first and put it on, her hands trembling. Hurt welled inside her. "You have another child?"

"No." He leaned against the doorjamb and scrubbed his face with his hands. "I took a kid under my wing once, joined this Big Brother program. This boy named Rodney."

"What happened?"

He turned his back to her, staring out the window, his shoulders rigid. "He'd been getting in trouble, possession of drugs, fights, minor stuff, but I thought I could help him."

"I'm sure you did."

"He died, Lindsey." He faced her then, the strain and horror of the boy's loss written in every craggy feature of his face. "He thought tagging along with me on a case would be fun so he followed me one day. Walked right into a bust. Got shot three times." His voice broke. "He was only fourteen."

Lindsey resisted the urge to react. Instead she reached out to comfort him, but he pulled away. Guilt darkened his eyes, tore at her own heart. "I'm sorry, Mac. But the boy's death wasn't your fault."

"Tell that to his parents," he murmured. "He was their only child."

As Cory was theirs. The magnitude of Gavin's guilt struck Lindsey full force.

"So you see, I don't deserve to have a family—"

Lindsey opened her mouth to argue, to tell him she refused to buy into his misguided theory, that everyone deserved love, but the phone trilled, cutting her off.

She raced to the den and picked up the handset, her hands trembling.

"Hello?"

"Miss Payne?"

"Yes, who is this?"

"It doesn't matter. But if you want your baby back, you'd better listen."

Chapter Eighteen

"We want Jim Faulkner released from prison."

"What? Who are you?"

"Just shut up and listen, Miss Payne. Faulkner's parole hearing is coming up. You and your cop buddy move it up to today. Then you go public and recant your testimony. When Faulkner walks out of the pen, you'll receive instructions on how to get your baby back."

Lindsey's heart was pounding so loudly the blood roared in her ears. She didn't recognize the man's voice.

"But how do I know you really have my baby?"

A low chuckle rumbled over the line. "I guess you'll just have to trust me."

Not good enough, Gavin mouthed.

"Tell me something, anything…"

"He has your brown eyes, Miss Payne, and a little square chin and a pug nose. And this crooked toe. Dr. Cross handed him to us right there at the clinic in Maple Hollow."

Lindsey bit her lip not to cry out. She saw a muscle tick in Gavin's jaw but he whispered for her to stall for time. Jim's parole hearing might have been coming up, but Gavin had assured her he'd never be released the first go-round.

''All right, but I don't know if we can do it today…it'll take time—''

''Today, Miss Payne. And we want Faulkner's record wiped clean.''

''I—''

''We warned you to call off the feds too. This time you'd better listen.'' The phone clicked and the line went dead.

Gavin muttered a curse.

''So Jim orchestrated this whole thing?'' Lindsey whispered in shock.

''It sounds like it,'' Gavin agreed. ''But I don't understand why he'd wait so damn long to contact us. If he arranged to kidnap our baby to free himself, why not make the demands right off?''

''Maybe he wanted to wait until nearer his parole date.''

''Parole dates can be changed.''

Lindsey's throat ached. ''Maybe he wanted to torment me.''

''Maybe, but every day he waited was another day he spent in jail.'' Gavin shook his head in thought. ''Something doesn't fit.'' He could see Faulkner or his parents paying someone to kidnap the baby, but why would Lindsey's ex go to so much trouble for a child he didn't want? And kidnapping would definitely eliminate any possibility of parole. What about the Faulkners—why would they risk a felony when they could have simply paid a judge to give their son an early parole or fight for visitation rights?

Lindsey swung her gaze to him in concern. ''You mean you don't think the caller has our baby?''

Gavin hesitated a fraction of a second too long. ''I don't

know. After our visit to Faulkner and his folks, it's possible…''

Oh, God. "It's possible they saw how distraught I was and decided to use our son's disappearance against me to get Jim freed from prison.''

He nodded curtly.

Lindsey's hopes disintegrated. "But if we arrange his release and they don't have our baby, can you have him arrested again?''

"Sure, unless his family whisks him off to some foreign country.''

Which they could easily do with their money and connections. "Then what do we do now?''

"We'll have to play along, see what they do when we free Faulkner.''

"Can you really arrange for his release today?''

Gavin picked up the phone to call Simon. "I'll have to have help. Let me talk to Simon, see if we can pull some strings.''

"No FBI, he said—''

"We'd be crazy not to accept their help. They know what they're doing.'' He reached for her, seemed to remember the night before and backed away. Lindsey fought off the hurt, knowing she didn't have time to dwell on the problems between her and Gavin. "There are no guarantees that whoever has the baby will give him back to us if we meet their demands. If they do have our baby and try to run with him, we'll need back-up. Timing will be crucial.''

"What if they see the FBI and something goes wrong?''

Gavin fisted his hands by his side. "I'll wear a mike, make sure they're a safe distance away. Trust me, Linds, it's the only way.''

Lindsey frowned. "I'll go shower and get dressed."

Gavin was punching in his partner's number as she left the room. Lindsey cradled her stomach and decided to call her mother and let her know the latest. She'd rather explain her plan than have her mom hear her apology to her ex on the radio or TV. Then she'd sit down and plan her speech to set her ex-husband free.

THE PLANS had changed. First, the boss had agreed the Payne woman should die and so should that detective because he wanted the baby. Now, he no longer wanted the child; he wanted him to hold off with the murders, too, until he got Faulkner out of jail. Once again, the boss had ordered *him* to do the dirty work so he'd called and bargained for Faulkner's release.

All because they'd learned who the baby's real father was. Damn.

The little detail was insignificant to him. For all intents and purposes he'd fathered the little boy himself, had planted the seed that had given him life. She had gone through labor and delivery.

But to him it meant a way to get to McCord and the Payne woman.

He lit a cigarette and closed his eyes, letting the sweet melody and sound of her voice wash over him as she rocked and sang to their baby boy.

"Rock-a-bye baby, in the tree top...down will come baby, cradle and all."

Unfortunately the cradle was about to fall.

He took a drag of the cigarette and inhaled, grateful for the nicotine's calming effect. He'd be glad when this whole ordeal was over, when they could leave and escape to some unknown place and be rid of the problems.

"I love you, sweetheart," he heard her say. "You'll always be my precious angel."

He crushed the cigarette beneath his boot, grinding the last of the embers into the dry dirt. She would die without the baby just as the fire died without oxygen.

He'd follow along with his boss, lure Payne and that detective to the cabin, then kill them and take the baby. His boss wouldn't care what happened to the little boy now, not as long as he got Faulkner back. And he didn't care what happened to Faulkner as long as he ended up with the child.

Chapter Nineteen

Three hours later Lindsey and Gavin entered the judge's chamber. With Special Agent Barnes's connections, a private hearing had been arranged—a formality that would exonerate Jim Faulkner, the man who'd tried to murder Lindsey.

Gavin and Agent Barnes both made brief statements, explaining the situation to the judge.

"You realize I'm releasing him into your custody, Mr. McCord?" the judge said with a stern warning about rights and responsibilities.

"Yes, Your Honor."

The gavel came down hard. Gavin, Lindsey and Barnes rose and exited the chambers to meet the press for part two of the ordeal.

Perspiration beaded Lindsey's forehead as she stared through the blinding camera lights to address the reporters.

Gavin spoke first. "We're here today to announce Jim Faulkner's release from prison. A little over a year ago, Mr. Faulkner was accused of money laundering as well as attempted murder. Today we have new evidence which we presented to Judge Townsend in chambers. Mr. Faulkner has been cleared of all charges. He will be released today, his record wiped clean.''

He turned slightly and Lindsey gripped the microphone.

''Miss Payne, who was married to Mr. Faulkner for a brief time and served as the key witness in the case, has an official statement to make.''

Reporters' hands jutted into the air, several yelling out questions. ''Is it true you lied under oath, Miss Payne?''

''Were you out for revenge?''

Gavin cut in, ''Hold the questions. Please let Miss Payne give her statement.''

Lindsey wet her lips and began. ''First of all, I'd like to tell Jim's parents, Mr. and Mrs. Faulkner, how sorry I am for putting them through this difficult time. And I'd like to apologize to my ex-husband, Jim.'' She paused, the microphone amplifying the tension in her voice. ''And yes, I admitted that I lied under oath.''

A collective gasp reverberated through the room. Several more hands flew up but Lindsey tightened her grip around the edge of the podium to steady herself.

''I was distraught in our marriage, having some…some emotional problems of my own. I…I regret to say I fabricated the story about him trying to kill me.'' She lowered her head, every vile word like a knife twisting in her throat as she remembered his hands tightening around her neck.

More questions surged through the audience. ''Are you in therapy?''

''Have you seen your ex-husband?''

''Are you facing charges for perjury?''

''Are you two planning a reunion?''

''We haven't discussed a reconciliation at this time. I only pray God will forgive me.''

Cameras flashed and two reporters on the front row

dashed forward, but Gavin and Barnes whisked Lindsey from the room before the stampede could hound her further.

THIRTY MINUTES later, Lindsey and Gavin met the warden at the Central Prison in Raleigh and prepared for her ex-husband's release. Gavin tried to control the rage building within him as he saw Faulkner's handcuffs removed. Faulkner should have served twenty years for his crimes. At best, at his first hearing, he might have been moved to a minimum security prison. He'd barely served a year though, and here he was walking free.

Gavin had asked Lindsey to trust him, yet she'd trusted him to make sure Faulkner stayed behind bars and he'd let her down. He'd let the feds wire him, but he still wasn't sure he was doing the right thing. What if this caller wasn't the kidnapper? Or what if something went wrong? What if the kidnapper didn't return their son?

The moment Lindsey saw Faulkner, a mask slid over her face, concealing her emotions. Thank God. She would have to be strong.

"Well, darling, you looked mighty fine on TV." Faulkner sauntered toward Lindsey and bent to kiss her cheek but Lindsey pulled back.

Gavin twisted Faulkner's arm behind him. "Listen here, you prick. We're only going along in exchange for Lindsey's baby, so keep your slimy hands off Miss Payne, you got that?"

"How could you lie to me, Jim? How could you have stolen my baby and kept him from me all this time? Was this some sort of sick plan for revenge?"

Anger flashed into Faulkner's cold eyes. "I told you I didn't know anything about the baby's disappearance."

He gestured around the warden's office. "I didn't set this up."

Gavin twisted Faulkner's arm harder. "Don't lie now, Faulkner. Just tell us where we can find the baby."

Faulkner shrugged. "I told you I didn't arrange this," he said, enunciating each word louder. "Not that I'm arguing with your change of heart, Lindsey darlin', but I had no idea I was being released until a few minutes ago."

Gavin frowned. Normally he'd have thought Faulkner was lying. He watched for that telltale sign, that little nostril flare. But Faulkner's expression remained controlled, steady. If Faulkner hadn't set up his own release, who the hell had?

"IT WAS YOUR father, wasn't it?" Lindsey asked a few minutes later as they left the prison walls behind them.

Faulkner stepped into the fresh air and inhaled, a smile beaming on his face as he stroked the lapel of his new suit. "Daddy dearest would be my best guess."

"I should have known," Lindsey said. "Your parents always disliked me. But I never thought they'd do something so cruel as to kidnap a child."

"Our son is their grandchild so I'd hardly call it kidnapping," Faulkner said harshly.

Lindsey glanced at Gavin, desperate to set the record straight. Jim had never wanted kids. Even now he was so cold she couldn't believe she'd felt guilty for letting him think the baby was his. If anything, prison had hardened his heart even more than before.

He gestured toward the parking lot. "Hey, where's my limo? I expected to be escorted home in style."

Lindsey rolled her eyes. Gavin growled and shoved him toward his car. "You're not going home."

Faulkner laughed as he climbed in the back seat. "Then where are you taking me?"

Gavin started the car and pulled from the parking lot. "We were hoping you could tell us."

Faulkner shrugged. "I told you I don't have a clue." He brushed a hand across the worn fabric of the seat. "But I certainly hope my next mode of transportation is a little more upscale than this."

"If you think I give a rat's ass about your comfort, Faulkner—"

The phone jangled. Gavin glanced at the number on the screen, realized it had been directed through Lindsey's home line, and indicated for her to answer it.

"Hello?"

"You did a fine job, Miss Payne." The voice sounded muffled, as if the caller were speaking through a handkerchief.

Lindsey clamped her hand over Gavin's to alert him the kidnapper was on the line. "I did what you asked, now tell me where my baby is."

"Is Jim Faulkner with you?"

Lindsey glared at her ex-husband. "Yes, he's here. Tell me if my baby's all right, please."

"The baby's fine. Now put Faulkner on the line. I'll give him directions. He'll tell you where to go."

Lindsey seethed, but lifted the handset. "He wants to talk to you."

Faulkner had the grace to look surprised, but accepted the phone in silence.

"Dad?" He paused. "Wait a minute, who is this? Yes. Yes, I know where that is. Yes, I'll bring them there."

When he hung up, he rubbed his neck. "It wasn't my father."

"Then who the hell was it? Someone who works for him?" Gavin asked through clenched teeth.

"I don't know, maybe. I didn't recognize the voice, he sounded as if he was speaking through a vacuum, like he was disguising it." Faulkner paused and stroked his chin. "We're supposed to go to a little hotel outside Asheville and wait for further instructions. Do you have a map?"

Gavin pulled one from the glove compartment.

"How about a gun?"

Lindsey heard the slight tremble in her ex-husband's tone. Gavin obviously picked up on it, too. "Why do you ask? Worried someone might have arranged your release to set *you* up for a hit?"

The frightened expression on her ex-husband's face would have been laughable if Lindsey hadn't realized Gavin had zeroed in on the truth. And if he had and his fears were real, were they going to get her baby back? Or were they walking into a trap?

Chapter Twenty

Gavin stewed over the long night ahead with Lindsey and Faulkner, finally deciding the three of them would have to share a room. With Lindsey's life in danger, he didn't feel comfortable leaving her alone, and they couldn't afford for Faulkner to escape before they negotiated the trade-off for the baby's return.

Faulkner apparently was contemplating his options— had his release been orchestrated by his family so they could save him or as a setup for someone who meant to hurt him? Damn, he wished he could shake this awful feeling. They didn't need another complication at this stage of the game.

He had to believe they were going to find his son or he would go crazy. Gavin grimaced when he finally found the Hotel Flamingo. The only comfort he took in seeing the dilapidated two-bit dive was Faulkner's reaction. Faulkner obviously hadn't reserved the accommodations. Of course, that also meant Faulkner's parents might not have orchestrated the release and they were walking into a trap.

"I suppose you'll reserve us separate suites," Faulkner said sarcastically as Gavin parked in front of the blinking neon sign.

"Yeah, right." Gavin hurried to help Lindsey from the car. She'd been uncomfortably quiet and he was worried about her, especially after their interlude in the bedroom the night before. He still didn't understand why Lindsey didn't hate him for putting them in jeopardy in the first place.

Faulkner stared at him blankly as he handcuffed him inside the car and locked the door. Gavin quibbled with the clerk at the front desk about one room, grimacing at the thought of Faulkner ogling Lindsey while she slept. Finally he opted for two connecting rooms. She simply glared at him but said nothing as they started back to the car.

"I don't understand, why not meet us tonight?" she asked as the bell above the door clinked, marking their exit from the lobby.

"My guess is whoever has the baby needed time to prepare a getaway."

Lindsey stopped midstride. "So you think they're planning to fly out of the country?"

"I can't imagine Faulkner staying in the U.S. now. His family isn't stupid. They know once we have the baby back, we can come after him."

"Shouldn't you have someone watching the Faulkners?"

"It's taken care of," Gavin said quietly. "If they do have our son and make a move, my partner will be right behind them."

"Then they might lead him to Cory?"

Gavin nodded. "That's the plan. But I doubt they'll do anything until your ex is free."

A shuddered look crossed Lindsey's face but she continued walking. "I hate to see Jim get away with all this."

"So do I."

They both fell silent as they arrived at the car. Seconds later they shuffled into the tiny rooms, the tension thick. A lumpy double bed with a worn spread occupied one room, while twin beds with similar faded spreads were in the other. Both rooms were painted dingy off-white with brown shag carpet.

"Not exactly luxurious," Gavin commented to Lindsey.

Lindsey shrugged. "I wish we could keep going tonight."

Faulkner stared at the furnishings in dismay. "My father definitely didn't arrange this. He has too much class to send us to a dive like this."

Gavin frowned. "It's a step up from your cell."

Faulkner's face turned harsh. "I never should have been put there."

Lindsey's eyes darkened with fury but she didn't reply.

Gavin simply gave him a cold look and decided if Faulkner didn't like the room, he certainly wasn't going to like the room service. But he'd sure as hell better enjoy it because Gavin had every intention of sending Faulkner's butt back to jail when they found his son. And if Faulkner had orchestrated the kidnapping, he'd make sure the man sat in the cell for the rest of his life.

Later, Lindsey lay in the big lumpy bed by herself, thinking of Gavin and her ex-husband sharing the neighboring room. Ironic that the man she'd once been married to was now sleeping in the same room with the man she loved.

There was no doubt in her mind that she loved Gavin.

Gavin was strong and protective, a gentleman at heart. A man who risked his life for strangers every day, then risked his own happiness to keep the ones he loved safe. How could she not love him?

Sure, last night she'd been hurt when he'd pulled away, even angry when he'd had his little outburst. But now she knew the reasons Gavin had refused her love.

He didn't think he deserved it.

He thought by pushing her from his life, he was protecting her.

He was wrong. She'd sure as hell found trouble before she'd met him. She'd been young and foolish and had been taken in by Jim Faulkner's charisma and charm. But she'd matured during their short marriage and now surface beauty no longer attracted her—the true grit she saw in Gavin did.

The problem remained—how could she convince Gavin he was wrong about marriage and family, especially when he'd grown up with a cop as a father and a neurotic alcoholic mother who hadn't been able to handle life? No wonder he harbored such doubts.

She suddenly sensed someone was watching her and bolted to a sitting position, pulling the covers to her chin. A hulking shadow filled the doorway, the hiss of breathing echoing through the room. Had her ex-husband come in while Gavin was in the shower?

"Linds?"

Her breath quivered when she recognized the gruff voice. "What is it, Gavin? Did you hear something?"

"No, I just wanted to make sure you're all right."

His footstep faltered in the doorway. She saw him struggling over whether to move closer, and she silently willed him to come to her, to crawl in bed and hold her all night.

"Linds?" His voice sounded weary, clipped.

"I'm fine. Where's Jim?"

"He's not going anywhere. I handcuffed him to the bed."

His words brought reality crashing back. His admission the night before had created a deep, wide chasm between them. His job meant he could not have her and a family. And she didn't have any answers to solve the problem. So she simply said good-night and watched silently as he retreated to the other room.

THE PHONE CALL came at 5:00 a.m. By five-thirty, he and Lindsey and her ex-husband climbed in the car for what he hoped was the final leg of their journey. Faulkner shifted in the back seat, grumbling at the confining handcuffs, but Gavin ignored him. As far as he was concerned, Faulkner was still a prisoner. He'd told him that he didn't intend to release him until Lindsey was holding her baby in her arms.

Two hours later, Gavin grew uneasy as they wound around the Blue Ridge Parkway, but Faulkner seemed to know the roads well, signifying they were headed to a familiar place. He'd already radioed for backup, checked his mike, set everything in motion. They would find the cabin, make the exchange, then the feds would swoop in. Hopefully, the switch would go off as planned.

But if this was a setup to hurt Faulkner, he'd have to protect the bastard.

Lindsey remained silent, simply staring out at the scenery as if they'd gone for a relaxing Sunday afternoon drive, but her face was drawn, the tension between them humming through the car.

The lush green mountains rolled in front of them, caverns sprawling from the cliffs like a magazine promo piece selling mountain property. Wildflowers swayed in the breeze and the colorful fall leaves painted a parade of colors along the horizon. Picnic spots sprang up along the outlook areas, along the river banking the highway. Families parked on the overlook paths, sightseeing, lounging on the banks to cook breakfast over campstoves, settling in for a long morning of fishing.

But the mood in the car was anything but relaxed. And if he were right, they seemed to be heading in the direction of the Johnsons' cabin. He'd discounted Johnson, but could the man have forged a deal with the Faulkners? The connection seemed far-fetched. Then again, the Faulkners had money. If they had hired a detective to find his Achilles' heel, they would have eventually ended up at Dwight Johnson's door.

Too bad Cross was still in the coma, although his prognosis indicated he would recover so maybe he would wake soon and talk. Swain hadn't confessed yet, but he'd just gotten out of prison, probably needed money. Maybe old man Faulkner hired him to do his dirty work.

"Down that graveled road." Faulkner pointed toward a narrow dirt road winding through the hills.

Gavin made the turn, checking around him for signs of an ambush but saw nothing except greenery and wildlife. The river thinned and tapered into a creek, then a trickle of a stream, the picnic spots non-existent on the isolated stretch. His ears popped as they climbed altitude, the brush growing thicker, the road more narrow, until finally they hit a dead-end.

"What the hell?"

"Guess we have to walk the rest of the way," Faulkner said dryly.

"Walk where?" Lindsey asked, suddenly looking nervous.

Faulkner gestured toward the rising hills. "To the cabin. It's up there a few miles."

Gavin should have known the caller would have sent them the most indirect route. He'd figured the kidnapper would choose a remote spot to make the trade and praised himself for his logic in suggesting Lindsey wear jeans and sneakers. He'd even grabbed some bottles of water and slung them into a backpack.

Weeds and sticks crackled beneath his boots as he climbed out. Lindsey shucked her long-sleeved shirt and tied it around her waist over her T-shirt while he helped Faulkner from the car.

Faulkner shoved his hands toward Gavin. "I could hike easier if you'd unfasten these."

Gavin simply gave him a push. "Now, why would I want to make things easier on a guy like you?"

Faulkner's glare promised retribution, but Gavin remained unfazed.

"Lead the way, Faulkner, this is your show." Gavin moved his gun from his jeans and flicked it in the air. "And remember, I'm right behind you."

"You think I don't want to see my baby?" Faulkner asked.

"You never wanted children," Lindsey said stiffly.

"Not back then, but maybe I've changed. Maybe I've decided I need a legacy."

"You'd make a lousy father, Faulkner, and you're not running off with Lindsey's son," Gavin snapped.

Faulkner muttered a curse at Gavin, then scanned the countryside, obviously getting his bearings. Lindsey bit her lip in worry as they waited, the early morning sun beaming down. Faulkner gestured toward an overgrown trail and began the hike. Gavin ushered Lindsey in front of him, following closely behind.

The stench of a dead animal wafted around them as they hiked deeper into the grove of trees. Thick weeds clawed at their legs, overgrown tree branches pricked at their hair and faces. Forty-five minutes later, the sun grew hotter, the hill steeper. Gavin was in good shape but he worried about Lindsey. It hadn't been long since she'd left the hospital.

"Stop a minute, Faulkner, let's rest on these rocks." He indicated a small clearing where a storm had obviously destroyed some of the older trees. They lay in half-rotted mangled positions, their trunks splintered. Chipmunks had created a home in one, in the other a nest of beetles attacked the bark. Gavin moved toward a large, smooth rock, then leaned against it.

Sweat dripped down Faulkner's face. "What's wrong, McCord, out of shape?"

"Lindsey was just released from the hospital."

"I can go on," Lindsey said stubbornly.

Gavin glared at her. "You need fluids." He handed her a bottle of water, took one for himself, then released his cuffs for him to drink and gave one to Faulkner.

Lindsey sipped hers, then blotted the end of her shirt with water and wiped at her face. Faulkner wasn't so polite. He poured some in his hand and sopped his neck with it.

"How much farther?" Gavin asked.

Faulkner shrugged. "Another couple of miles, I guess."

Lindsey recapped her water and handed it back to Gavin. "Let's go."

Gavin nodded and stored the water bottles when suddenly a shot rang out. Faulkner dropped to the ground behind the rock and Lindsey screamed. Gavin dove to protect her, but he felt the sting of the bullet zing through him as he hit the dirt.

Chapter Twenty-One

The gun slipped from Gavin's hand as he went down. His boot skidded on the raw dirt and sent his weapon skittering a good foot away in the gravel. Faulkner reached for it, but another shot pinged off the rock above him and Gavin crouched to the ground. A forest of trees shadowed the clearing, setting an ideal hiding spot for the assassin, a perfect trap. Blood spurted from Gavin's shoulder, pain slicing through his upper body and arm.

"Oh my God, you've been shot," Lindsey cried.

He ignored the horror in her voice. "It's just my shoulder. Hand me my gun."

She stared at him in shock, but Faulkner quickly lurched for the loaded weapon. She swiped it before Faulkner could, then raised it without wavering and pointed it at her ex-husband. "Don't move, Jim."

He froze, obviously surprised at her lethal tone. She calmly handed Gavin the gun, her gaze never straying from her ex-husband. Ignoring the pain in his body, Gavin pivoted to scan the bushes, trying to estimate how many shooters were in the woods, but another shot zoomed daringly close to Lindsey's head. He shoved her down behind him.

"Who the hell is doing this?" he barked at Faulkner.

Faulkner shook his head as Gavin rose on his knees and fired a shot in the direction of their assailant. He saw a movement, a shadow darting through the bushes, fleeing, just as the gravel crunched behind him. Faulkner raced into the sanctuary of the trees, running for all he was worth.

"He's getting away," Lindsey yelled.

Gavin grabbed her hand to keep her from chasing him, scanning the distance in case another shot was fired. Trees rustled, the shadow of a person disappeared into the thick woods cresting the canyon. The shooter must have accomplished his purpose. Faulkner had escaped and run ahead, leaving Gavin injured.

"We'll catch him," Gavin said through gritted teeth.

"But we can't go on, you're hurt," Lindsey said, her voice quivering. "We have to get you to a doctor."

Dust assaulted him as a wind stirred the rocky terrain but he focused on calming Lindsey. "I'll make it. We can't go back now, Linds, or we'll lose him for sure."

Her tear-filled gaze made his heart squeeze. No one had ever cared that much for Gavin McCord.

He pressed his hand over the open wound, the crimson stain rapidly spreading across his chest. His head spun as he wrestled to remove his shirt. Lindsey jerked at his clothes, trying to help him. Finally she rolled his T-shirt into a ball and pressed it against the wound.

"Let's tie this on and get going," Gavin ordered.

Lindsey's frightened eyes met his but a wall of courage went up and she nodded. She removed her shirt from her waist and tied it around his shoulder, creating a makeshift sling to keep pressure against his injury and support his arm.

As soon as she finished, he gestured for her to go. She gave him a hesitant worried look, then followed behind as he crept toward the bushes, trailing Faulkner. Overgrown weeds and tree stumps marred their path. They passed a carcass of a decaying deer, a beaver-engineered dam across the creek, then twisted through briars and poison ivy and wild mushrooms. Gavin followed Faulkner's footsteps when he could find them, a broken patch of grass, the movement of branches swaying in the trees as if Faulkner had just fought his way through them, the entire time dodging the question echoing through his mind—what if they were too late? What if Faulkner had made it to the cabin and had escaped with their son?

LINDSEY PLUNGED through the brush, shoving tree branches out of her way, trying not to stumble over the vines and battered tree roots as she hastily tried to keep up with Gavin. For an injured man, he possessed amazing strength. She prayed they weren't too late.

Her mouth was dry, her limbs ached, her fingers felt raw from swiping at the rough tree bark. But her baby was up there somewhere and she'd be damned if she'd let her ex-husband cart him off to some foreign country and raise him as his child. She pushed harder, forcing herself to breathe out of her mouth to keep up the pace. Finally, Gavin paused. He'd heard something. She listened and heard it, too. The soft sound of someone singing. Humming a lullaby. Whoever was singing had her baby.

Gavin steered her behind a cluster of pine trees. She looked through the clearing and spotted a small log cabin, nestled in the woods like a cottage out of an episode of *Little House on the Prairie*. A white van was parked beneath a crudely built carport, a black Mercedes hidden behind the frame of the house.

On the wooden porch Lindsey spotted an elderly

woman wearing an old-fashioned housedress. She sat hunched over in a straight chair rocking a tiny wooden cradle back and forth, humming in a sweet voice. Lindsey's lungs tightened.

Her baby was in the cradle.

But who was the woman?

She rose to run to her son but Gavin yanked at her hand. "No, Linds, wait. Backup should be here soon."

The baby began to wail, drowning out his words. Her son's cries reminded her of all the nights she'd heard him in her sleep. All the days and nights she'd already missed being with him.

The old woman picked him up, cradled him in her arms, swaying back and forth and humming, softly. "Rock-a-bye-baby, in the treetop..."

Lindsey's arms ached. Cory was her baby, she should be holding him, giving him comfort. Not a stranger.

Her ex-husband staggered from the edge of the woods and walked toward the porch, his arms outstretched. "Nora, let me have him now."

Nora. The old woman had been Jim's nanny when he was little. Lindsey couldn't stand the thought of her ex-husband touching her son. She bolted forward, ignoring Gavin's pleas to wait, and ran for the porch.

But another man, Jim Faulkner's father, stepped from the shadows of the woods and grabbed her. He thrust a gun in her face just as her ex-husband started to lift her baby from the old woman's arms.

"No, give me my baby!" Lindsey cried. "You got what you wanted, so pl-please give me my son."

GAVIN'S PULSE raced as he forced himself to think, not to allow his own explosive emotions to cloud his actions. Simon had followed the Faulkners; he'd be here somewhere. A wrong move might push Faulkner's panic button and he'd end up getting Lindsey or his son hurt. He slowly emerged from his hiding place.

"It's over Faulkner, let her go," he said calmly.

The older Faulkner, an aged version of his son with gray hair and small, dark bifocals, glared at him with controlled rage. "It's not over until my son is out of here."

Lindsey strained against the man's arms but he tightened his hold around her neck until she stilled. Gavin clenched his hand by his side. "Okay, we did everything you asked. Now, why don't you hand the baby to Lindsey and take off."

"It's not as simple as that anymore." The screen door opened and the elderly Faulkner's wife slid through the door. Diamonds glittered off her earlobes and hands in the bright sunlight, her expression hard and cold.

Jim Faulkner gently lifted the infant in his arms. Lindsey nearly doubled over. This evil, heartless man who had never wanted children was holding her son. "I'll take good care of him, Lindsey. I'll make sure he has the life only a Faulkner could give him."

"No—"

"He's not your son," Mrs. Faulkner stated baldly.

"What?" Faulkner turned to Lindsey. "You let me think he was?"

"How many times did you lie to me?" Lindsey snapped back. "This is my son's life we're talking about, Jim. You got your freedom, now give me my baby."

Faulkner's eyes turned icy, his voice harsh. "If he isn't my child, then who the hell is the father?"

Lindsey bit down on her lip. Faulkner turned to Gavin, rage darkening his eyes as he put two and two together. He slowly handed the child back to the elderly woman and started for Gavin, but his mother grabbed his arm.

"Wait," Mrs. Faulkner said. "It's going to be all right, Jim. It's really better this way. Now you can leave without any ties to that little witch."

Faulkner waved his fists, glaring at Lindsey. "How long were you sleeping with him? Were you making it while we were still married?"

"No, I never—"

Jim flashed his father a look of disdain. "If you knew, why didn't tell me?"

"You have to believe us, son, when we first arranged to take the baby, we thought he was yours," Mr. Faulkner said. "Our grandson."

"We had her followed. When we found out she was pregnant, we assumed the baby was yours. We figured we'd already lost you. We didn't want to lose our only grandson. So we had Walt arrange things with Dr. Cross—"

"Your butler blackmailed Cross into helping you," Gavin supplied. "Did he try to kill Lindsey, too?"

"Walt is very loyal," Mr. Faulkner said. "He's always done what I asked. In turn, I take care of him and his wife."

"Whose idea was it to fake the baby's death?" Gavin asked.

"Cross's," the old man said matter-of-factly. "Rather ingenious, I thought. When that other baby was stillborn, he decided to induce Lindsey. He called us right away so we could be there when the baby was born. Everything fell into place, we hired that ex-con to help tail Lindsey—"

"Danny Swain?" Gavin interjected.

"Right, he spent some time with little Jim here when you first locked him up. They had a good time comparing notes on you, Mr. McCord."

So Swain had been involved. Gavin would make sure he paid for it, too. He massaged the ache in his arm, realizing the wound had started to bleed again. He wasn't sure how much longer he could hold out but he had to stall. "Why wait so long to make your demands?"

"Yeah, why did you let me rot in that cell?" Faulkner asked harshly. "You knew every minute I spent in that hellhole was torture."

Mrs. Faulkner clutched her son's arm. "We...we didn't think of using the baby to win your freedom until we found out the baby wasn't yours. At first, we...only wanted our grandson. It was fitting, you know. She took our son and put him away so we'd take her son. So we had Walt get him for us. And he was supposed to kill that...that woman, but he kept messing up. Then this stupid cop showed up." Mrs. Faulkner lay a shaky hand against her neck. "And a few days ago Dr. Cross phoned us, said this detective was asking a lot of questions, that he claimed the baby was his son, not yours, Jim."

"So, you knew he was the father," Faulkner spat in disgust. "And you changed your plans."

Gavin grimaced, remembering how he'd blurted the truth to Cross. "You tried to have Lindsey killed so she wouldn't come looking for the baby. But when you discovered the baby wasn't your son's, you decided to use the baby to arrange for his release, then kill us all." Gavin fought a wave of dizziness. He glanced at Lindsey, saw the fear in her eyes, and something else...trust.

She trusted him to save them. He couldn't let her down. *Family is the most important thing in the world....*

"I don't understand," Lindsey said. "Why go to all that trouble when you said yourself you would have taken me to court? You have so much money—"

"We *had* money," Mrs. Faulkner said bitterly. "Do

you realize how much we went through trying to keep Jim out of prison? We wasted half a fortune and it didn't save him. No, this time we weren't going to take any chances.''

"Plus, grandparents rarely win in custody suits involving the birth mother," Gavin added. "Right, Mrs. Faulkner?''

"That is what our attorney said," she replied curtly. She quickly turned to her son. "We can fly away now. Leave the child, you can start over in Brazil—''

"I'll take the baby with me," Faulkner roared. "Kill them both for what they did to me, then I'll raise this baby as mine—the son I would have had if Lindsey hadn't betrayed me.''

"I never betrayed you. And you never wanted a child, remember?" Lindsey whispered hoarsely.

"You won't get away with our murders," Gavin said, gauging both the young and old Faulkners' reactions. "The FBI knows where we are.''

"Then we'd better hurry, hadn't we?" Faulkner said snidely.

"No, Jim, please," Lindsey pleaded. "Just leave Cory with Mac. I'll go away with you, we'll start all over, I'll give you a son of your own—''

"Give me the baby.''

All heads turned in shock as another man stepped into the picture. A beefy, bald man with a double chin and a dark mole on his upper lip. His hand shook as he raised a .38. "No one is going to raise this baby but Nora. She's his mother now." He gestured toward the nanny clutching the baby in her arms, a distant expression in her glazed eyes.

Mr. and Mrs. Faulkner both appeared shocked, their son

furious. "What the hell are you doing, Walt?" the older Faulkner asked.

The old man took a step toward Jim. "Put down your gun, Mr. James, you don't want me to hurt your son, do you?"

The old woman drifted into another lullaby, rocking the infant gently.

Gavin kept his gaze on the .38 and the butler. Lindsey's ex tried to reach for the gun but the old man waved it toward him. "Stop, Mr. James or I'll shoot." He gestured toward his wife. "Nora here's been taking good care of the little boy. She couldn't have babies of her own, suffered so much trying to have a child, then you came along, Mr. Jim, and your mama was too busy to raise you, so Nora cared for you like you were hers. She sung to you at night, changed your diapers, cooked you soup when you was sick. She should have been your mama."

Mrs. Faulkner pressed a shaky hand over her heart, her face bloodred. "James, do something. Walt has completely gone mad."

The elderly Faulkner held out a hand to calm him, but the old man spoke again, more fiercely. "I'm through taking orders from you, Faulkner, doing your dirty work." He shot Jim a pained look. "You were a disappointment, Mr. Jim. Broke Nora's heart. She thought she'd raised you better than to rob all those people."

Jim Faulkner started to sputter an excuse but the old man silenced him with a menacing glare, then turned to the elderly Mr. Faulkner.

"I said put down your gun, Mr. James. You got what you wanted, your son back. I intend to have what I want, this baby for Nora." He gestured toward the door. "Now, everyone, go inside."

Lindsey's panicked gaze flew to Gavin's. Where was his backup?

"How do you think you'll get away with this?" Gavin asked.

"Mr. Faulkner has his private jet all ready to roll. Me and Nora and little Tommy here will just fly on out of here, just like Mr. James planned to do."

"But what about us?" Mr. Faulkner asked. "You can't leave us here. They'll come back and get Jim—"

"I told you I'm through taking orders from you and doing your dirty work. All I want is for Nora to keep the baby, our little Tommy."

"His name is not Tommy, it's Cory, Cory Adam Payne," Lindsey said, enunciating each word clearly.

The old man frowned, then brushed off her words. "He'll go by Tommy from now on. Don't worry, Miss Payne. Ain't no one gonna love him or be better to him than Nora. You're still young enough to have another baby, my Nora and me, we can't...." His voice broke, a single tear slid down his cheek. "And we get so lonely sometimes."

The old woman nuzzled the baby to her cheek, humming again so softly it raised the hairs on Gavin's neck. The man's expression hardened and he pointed the gun toward the door. "Everyone inside now."

Faulkner's father clutched Lindsey in front of him and raised his gun. "You can take the kid, Walt, but don't hurt my son."

"You can't leave us here to go to jail," Mrs. Faulkner cried. "Not after all we've done for you—"

"All you've done for me! I've been doing your dirty work for years, listening to your orders, heeling left and right and watching Nora work her fingers to the bone cleaning for you. It stops today."

Faulkner's father raised his gun in panic. Gavin saw Lindsey's determination and hoped he could defuse the situation, but Lindsey suddenly raised her foot and kicked her father-in-law's knee. He yelped in pain and immediately released her. Just as she dropped to the ground, Gavin dove toward him to grab his gun. But the gun fired just as Gavin tackled him and another bullet slammed into Gavin's chest, knocking him to his back.

Within seconds, the FBI swarmed. Gavin rolled sideways and knocked the gun from old man Faulkner's hand, then rammed his fist into the man's face. Blood spurted from Faulkner's nose, his eyes lolled back in his head, then he groaned and passed out. Gavin tried to stand up, saw Simon and Barnes and Jernigan quickly subdue the butler and Lindsey's ex. Where was Lindsey? Had she been shot?

Sunlight blinded him as he searched the area for her. The sky was blue, then turned blurry. Tree branches swam in front of his eyes. Blackness quickly drowned out the blue. Gavin's last pain-filled thought before the darkness sucked him in to its long tunnel was that he wanted to see his son's face just one time before he died.

Chapter Twenty-Two

Lindsey heard the shots behind her and prayed Gavin hadn't been hit again as she darted up the steps toward her baby. Jernigan tackled the butler while Barnes and Gavin's partner grabbed her ex-husband and his parents. Her heart fluttered at the sight of her son nestled in the blue blanket, held so lovingly in the old lady's arms. Dark fine hair covered his head while his small fists lay curled up to his chin in his sleep. His eyelashes suddenly fluttered, then he opened his eyes—the biggest, brownest, most beautiful eyes she'd ever seen. Her son had creamy skin, a chubby cherublike face, a square chin like his father's.

The woman named Nora turned tear-filled eyes toward Lindsey. "I knew you'd come for him one day. You're his mama, aren't you?"

Lindsey nodded, her own eyes moist.

"They said you didn't want him, but I thought different. A mama has a fine little guy like this, she couldn't give him away."

"I always wanted him." Lindsey ached to reach out and pull her son into her arms, but Nora seemed disoriented, as if she wasn't fully aware of what was going on around her. "Thank you for watching him, Nora, for loving him."

"I took real good care of him, miss, just like I always did little Jim." She angled her head to look at the baby, brushing her fingers across his small forehead. His big brown eyes gazed back at the woman, a tiny little dimple pulled at his left cheek. He'd already grown so much.

And he didn't even know her.

Then he turned his small round face toward her and a big toothless smile spread onto his face. Tears filled Lindsey's eyes at the immediate bonding.

"I loved him just like he was my own little boy." Nora leaned over and kissed the baby's forehead, then surprised Lindsey by placing him in her arms. "He belongs with his real mama. Will you bring him to see me every now and then, miss? My house is so awful quiet without little feet pitter-pattering."

Lindsey hugged the old lady's neck as she accepted her son back into her arms. "Thank you again for taking such good care of him, Nora. And, yes, I'll bring him to see you," she whispered in a choked voice.

"He likes to be sung to." Nora blushed. "He loves it when I sing lullabies."

"I promise I'll sing to him every night." The tears flowed freely as she stared at her son in amazement. "Hi, Cory, I'm your mommy." She traced a finger over his soft skin, memorizing every feature of his face. He was the most beautiful little boy in the world. How could she have thought she might not recognize him? Sure, he'd grown a little but he reminded her more of Gavin than he had the day he was born. She planted soft kisses all over his face, nuzzled her nose against the baby powder scent of his blanket, laughed when a tiny smile formed on his pink mouth.

But reality around her returned, and she realized the shots had died and the Faulkners were in custody. But Gavin hadn't appeared beside her. She frantically scanned the area for him, then spotted his partner kneeling on the ground over Gavin's still body. Fear bolted through her. She could get her son back only to lose Gavin.

She clutched her baby in her arms and barreled down the steps, racing for the man she loved.

"I've radioed for the EMTs," the agent said. "They should be here any minute."

Lindsey knelt beside Gavin, her heart clinching at Gavin's chalky pallor. Blood seeped from the makeshift bandage she'd created earlier and she gasped when she noticed a small towel pressed over a second wound.

"How bad—" She couldn't finish the sentence.

"I don't know, but he's tough, ma'am. He'll make it."

"He damn well better," Lindsey said, earning a smile from Gavin's partner.

Gavin's dark eyelashes fluttered. Another flutter. His eyes slowly opened. He blinked again as if to focus. His lips twitched, formed a smile.

"Linds?"

"I'm here, Mac." She lowered her mouth and kissed his forehead, brushing a damp strand of hair from his eyes. "And so is your son."

Then she angled the baby so he could see his little boy's face for the first time.

MOISTURE GLITTERED in Gavin's dark eyes as he focused on their baby. Cory was a beautiful, healthy-looking little guy, a smattering of dark hair like his own, a round chubby face, an adorable toothless smile. Pain from the gunshot wound knifed through him but joy over seeing his son made it worth it. Love for his baby was so evident in Lindsey's eyes, but he thought he saw love for him there as well. Could they all somehow come together as a family?

Family is the most important thing in the world. Sometimes you don't realize it until it's gone.

Did he have to lose Lindsey and his son again to realize how important they were to him? No, he—

A loud whirring noise burst into the air, leaves and dirt swirled around him filling his eyes with grit. The helicopter, he realized, coming to take him to the hospital.

"You hang in there," Lindsey whispered. "You have a lot of birthdays to celebrate with your little boy."

Gavin imprinted the words in his brain right before the pain and darkness drove him over the edge and swept him into an empty void.

HOURS OR DAYS later, Gavin didn't know which, he awakened to the scents of antiseptics and alcohol and the droning of hospital machines. He had been in surgery, he realized—they'd had to remove the bullets. He didn't remember much of the shooting at all, except the soft sound of Lindsey's voice urging him to wake up. And the beautiful melody of his son's occasional cry. He finally opened his eyes and tried to ignore the fact that he was in pain and could barely move. He didn't care. Lindsey was sitting beside him, his son cradled in her arms.

He'd been dreaming about them, the three of them together as a family.

"How long have you been here?" he asked, struggling to speak loud enough for her to hear.

"A couple of days."

"You should have gone home—"

"We're family, Mac. I love you. How could I be anywhere else?"

"Lindsey—"

"So don't think you're going to get rid of us so easily," Lindsey said, refusing to listen to any arguments. "This baby and I need you and we love you. Both of us." She pounded her heart with her fist. "And I don't care what you say about keeping us safe—I'm a strong woman. God knows if I survived the last few weeks I can survive anything. And we're much safer when you're around to watch over us. You found Cory."

"You are strong," Gavin agreed, remembering how hard Lindsey had fought to make him believe their son was alive.

"Then are you going to stop blaming yourself for that boy's death?"

He blinked, inhaling her scent—fresh flowers and rain.

"Are you?"

He nodded slowly. Somehow, in Mrs. Johnson's own grief and motherly wisdom, she'd given him the forgiveness he needed. And also the foresight not to let his own family slip through his hands.

"And are you going to stick around and teach Cory how to throw a baseball?"

He hesitated, remembering all his reservations. But Lindsey leaned over and teased his mouth with her tongue and all rational arguments vanished. "You'd better say you are, because I know ways to torture you in here. I made friends with the nurses. And I know how you hate needles."

"I knew I shouldn't have told you that." He tried to laugh, but his chest hurt too much. God, he loved her.

His reservations no longer seemed important. With Lindsey and the strength of their family, they could get through anything.

"I…I love you, Lindsey. But there's my job—"

"I don't want you to give up your job. Your work is as much a part of you as my teaching is a part of me. It's one of the reasons I love you, Mac." Lindsey stroked a lock of hair away from his forehead, her voice soft and loving, "Either one of us could get hit by a bus or have a car wreck at any time, so your job is not an issue, do you understand?"

The truth of her words finally hit him. After all his mother's fears, his father had died in an ordinary accident, just the way anyone else could.

"Gavin?"

"Yes, I understand. And I love you so much, Linds." Tears stung his eyes. Unable to blink away the moisture, he felt a teardrop slip down his cheek. Lindsey gently wiped it away with the pad of her thumb and kissed his cheek, then nudged his good arm up, enough to lie his son in his arms. The baby cooed and gazed at him with innocent brown eyes. Trusting eyes exactly like his mother's.

Gavin knew he'd never be able to let them go.

He looked up and saw Lindsey smiling at him, a self-satisfied, smug smile, a wicked glint to her eyes. "Well? What do you think of your son?"

"He's beautiful." He pulled her hand in his and lay them both gently on top of their son's chest. "And I'm not only going to stick around but I'm going to marry you, Lindsey Payne. That is if you'll have me."

Lindsey smiled tenderly. "I'll have you."

His voice choked again, "For our honeymoon, we're going to take this little guy on a train ride around the world."

Lindsey smiled through her tears and kissed him tenderly. "I'd settle for taking our baby home, Mac—together, forever and always."

Epilogue

"The wedding was beautiful, Linds. And so were you."

Lindsey leaned on her tiptoes and kissed her husband's cheek, laughing when Cory swiped a hand out and tried to latch on to the flower in her hair. Today had been the happiest day of her life, the day she and Gavin had said their vows. She had her son and his father home for the first time—together.

"Lindsey, dear, do you want me to rock him to sleep while you say goodbye to your guests?"

Her mother's soft voice broke the moment, but Lindsey turned and placed the baby in her mother's arms. "Oh, Mom, he's smiling at you," Lindsey said softly. "I wish you could see him."

"Don't fret," her mother whispered with a laugh. "I can see him in my mind."

Gavin gently guided Lindsey's mother to the rocking chair in the corner. Her mother sat down and began to sing softly to her grandson. Andy pulled a chair up and chatted with her mom, admiring the baby.

JoAnn rushed up and hugged Lindsey. "The ceremony was wonderful, you guys. I'm so happy for you, Linds."

JoAnn's husband Paul slid a protective arm around JoAnn and grinned. "Did Jo tell you the good news?"

Lindsey shook her head, her mind spinning. "What news?"

"I'm pregnant." She lay a hand over her still-flat tummy. "With twins!"

"Oh, JoAnn that's great!" Lindsey hugged her, both of them crying and laughing at the same time.

Gavin shook Paul's hand. "Congratulations."

Paul beamed like a proud expectant father. "Well, we'd better go. Jo has to get her rest these days."

JoAnn laughed but rolled her eyes. "The doting, over-protective father."

When the couple left, Gavin lowered his head to kiss his bride.

"I think he's sleeping," Lindsey's mom called.

Lindsey and Gavin pulled apart and laughed. "Come on, let's put him in his own room."

Gavin's gaze strayed to the nursery. "He hasn't been sleeping in there?"

Lindsey shook her head. "No, I've been keeping him in the bassinet in my room. I didn't want him to be too far away."

He brushed her hair with his fingertips. "I know what you mean. I can't stand being away from either of you."

"And I wanted you to be here when we showed him his room for the first time, Mac."

Gavin arched a brow but followed, snuggling his son in the crook of his arm as Lindsey opened the door. When Gavin saw the room, his eyes grew suspiciously moist. Trains.

Everywhere. A wide blue border with a train track and a choo-choo train ran around the ceiling. Plastic toy trains filled a bright red toy bin. A mobile with different colored soft-sculptured trains dangled above the baby's crib. And his favorite childhood book, *The Little Engine That Could,* sat on a white child-size table.

"When did you do this?" Gavin turned to Lindsey.

"Before Cory was born."

The magnitude of Lindsey's love humbled him. She'd planned to give Cory a part of him even though he'd hurt her and sent her away.

She eased the baby from his arms and settled him in the baby bed, and he pulled her into his arms. "I love you, Mrs. McCord."

"I love you, too, Mac."

He removed a shiny silver whistle from his pocket and tied it to the mobile above the crib.

Lindsey slipped her arm around his waist and leaned into the curve of his arm. "What's that for?"

Gavin smiled and rubbed a thumb over his son's soft cap of hair. "So if he ever gets lost again, he can let us know where he is."

Lindsey kissed him through her tears, then handed him a small envelope. He narrowed his eyes, then opened it and discovered another surprise waiting inside. Cory's birth certificate.

Printed clearly on the form, he read his son's name—not Cory Adam Payne as Lindsey had plainly told her ex-husband—Cory Adam McCord.

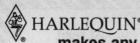

HARLEQUIN®
makes any time special—online...

eHARLEQUIN.com

your romantic
books

♥ Shop online! Visit Shop eHarlequin and discover a wide selection of new releases and classic favorites at great discounted prices.

♥ Read our daily and weekly Internet exclusive serials, and participate in our interactive novel in the reading room.

♥ Ever dreamed of being a writer? Enter your chapter for a chance to become a featured author in our Writing Round Robin novel.

• • • • • • •

your romantic
life

♥ Check out our feature articles on dating, flirting and other important romance topics and get your daily love dose with tips on how to keep the romance alive every day.

• • • • • • •

your
community

♥ Have a Heart-to-Heart with other members about the latest books and meet your favorite authors.

♥ Discuss your romantic dilemma in the Tales from the Heart message board.

your romantic
escapes

♥ Learn what the stars have in store for you with our daily Passionscopes and weekly Erotiscopes.

♥ Get the latest scoop on your favorite royals in Royal Romance.

If you enjoyed what you just read,
then we've got an offer you can't resist!

Take 2 bestselling
love stories FREE!
Plus get a FREE surprise gift!

Clip this page and mail it to Harlequin Reader Service®

IN U.S.A.	IN CANADA
3010 Walden Ave.	P.O. Box 609
P.O. Box 1867	Fort Erie, Ontario
Buffalo, N.Y. 14240-1867	L2A 5X3

YES! Please send me 2 free Harlequin Intrigue® novels and my free surprise gift. Then send me 4 brand-new novels every month, which I will receive before they're available in stores. In the U.S.A., bill me at the bargain price of $3.57 plus 25¢ delivery per book and applicable sales tax, if any*. In Canada, bill me at the bargain price of $3.96 plus 25¢ delivery per book and applicable taxes**. That's the complete price and a savings of at least 10% off the cover prices— what a great deal! I understand that accepting the 2 free books and gift places me under no obligation ever to buy any books. I can always return a shipment and cancel at any time. Even if I never buy another book from Harlequin, the 2 free books and gift are mine to keep forever. So why not take us up on our invitation. You'll be glad you did!

181 HEN C22Y
381 HEN C22Z

Name	(PLEASE PRINT)	
Address	Apt.#	
City	State/Prov.	Zip/Postal Code

* Terms and prices subject to change without notice. Sales tax applicable in N.Y.
** Canadian residents will be charged applicable provincial taxes and GST.
  All orders subject to approval. Offer limited to one per household.
  ® are registered trademarks of Harlequin Enterprises Limited.

INT00

MAITLAND MATERNITY

Where the luckiest babies are born!

In March 2001, look for

BILLION DOLLAR BRIDE
by Muriel Jensen

Billionaire Austin Cahill doesn't believe in love or marriage—

he only wants to marry in order to produce an heir. Single
mom and wedding planner Anna Maitland is horrified by his
old-fashioned attitude. So when Austin proposes a marriage
of convenience, will Anna be able to refuse him...
now that she's fallen in love with him?

*Each book tells a different story about the
world-renowned Maitland Maternity Clinic—
where romances are born, secrets are revealed...
and bundles of joy are delivered.*

Silhouette®
Where love comes alive™

HARLEQUIN®
Makes any time special ™

#1 *New York Times* bestselling author

NORA ROBERTS

brings you more of the loyal and loving,
tempestuous and tantalizing Stanislaski family.

Coming in February 2001

The Stanislaski Sisters

Natasha and Rachel

Though raised in the Old World traditions of their
family, fiery Natasha Stanislaski and cool, classy
Rachel Stanislaski are ready for a *new* world of love....

And also available in February 2001 from
Silhouette Special Edition, the newest book in the
heartwarming Stanislaski saga

CONSIDERING KATE

Natasha and Spencer Kimball's daughter Kate turns her
back on old dreams and returns to her hometown, where
she finds the *man* of her dreams.

Available at your favorite retail outlet.